I0540928

LANDSFOR

DISCOVERIES AND REVELATIONS

Raj Bansal

LANDSFOR: DISCOVERIES AND REVELATIONS
Copyright © 2022 by Raj Bansal
ALL RIGHTS RESERVED

This book is a work of fiction. Names, characters, places, and incidents either in the narrative or pictured are products of the author's imagination or used fictitiously. The individuals on the cover are models and do not represent actual people. Any resemblance to actual events, locales, or persons living or dead, is entirely coincidental. All rights reserved, including the right to reproduce this book, or portions thereof in any form whatsoever. Contact author at tecolandsfor@gmail.com or www.grbauthor.co.uk

Publisher: Absolute Author Publishing House
Cover: Germancreative @Fiverr
Interior Formatter: Dr. Melissa Caudle
Maps Creator: Raj Bansal
Maps Illustrator: Tim Godfrey using *ProFantasy* software (licensed by Ralf Schemann) and used with permission

Library of Congress Catalogue-in-Publication Data
  Bansal, Gourav

Hardback ISBN: 978-1-64953-718-8
Paperback ISBN: 978-1-64953-719-5
eBook ISBN: 978-1-64953-720-1

Printed in the United States of America

TABLE OF CONTENTS

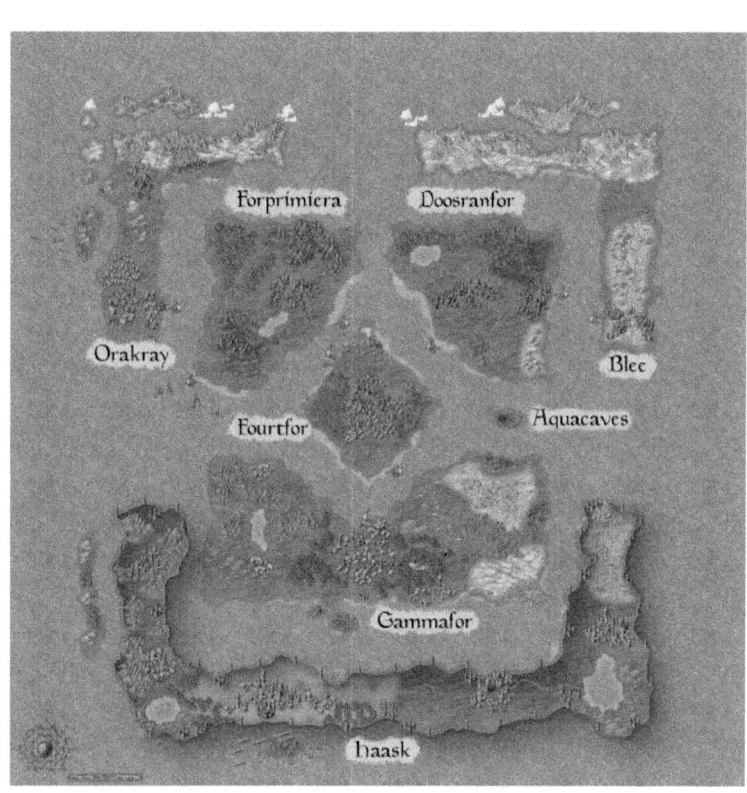

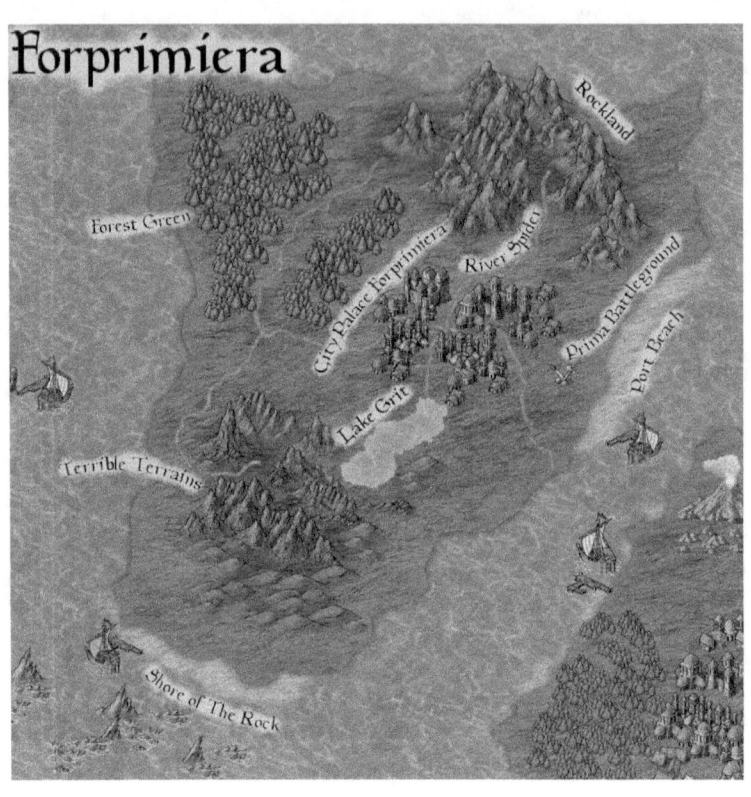

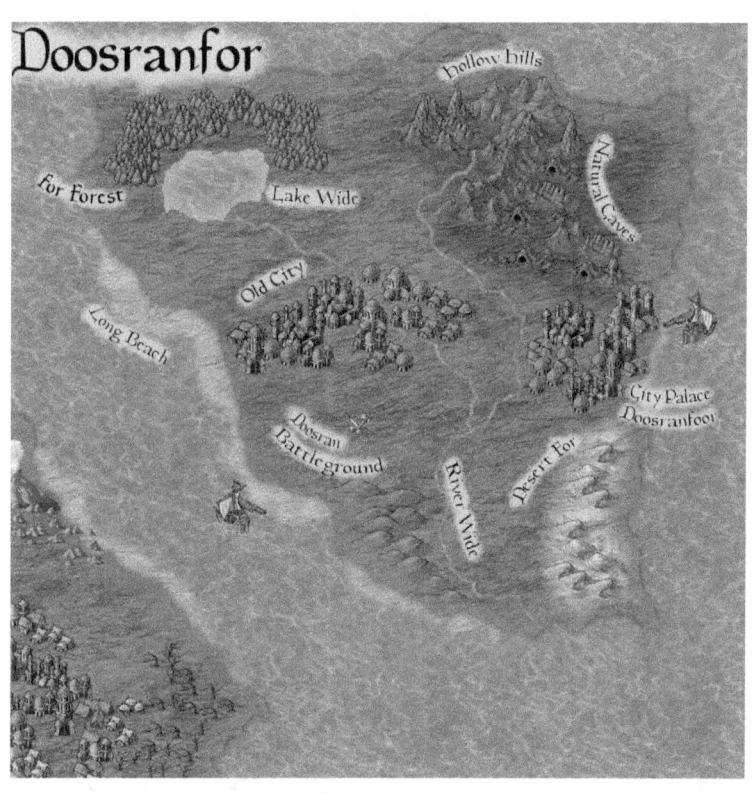

Gammafor

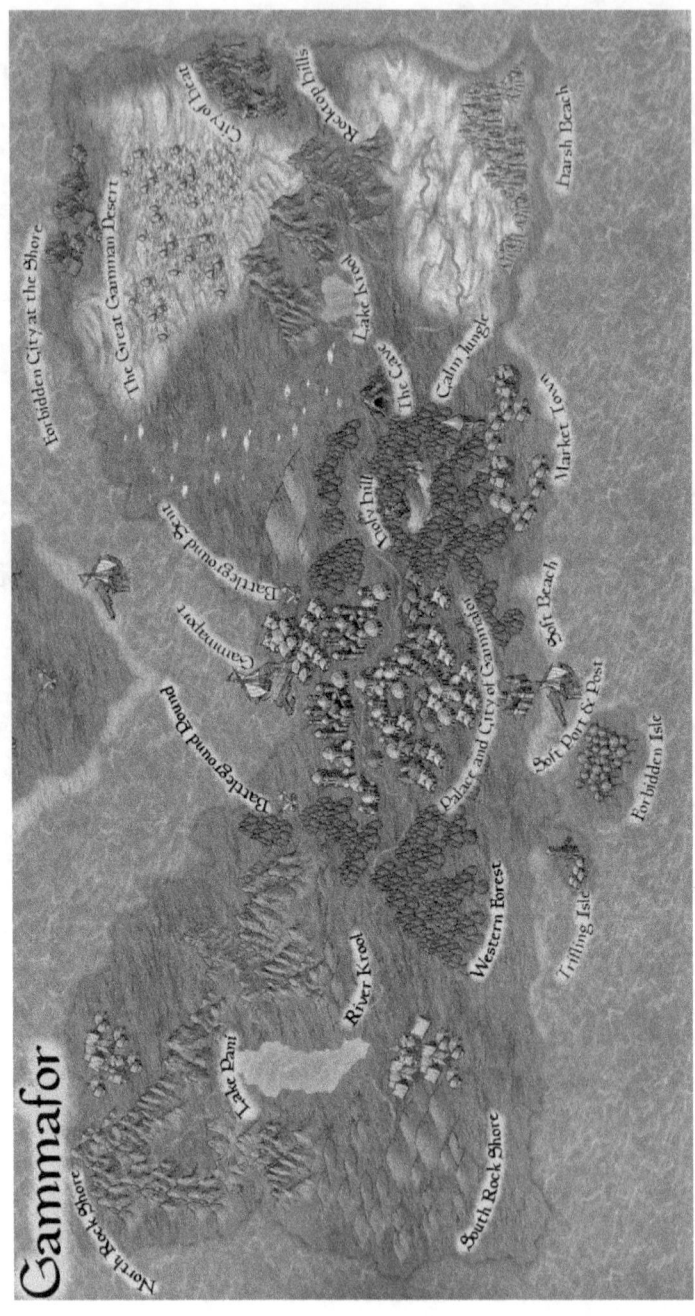

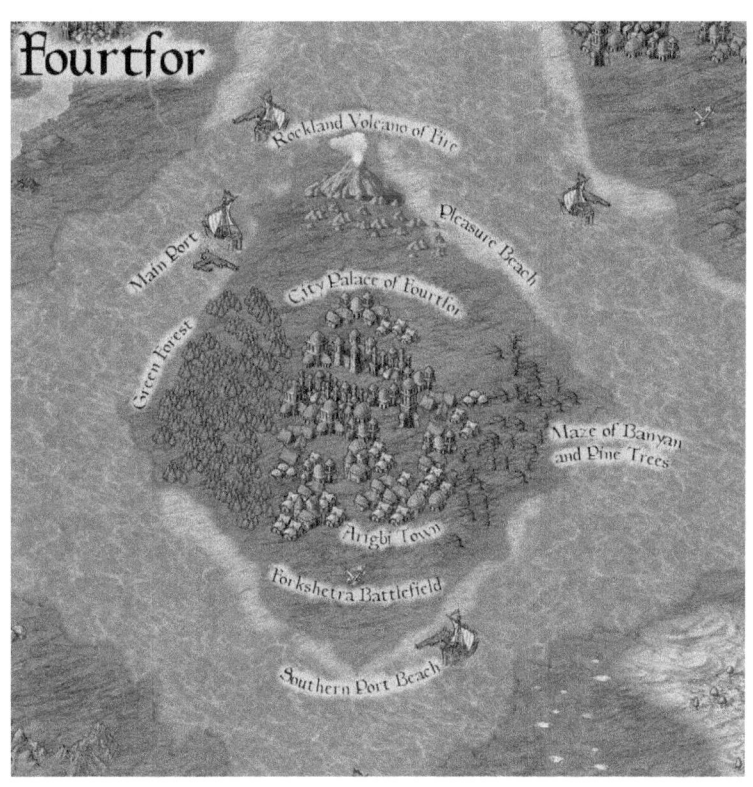

Fourtfor

Rockland Volcano of Fire

Main Port

Pleasure Beach

City Palace of Fourtfor

Green Forest

Maze of Banyan and Pine Trees

Arigbi Town

Yorkshetra Battlefield

Southern Port Beach

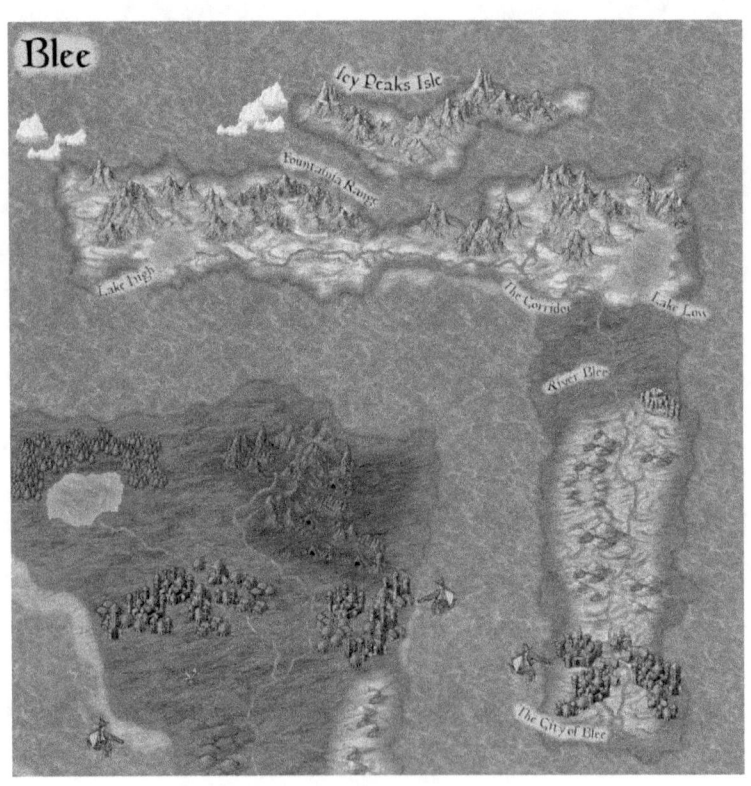

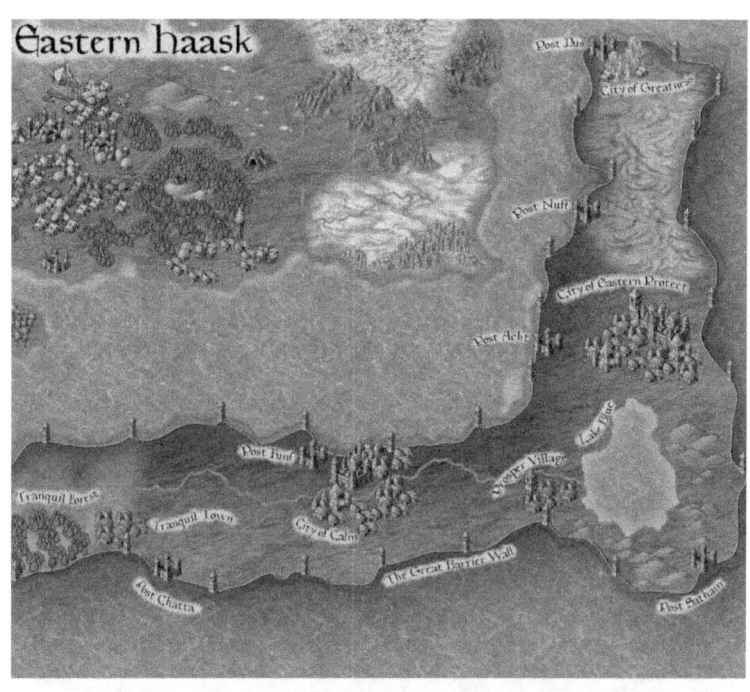

Eastern haask

Post Dia
City of Greatwa...
Post Nufi
City of Eastern Protect
Post Acht
Lake Tine
Deeper Village
Post Tund
Tranquil Forest
Tranquil Town
City of Calm
The Great Barrier Wall
Post Chatta
Post Satham

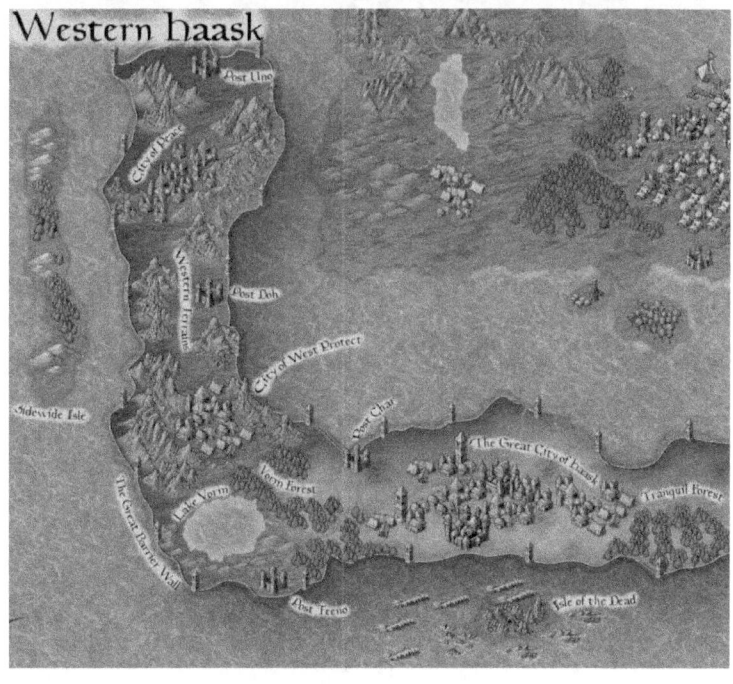

Western haask

Post Uno
City of Peace
Western Terrain
Post Deh
City of West Protect
Sideside Isle
Post Char
The Great City of haask
Town Forest
Tranquil Forest
The Great Barrier Wall
Lake Verin
Post Tecua
Isle of the Dead

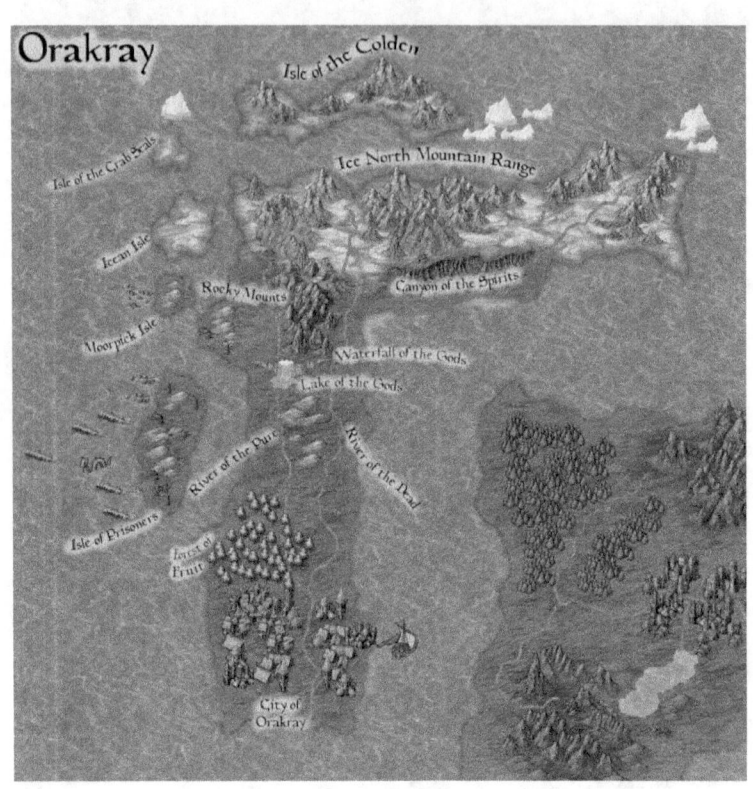

PROLOGUE

THE KING'S CHALLENGE

When King Balathaar of Landsfor grew old and his three sons and daughter became adults, he faced the grave dilemma and difficulty in naming his heir. As per tradition in Landsfor, his eldest son, Shilathaar Rain, was next in line for the throne and Balathaar himself favoured and loved the boy the most out of all his children. But he also knew the citizens of Landsfor would revolt against this decision as Shilathaar lacked many of the qualities that a King should possess. To console his heart and demonstrate his impartiality, King Balathaar decided to set a challenge.

For an entire year, he divided his kingdom into four parts. He gave Shilathaar the North-Western Island of Forprimiera, he gave his second son, Grygerious, the North-Eastern Island of Doosranfor, and to his youngest, Dymondo, he gave the Southern Island of Gammafor. He kept the central island, Fourtfor, for himself, where from the capital city, he and his Queen, Ohio, monitored the progress.

Fourtfor was the smallest of the four islands, but undoubtedly the most beautiful and affluent. As such only the rich and elite could afford to live there. It had beautiful markets, selling exotic food, lavish clothing and many other sought after household items. It contained the royal palace and royal mansion and was filled with marvellous restaurants, baths, and watering holes. It was a place of peace and enjoyment.

Nevertheless, that year King Balathaar endured many sleepless nights, dreading the day when he must decide, which of his three sons had emerged as his worthy heir? He had split his kingdom and set this challenge to please the people of Landsfor and portray himself as a fair and just King. But he knew deep inside he wanted Shilathaar to win. He prayed day and night for the results to fall in his beloved son's favour, and that Shilathaar would turn out to be the most beloved prince among the three. In truth, King Balathaar had already made his decision. He would coronate Shilathaar Rain regardless of the result. But what if one of the other two princes performed well and overshadowed Shilathaar's performance? King Balathaar was certain the womanising Grygerious would not be the one. Yet, he did not know much about his youngest son, Dymondo.

Thus the three principalities of Landsfor were ruled—three different princes with three different approaches—and all three islands prospered in their own way, though Shilathaar did not fare as well as Dymondo. Eventually the year passed and the time came for King Balathaar to assess the results of the contest. King Balathaar called his three sons into his chamber, one by one, his beloved son, Shilathaar, first.

"You have been ruling the island for a year now, Son. Tell me…are you worthy to rule the entire Kingdom? If yes, then tell me why and what would you change going forward?" asked the old King in his withering voice.

"I would change nothing, Father, but I should be King! I rule like a true sovereign. I am feared by all and I have everything under my control. My army is strong and my decisions are final. My people have all they need. They have food, education, safety and freedom. All is well in my kingdom, so I completely deserve to be King," proclaimed Shilathaar in his deep voice.

"Freedom? But they cannot leave the island!" exclaimed King Balathaar.

"They are free to do whatever they wish! But in my land, they have everything! Why should they wish to leave?" cried Shilathaar.

"But that is not your decision, Son."

"I believe it is!"

After much discussion and debate, King Balathaar ended his conversation with Shilathaar. Shilathaar was firm in his beliefs and remained adamant. King Balathaar dismissed him and called in Grygerious next.

"I would not change my ways, Father. I have brought peace, joy, happiness and harmony to my land. Everything is completed on time with love, care and patience. There is a song and dance in every street and a jovial mood all around. All the people are happy and relaxed and enjoy their lives and their work. This is what a King should give to his people and that is exactly why I should rule," said Grygerious in his melodious voice.

"Completed on time? Your ministers inform me many tasks were left unfulfilled—always left till the next day," said King Balathaar.

"You have heard incorrectly, Father," lied Grygerious. "Everything on my island is done on time!"

Once King Balathaar had heard enough from this insincere fool, he dismissed Grygerious and finally called in Dymondo, asking the same question.

"Change is inevitable, Father, but everyone must be adaptable to it. I will always attempt to do what is necessary, remaining open to a different approach the next time round if it means improvement. For now, I have done what I think is right and have done it to the best of my ability."

"Should you be King of the entire realm?"

"I am no one to judge that, Father. You must ask the people on my island – are they happy under my rule? I have only been King of Gammafor for a year and I feel I still have a lot to learn. I know that all three islands are prospering, so it must be a difficult decision for you. But perhaps there is a way the people of Landsfor can know who is best to rule them."

"What do you suggest?"

"The people from brother Shilathaar's island and brother Grygerious's island should also get an opportunity to experience life for a month or two on my island, and my people should live a month or two on theirs. After this experiment is complete, both you and I should be able to gauge which island is best. We can deliberate then. But I insist you should only choose a handful of people from each island who are willing to become a part of such a trial as it is difficult for most to uproot their home."

The frail old King Balathaar pondered his son's words gravely, with his brow wrinkling in consternation. He saw Dymondo out from his chamber and walked back to his large, emerald throne, his light green eyes struck with fear and dismay for he knew that Dymondo would no doubt be the best King for the nation. Still, his blind filial love for his eldest son held his tongue from uttering those words. To buy himself some time, he decided to heed Dymondo's suggestion.

So some of Dymondo's people went to live on Shilathaar's island for a month or two and others went to Grygerious's island for the same period. In return, Dymondo hosted citizens from Shilathaar's and Grygerious's islands. This was not a smooth exchange of populations, and it took some time, but it helped the father avoid doing complete injustice to the realm by making a hasty decision.

King Balathaar found flaws in both Shilathaar's and Grygerious's approach. Shilathaar failed to show compassion, and Grygerious failed to show assertiveness, giving little concern to warfare and land security.

Dymondo, he faulted the least out of the three. He appreciated his youngest son's approach, and his mind was constantly persuading him to coronate him as the King, yet his heart still beat for Shilathaar. By God Aquinious he wished his eldest could be more like his youngest! But that just wasn't the case. His love for his eldest son had become a curse. He had showered Shilathaar with too much love and, therefore, spoilt him. It was his own fault, not his son's. He knew this. Nevertheless, King Balathaar wanted to give Shilathaar a chance and waited six months more for the respective people from each of three islands to return to their homes.

The subjects from Shilathaar's island were glad to experience freedom and for once live without the fear of a tyrant. They enjoyed their time on Grygerious's island as for them it was a holiday, yet it felt unproductive. They preferred life in Dymondo's kingdom where they could be both free and industrious. The people from Grygerious's land despised their time under Shilathaar's rule as they lived in fear most of the time. They too enjoyed the freedom on Dymondo's island, while also developing an appreciation for work. When they returned home, they felt lazy and longed to go back to Dymondo's kingdom.

Dymondo's subjects who went to Grygerious's island became overweight and useless. It was like one long holiday, and though they enjoyed it at first, they preferred to be back home where they could be productive again. And for those who travelled to Shilathaar's island, they did not like the atmosphere of constant fear. Some even escaped, secretly returning earlier than anticipated.

This exercise proved that life was much better on Dymondo's island, and as such, everyone wanted to live there. Even before the King could make his choice, a great migration began as most of the people from Grygerious's island moved to Dymondo's island for a better, more productive lifestyle. Those who remained tended to be the lazy ones, who simply enjoyed being on a lifelong holiday.

Grygerious paid no mind to the departing subjects as he still had his maidservants; his mistresses; his music and his wine and the protection of two strong brothers. Nonetheless, he still longed to be the ruler of all Landsfor—an effect of the constant incitement by the maidservants and mistresses in his company. But political ambition was not high on his list of priorities. For Grygerious, his kingdom was his playground; where he made his own rules, and got to play all the games *he* enjoyed.

Meanwhile, the least-liked island was that of the King's favourite son, Shilathaar, where people were still not allowed to leave. Even when it became evident to them that Dymondo was the better ruler, Shilathaar's subjects had no choice but to remain and accept their fate.

It was evident to King Balathaar as well, and the old King grew increasingly distraught. He loved Shilathaar with all his heart and would do anything to behold the sight of him on the throne and place the legendary golden crown of Landsfor upon his head. But he knew the people would not be happy with Shilathaar as their sole King. He knew Dymondo had won the contest. Still, King Balathaar had to give Shilathaar something, and if he did that, he also had to think about the useless idiot that was his middle son.

King Balathaar knew the citizens of Landsfor would only be pleased if Dymondo sat on the throne as King, but he also knew Shilathaar would revolt and raise an army against his brother to overthrow him. If that happened, Dymondo would protect his rights and a bloody civil war would ensue with Grygerious getting crushed between the two. Dymondo would stand his ground, but he was not ready to battle Shilathaar...not yet. King Balathaar did not wish to behold such a sight in his lifetime.

If Shilathaar became King, there would be no revolt. The people would simply be too afraid. Grygerious would not stand up to his brother, and Dymondo would not revolt against what he would see as a traditional move of naming the eldest by his father. But he would most definitely question his father, as to the reasoning behind his imprudent spectacle of laying the task of comparing the kingdoms, just to end up announcing the eldest as supreme ruler after all. Balathaar did not want to face such an interrogation as he would not have an acceptable answer for him. But he also did not want to give Shilathaar total control. Shilathaar had proven that if given rule of the nation, he would destroy the people.

Dymondo had clearly won the challenge, but King Balathaar could not bring himself to name him as his sole heir. To console his heart, he decided that everything would go on as it currently was. Shilathaar would remain King of the North-Western Island of Forprimiera, Grygerious would keep control of the North-Eastern Island of Doosranfor, and Dymondo would continue ruling the Southern Island of Gammafor. The old King and Queen would remain on the smallest island of the four, the capital, Fourtfor, where they would see out their remaining days.

This was an injudicious and unwise decision by the King. Shilathaar fumed over not receiving the entire land, as he truly believed he deserved it, but after much deliberation with his son, King Balathaar explained that he had three sons and he had thus divided his land equally among them. Shilathaar was temporarily appeased by the fact that neither brother had more than him, but the fire raged in his heart day and night with the thought that he should have it all.

Two more years passed and the time came for King Balathaar to enter the afterlife. Once again, he was left with the horrendous decision about who would rule the fourth island of Fourtfor. This time on his deathbed he made the correct decision by handing over control of Fourtfor to Dymondo. It was a decision made with pragmatism, and not out of his love for Shilathaar.

The people of Fourtfor cheered and celebrated the announcement for many days, but the decision infuriated Shilathaar and emotionally wounded Grygerious. Another argument ensued between King Balathaar and the two elder brothers on the King's deathbed. Dymondo decided not to partake in the discussion out of respect for his dying father.

Grygerious lied to his father that he would have been content if Shilathaar received the extra island, but that it wasn't right to choose Dymondo because he was the youngest of the three. By expressing this, Grygerious, as intended, established a special place in Shilathaar's heart. Grygerious's goal, of course, was to be King of all four islands, but he knew this was not the correct moment to enrage Shilathaar further.

For now, it would suit him to see Shilathaar get more land than their younger brother. Shilathaar relentlessly argued the same old point of him being the eldest, but the King's decision was final. King Balathaar ultimately gathered the courage to tell them both the truth: Dymondo was a far better person and would make a far better King. He advised them to learn from him and become better men themselves. With that, the furious brothers left the King's chamber. Queen Ohio who wanted her husband to spend his final moments in peace followed the brothers out and scolded them, telling them she did not want them to raise the topic again.

With that, Dymondo took possession of Fourtfor, and a day before King Balathaar drew his final breath, he called Dymondo to his bedside, along with his beloved wife, Ohio. The King folded his hands and begged for forgiveness from his son for the injustice he had done to him and the people of Landsfor. Dymondo was humbled before his father and assured him he would do all he could within his power to keep the family together and bind his brothers to him through love and affection. King Balathaar also sought forgiveness, for loving one child more than his other children. Dymondo explained to him that the realisation was penance enough; therefore, his father should be at peace knowing that his youngest son forgave him and would continue to love him even after his death. With that, King Balathaar left the world as the proud father of Dymondo, the rightful heir to the throne.

A royal funeral took place with pomp and grandeur, and towards the end of the rituals, Dymondo made a special effort to bind the three brothers together, and the two reciprocated his gestures, insincerely. Dymondo could understand their half-hearted response, yet he believed the day would arrive when all three brothers would love one another truly from the heart. But as is often said in Landsfor, human desire is like water. It keeps flowing without hindrance. But now the water had become fire as the unacceptable arrangement by the departed King had enraged the two elder brothers, stoking an inferno of hate in their greedy hearts.

CHAPTER 1

THE BANQUET

After the death of old King Balathaar, the people from the four islands were no longer hailed as Landsforians. Those who hailed from Forprimiera, ruled by King Shilathaar, were called Primierans. People from Doosranfor, ruled by King Grygerious, were called Doosrans. People from Gammafor or Fourtfor, where Dymondo reigned, were called Gammans and Fourtans respectively.

Neither was the realm referred to as Landsfor. Shilathaar, during the renaming of the islands, announced that no one would be allowed to utter the name Landsfor in the entire kingdom as that name had died with his father, King Balathaar. Anyone who did so in public would be seen as disrespecting their King and would be punished. So a name of a nation, which had stood for centuries, died with the old King. Grygerious and Dymondo both remained silent when Shilathaar issued his edict, but neither served the punishments recommended by their older brother. Nevertheless, the people gradually refrained from using the name after hearing of the horrible fates of those who had done so on Forprimiera. Only one person could call it Landsfor, and she always did: the old Queen Ohio. She outlived her husband King Balathaar and always despised the spineless decision her husband had made to split Landsfor. She believed that her youngest son, Dymondo, deserved to rule the entire kingdom as he was worthy, and she had argued with her husband for days on end to revoke his decision. All her

1

reasoning fell on deaf ears, as the King's love for his eldest son blinded him to the correct course.

After her husband's death, Queen Ohio remained in Fourtfor, residing in the royal castle, where the King had lived out his final days. The royal palace and royal mansion of Fourtfor were now empty as Dymondo chose to rule from his own royal palace and mansion on Gammafor. Nevertheless, he ensured that his mother got treated and looked after well. He had insisted she live with him on Gammafor, but she had refused due to her promise to her husband that they would remain in Fourtfor as a symbol of their impartiality.

Dymondo gave strict orders to the citizens that Queen Ohio was to be respected more than he himself. She was given the right to overrule any command or decision he gave. But Ohio was an understanding and considerate woman, and she never interfered in Dymondo's royal matters or decisions. She just enjoyed her peace and quiet in her royal castle living with the fond memories of her husband and their time together. When visitors came to pay their respects, Queen Ohio would wave to all of them from her chamber window to show her love as she did the day she married King Balathaar.

The Queen made many attempts to bring her family closer by holding royal banquets in Fourtfor. Her latest banquet was a marvel. The banquet hall was decorated in the traditional Landsforian colours of blue and purple, and Queen Ohio ensured the crest of the golden lion was displayed everywhere in the castle, palace and mansion. Elite noblemen and courtiers were invited from all four islands, and the finest food was served and the best musicians in the realm were invited to play. Lance Sterferep and Lance Kor, two of Dymondo's most trusted men, stood guard at the entrance of the banquet hall watching over the festivities. As for the extended families of the outer islands of Orakray and Blee, they were not in attendance.

The banquet was underway and Queen Ohio sat at the royal table with Shilathaar and Grygerious on either side of her. Next to Shilathaar sat his magnificently beautiful wife Silvenia, the princess of Orakray and now the Queen of Forprimiera.

Silvenia was very beautiful with her auburn hair and piercing blue eyes. Normally she was very fidgety, moving around constantly whether she was alone or in the company of family and friends, but now in a public setting, she remained calm and collected. She looked slightly mature for her age and this feature made her a good match for Shilathaar who too looked older with his beard. She had a short but slender body and would often wear long, brown dresses. The lower neck line on the dresses would always display her cleavage and, from time to time, "accidentally" expose her nipples. Some murmured that Silvenia knew perfectly well her bosoms were on a never-ending exhibition. In fact, she liked people staring at them whilst they talked to her. If she was by any chance made aware by another of her slippage, she'd deny any knowledge of it and wrap herself up and say, "Oh my! When did they get out?" and laugh it off and act shy.

Next to Grygerious sat his wife, Gilgenia, the gorgeous princess of Blee and now the Queen of Doosranfor. Though she was married to Grygerious, Gilgenia was Dymondo's childhood friend. When he arrived, he went over to sit next to her, but the flirty Silvenia invited him to sit next to her. Dymondo could not refuse the gesture. Dymondo did not share a good relationship with Silvenia. He found her presumptuous and brazen and abhorred her style of dress. Silvenia knew very well Dymondo despised her behaviour and flirted with him on purpose to make him feel uncomfortable, especially when it was just the two of them and no one else was around.

Gilgenia remained remarkably elegant and wore decent dresses which mainly covered her shoulders and upper arms. She had a lovely oval face, medium-length, red, shiny and wavy hair. She was fair and often dressed in soft brown, dark red and occasionally green linen outfits with silver jewellery encrusted with either crystals, rubies, or emeralds respectively. She was slim and short, but it was her striking, light-brown eyes that made her so beautiful. Gilgenia remained quiet throughout the banquet as her husband touched and flirted with the maidservants who served him, to Queen Ohio and Dymondo's disgust and Shilathaar and Silvenia's amusement. From time to time, Gilgenia would move her eyes away from the wooden table and fix them upon Dymondo. Her eyes contained questions, anguish and anger, and Dymondo did his best to evade them. He had other problems to deal with since, under the table, Silvenia had discreetly placed her hand on his thigh and had starting moving it up and down, even over his crotch, squeezing occasionally. Dymondo sat there quietly and endured.

Shilathaar boasted throughout the banquet how his island was flourishing (as did Grygerious). Silvenia made the occasional comment to further her husband's words in an attempt to impress Queen Ohio.

Ohio was a traditional woman, though, wearing less colour and covering herself from neck to toe. She remained quiet, maintaining her angelic smile while her son continued his boasting.

"And the armory has many more weapons now, mother!" announced Shilathaar.

"That is great. Brother Shilathaar, you have truly done well. Forprimiera is no doubt a fortress," proclaimed Grygerious. Shilathaar enjoyed the flattery.

"It is indeed, Grygerious!" added Silvenia as she looked over at Dymondo and flicked her auburn hair. "Have you nothing to say,

Dymondo?" She grasped his crotch tight underneath the table.

Dymondo sat up straight and hesitantly smiled. "What can I add? No one in the realm can match the might of brother Shilathaar."

"I shall drink to that!" roared Shilathaar and raised his goblet and finished his wine. Everyone raised their glasses and drank except Gilgenia.

"Gilgenia dear, you have been rather quiet throughout the meal. What troubles you?

Gilgenia assumed her fake smile. "Nothing at all, Mother. I have not been well lately," she lied.

"Isn't my son taking good care of you?

"Mother I am the kindest person in the realm," boasted Grygerious, putting his arm around his wife to which Gilgenia smiled timidly. She raised her glass.

"To brother–in-law, Shilathaar!" she said and drank. Shilathaar nodded in acknowledgement. To Gilgenia, the wine tasted foul, as did everything at the banquet. Even the air smelt foul to her, but she was doing a sound job of holding in her discontentment. Even so, when others were not looking, her piercing eyes gazed upon Dymondo.

Queen Ohio grew bored of all the compliments, ordered dessert and decided to change the topic.

"So my sons, what amusements do you have planned for yourselves?" asked Ohio.

"Wrestling!" Shilathaar was the first to respond.

"Natural water baths and relaxation for me!" Grygerious was next.

"Silvenia? What about you? Perhaps watching a play from Julius Breaksteer?"

"Maximilian Shoves-Word is much better, Mother. But no, I find it boring watching the same play over and over again!" She indirectly mocked her mother-in-law as Ohio loved watching plays.

"Breaksteer is more famous."

"Not in Orakray, mother."

"This is Landsfor!"

"Mother, no one calls it that anymore," interrupted Shilathaar.

"Shila, I can call it anything I like!" she replied and turned to Silvenia again. "So then, dear Silvenia, what instead of plays?"

"Gladiators! I love watching them train. I will head to the ludus. Oh, the strength, the swords, the spears, the sand, the sweat and the blood!" Her grip again tightened around Dymondo's thigh as she spoke, digging her shiny nails in hard.

Shilathaar laughed at his wife's comments.

"Perhaps Gilgenia will enjoy a play or two with you, Mother," suggested Silvenia with a malicious grin.

4

Gilgenia smiled. "Yes, I would love to, Mother. Any playwright you prefer," she said with her soft yet assertive voice.

"Oh no, dear Gilgenia, I know you love riding. When you were young, you and Dymondo used to go riding all the time, sometimes all the way to the ocean! I shall have some of the finest stallions prepared for you both, and you shall go riding tomorrow."

Dymondo smiled.

"No, Mother. Times have changed. I no longer ride. We shall watch a play together enacted by some of the finest actors in Fourtfor and written by Julius Breaksteer," said Gilgenia, starring at Dymondo. Queen Ohio said nothing and lowered her eyes.

Another malicious smile formed on Silvenia's face.

"That would be best, Mother," she said. "Tongues would wag if these two were seen riding into the hot red sunset together. After all, she is Dymondo's sister-in-law," she added as she turned to face Dymondo whilst her hand was now upon his knee.

"Silvenia! There is no need—"

"I but jest mother!" she interrupted, rising from her seat and going behind Ohio's chair to put her arms around Ohio's neck.

"Your jests can hurt someone, dear Silvenia," corrected Ohio.

"I apologise. Gilgenia, dear, I do apologise."

"What fun would there be if there weren't zestful remarks exchanged between family members?" laughed Grygerious.

"Absolutely!" seconded Shilathaar and they both laughed.

Gilgenia smiled nervously. Dymondo was relieved that Silvenia's hand was no longer on his leg.

Soon after, Dymondo's chief researcher, the old scholar Lorca Loray approached Dymondo discretely at the table.

"My King, may I have a word?"

"Not now, Lorca," said Dymondo not looking at him.

"It is about the important research task you have assigned me."

Grygerious heard the words "research" and looked over at them.

Dymondo got up, subtly adjusted his trousers, and took Lorca to a corner of the hall. Queen Ohio was disgusted at Dymondo leaving the table to converse with Lorca. She did not deem it correct for Lorca to interrupt his King and for Dymondo to walk away from the royal table. Grygerious's eyes followed the pair to the corner. Lance Sterferep, who had been keeping a close eye on the royal table, noticed Grygerious's interest in Dymondo's conversation.

CHAPTER 2

SAPPHIRE-EYED ASSASSIN

C ourt had not yet begun in the land of Gammafor, yet King Dymondo Rain was bathed, dressed and ready. He was at his dark, wooden desk by his large window preparing his scrolls for the day's discussion when there was a knock at the door.

"You may enter!"

It was Lance Sterferep.

"Pardon me, my King, but I believe it is time we left for court."

"Thank you, Lance Sterferep, I am nearly finished scribing the last few actions. I will meet you outside when they are complete," said Dymondo.

"My King," said Sterferep as he bowed and started to close the thick, wooden door.

"Oh, and Lance…"

"Yes, my King?"

"'Good morning' is preferable to the boring 'Pardon me," said Dymondo winking at Sterferep.

"My King is kind," said Sterferep smirking back and bowing again as he closed the door.

Dymondo completed his scribing, rose from his chair and proceeded towards the door. As he opened the door, the two Lances snapped to attention. Lances, Gammafor and Fourtfor's elite fighting force, dressed in uniforms of gold and red, distinguishing themselves from the regular soldiers of the land. A guard or a soldier had to go through incredible amounts of rigorous tests and training to attain the title of Lance. When achieved, each was armed with a fear-inducing gladius or a menacing spear, sometimes both.

"Lance Sterferep Unknown … Lance Kor Grayish… shall we proceed?" Dymondo asked and began to walk.

"Yes, my King!" both shouted and followed closely behind him.

"Lance Kor, how is our new Lance training coming along for the younger candidates?" he asked.

"Very well, my King. Many of our guards are training to become Lances and have expressed an interest in going ahead to advanced training. And many young men from the public have already completed the preliminary classes. If they choose to continue, they will become guards or soldiers and eventually Lances themselves," Kor replied.

"So you have got young men to visit our training camps?"

"Yes. Those aged above nineteen."

"How many exactly expressed the desire to continue?"

"From one class, my King… a total of twenty."

"Twenty? But that's more than half the class!"

"Yes, my King."

"Well, that is very good. Very good, indeed. As you know, to become a Lance takes much dedication and commitment, but above all interest!"

"My King, this is all due to your excellent suggestion to run these sessions in the first place, and to invite all young men to take part. You have provided them the opportunity to experience life as a Lance and let the men themselves decide whether they wish to continue. By this method, most men in the land have received basic warfare training, and even if they decide not to continue to the advanced training and join the army, they will have at least learned something valuable and be able to wield a sword."

"Gratitude, Lance Kor, but this is all due to you running the classes so successfully. The numbers clearly suggest your sessions are sparking an interest in these young men's hearts to become a Lance. Good work!"

"My King," Kor said, nodding humbly to his King.

Lance Kor Grayish was a very pretty man with long, brown, wavy hair and dark brown eyes. He was the same age as Dymondo, and the King adored him for Kor was polite and clever, and always used diplomacy. He therefore could be trusted to send all the King's delicate messages. The Lance stood tall and broad but not as tall or broad as his best friend, Lance Sterferep Unknown. He knew that in most ways Sterferep was the better Lance, so he did not mind playing second fiddle. The only advantage Kor had over Sterferep was in his kind nature, which generally won him praise and the attention of many women. His body was muscular, and in battle he was known to be agile and swift, preferring the spear to the sword as it came to him more naturally.

"Lance Sterferep."

"My King."

"I heard that some young girls are been commanded by their fathers not to attend school and instead have been asked to help their mothers with daily household chores. Do I hear that correctly?"

Lance Sterferep paused.

Dymondo stopped walking and so did the Lances behind him.

"Lance...I am waiting for an answer."

"My King, apologies, but you hear correct. This is unfortunate. Fathers must not stop their daughters from attending school. As per your orders, all children of this land must be educated up to the age of eighteen at the very least."

"Yes, this is a grave matter. Have you taken any measures regarding this issue?"

"I have informed the education minister, Olivious...and Prime Minister Kriptus is also aware."

"Have they taken any action?"

"I do not believe they have."

"Lance, that is direct. You could have chosen your words more diplomatically."

"Forgive me my King, but I'd rather tell the truth and face the consequences than lie and save my skin. I am no diplomat, my King, nor a politician. I am a Lance. My weapons are my diplomacy."

Dymondo turned and placed both his hands on Lance Sterferep's shoulder. "Lance Sterferep... what are we going to do with you?" he smiled shaking him gently before turning and continuing to court.

The two Lances exchanged glances and smiled and followed their King.

"I like you, Lance, but you can at least learn to be more thoughtful when you choose your words. The ministers despise you. I am saying this for your own good. I respect you and fully trust you. You just need to get others to trust and like you as well."

"You respect me... I am honoured my King. Your trust is all I aim for. I have no care for others except you, your mother, princess Nilharia, fellow Lance Kor and Lance Tamaris."

"Hah! What of Dan and Dwarpal? Do you not care for them?" asked Dymondo.

"My King, Sterferep cares for many people. Deep inside him there is a warm heart," interrupted Kor.

"I am of aware that, Lance Kor," smiled Dymondo.

Sterferep Unknown too smiled and shook his head, choosing not to speak any more. He was the complete opposite of Kor. No diplomacy, no politics. He was brash at times, even with the King, but only in private, and Dymondo allowed that as he knew this tall, strong Lance was probably the most trustworthy man in the entire kingdom. Sterferep would not talk back to his King in public no matter how much he disagreed.

Sterferep had a large frame but not one inch of body fat. No other Lance stood a chance in a duel with him in training nor did any enemy on the battlefield. His body was like iron, and so was his tongue, able to utter any truth no matter how bitter. He was not the most handsome of men, but the ladies at court could not take their eyes off his brutish physique, his short, thick, dirty-blonde hair, and his chiselled face. He was older than Dymondo, more near to Shilathaar's age.

"Anything from Lorca yet?" asked Dymondo.

"No, my King. I was again asked to wait. He still needs to finish his investigations. Not entirely sure when he will respond," replied Kor.

"That man!" cried the King. "Very well...Admiration to you for gathering information before my prompt, but do not pay him a visit from now on. Let us see how long he takes to complete what I have asked of him. In the meantime, I shall speak with Olivious about why he has not yet dealt with the situation with those the poor, young girls."

"Are you certain you do not wish me to pay a visit to Lorca, my King?"

"Why do you ask, Sterferep?"

"He is an old man and has locked himself in a servant chamber for this task. He sleeps there and does not go home—just wanted to ensure that he yet draws breath."

Dymondo looked him up and down, and Sterferep looked right back and raised his eyebrows.

"Surely the servants that give him his food would have told us by now, Lance," said Dymondo.

Sterferep shrugged his shoulders.

"Very well! You head there first. Lance Kor and I shall head to court. You join us later."

"My King."

Lance Sterferep left the others and headed to Lorca's chamber through many corridors, passing many guards who greeted him as he went by. He finally reached Lorca's chamber and was greeted at the door by two guards in their mid-twenties: Dan Smoten and Dwarpal Kentish. Both wore black and golden attire and were of parallel height and strong build. Dan had dirty-blonde hair and Dwarpal's hair was light brown. They bore similar facial features and were often mistaken as brothers.

"Good morning guards, how do you both fare?" he asked.

"All is well, Lance Sterferep. How do you fare?" Dan pleasantly replied.

"I'm well, Dan…And I hear you shall be Lance very soon."

"I hope to, Lance Sterferep."

"Well, you've got the courage, Dan" said Sterferep and turned towards Dwarpal.

"Dwarpal!"

"Lance Sterferep!"

"I believe the chief researcher, scholar Lorca, is in?"

"Correct, yet his strict orders are that he not be disturbed."

"The King's orders are that I pay him a visit!"

Dwarpal was an arrogant man. Both stood staring at one another for a while. Finally Dwarpal turned and banged on the door and told Lorca of his visitor. Lorca assented to the visitor. Dwarpal then turned back to the Lance. "You may enter, Lance Sterferep."

"Damn right I will!" Sterferep said, barging past.

The stench in the room was unbearable. It smelt of urine, excrement and vomit. The lighting was dim; the lit candle on the researcher's table had nearly burnt out. There was a small bed set to the side of which the sheets had not been washed for months. Lorca sat at his desk with his face buried in a large, dusty book, peeking at the text through a small magnifier. His white, cotton linen had turned dusty and grey. He needed a bath and a sharp, hot blade and oil for his long, grey, greasy beard and hair.

Sterferep placed his hand upon his nose and got straight to the point.

"Scholar Lorca, hope you fare well. What is the progress on the task set to you by the King?"

The old man turned around to show his wrinkled face.

"Lance Sterferep is it?" he asked in his creaking voice.

Sterferep turned his nose up at the sight of the unkempt official. He never liked Lorca. Though knowledgeable, the man was peculiar.

"Yes, it is I."

"Well…it would not take so long, if the King didn't send his Lances to check up on me every other day! That friend of yours, Kor Grayish, was just here. And now here you are!" snapped the old man.

Lorca had good reason to be annoyed. Normally, he would go home every night, bathe and sanitise like the rest of the people, but this task had him confined to a room. Sure he was free to lock up every night and leave, but he was senile and passionate for his work, and the task the King had given him was particularly daunting. So he remained in that room, which no doubt would have to be aired out and scrubbed clean after he was finished.

"I am here to get a progress report and to find out how you are," replied Sterferep assertively.

"Well I am alright!" shouted the old man. "Now leave! I am not yet finished!"

10

"When do you expect to be?"

"How long is a piece of string, Lance? I do not know! Now away with you, I was near to something! But now I have forgotten what I was reading."

"You do know about manners and etiquette, don't you, Scholar? You have begun to behave like an animal, and you are surely living as one! And you certainly do not know how to address Lances!"

"And you certainly do not have any sense! Do you reckon I enjoy it in here? No! I am merely keeping myself away so I can get this done! I am not here to sweet talk you! I do not interfere in your tasks, so you keep your maw out of mine. You've got the update you needed; now be gone!"

Lorca hobbled over to a wooden bucket in the far corner and lifted his dirty toga and urinated in it. Sterferep looked away in disgust. Lorca finished and limped back to his desk, wiping his hands on his toga.

"Go, Lance! I shall send word when I'm done! Tell the King I may be near but not yet finished!"

"I will tell him, but scholar Lorca, see to yourself, please. Have a bath, and request for the chambermaids to clean this room and give you fresh clothes and bedding." Sterferep would not say this out of concern to anyone, but even a strong-hearted man like him felt the old man required some self-care.

"I will be done soon, you need not worry about me!" sneered the researcher.

Dwarpal knocked on the door and entered. "Food is here!" He let a women dressed in black enter with a large plate of olives, bread, fruit and fresh vegetables, and a large slab of cooked meat. She had her head covered as well as a face mask to cover her nose and mouth. Only her striking, sapphire-blue eyes were visible. She entered and waited.

"Ah! Yes! A man must eat," said Lorca and picked up the deceased candle from his work desk and took it to another table near his bed. The table was pure filth with bits of old rotten bread, olive pips and moulding slices of fat from old meat. The woman placed the plate on the table amidst the mess and swiftly turned to leave.

"Wait!" shouted Sterferep.

The woman halted, looked back at him, and her eyes widened in anger. They were very blue.

"At least give the man's table a wipe!"

"I am not a slave, sire!" exclaimed the woman in a voice that would provoke fear in any man. "I just deliver the food."

"Who are you? Why the mask? Remove it at once!"

"I am not bound by your commands, sire! Excuse me, but I must return to Fourtfor by nightfall! I do not hale from Gammafor. I am a Fourtan."

"Remove your mask!"

"I do not wish to catch disease from this room! Step aside, sire, and let me leave!"

"Dwarpal!" shouted Sterferep.

Dan and Dwarpal both entered. "Dan! You remain outside! I only called Dwarpal!"

"Yes, Lance," Dan said and swiftly returned to his position outside.

"Dwarpal! Who is this woman?" shouted Sterferep.

"This, Lance, is the lady who brings Lorca his food. She comes every day in the morning to deliver his plate."

"You see her *every day*?"

"Yes, I do. I would not suspect her—"

"Have you seen her face?"

"No, sire, but the chamber is scandalous, sire."

"When she came the first day, I am pretty sure it did not smell of piss and shit! Did she still have this concealment on her face?"

Dwarpal did not have an answer. Both he and Dan would occasionally check the maids and servants as they came in, but they had refrained from doing so over the past few weeks.

"Fool! So, you have had maids coming in every day with face garbs and you do not know their names, nor have you been asking them to remove their face masks. Have you at least been checking the food platter?"

Dwarpal lowered his head.

"Lance, go now," interrupted Lorca. "She gives me my food every day! You have nothing to be concerned about!"

"Vigilance! That is what a Lance must possess, Dwarpal! And you are training to become a Lance? You are an idiot!" Sterferep ground his teeth at Dwarpal and, completely ignoring the words of the scholar, continued to shout at him further shattering the young guard's pride.

Sterferep turned to the woman. "Now, madam…tell me your name and show me your face!"

"Aaargh!" screamed the scholar as he lifted his finger in the air. Clinging to it, was a bright yellow and red scorpion, which had administered its sting deep into the old man's weary finger. Lorca wailed in agony as he tried to shake it off.

Dwarpal and Sterferep both ran to his aid. Dwarpal drew a dagger from his waist and flung it, pinning the arthropod to the rotten, wooden desk, without scratching the researcher. Sterferep had to admit he was amazed by the precision of the throw. The scorpion's grip loosened as it suffered and eventually died. The researcher collapsed to the ground. The woman with the blue eyes made for the door, but before she could reach it, Sterferep drew his sword and struck it perfectly through the metal door ring and frame to seal it shut. This time it was Dwarpal who watched in admiration.

The woman struggled to open the door, but Sterferep advanced towards her, grabbed her arm, turned her around and struck the back of his hand across her face. One backhand from the brutish Lance was more than enough to send the woman to the floor unconscious. With one hand, Sterferep pulled his gladius free and opened the door.

"Dan, come, seize this woman! She has tried to assassinate Lorca! Dwarpal, see the chief researcher to medical aid!"

Dwarpal placed the stinking man on his shoulders and headed down the corridor toward the apothecary and royal physician. Dan grabbed the woman from the floor and held her in his arms as he locked the chamber and followed after Dwarpal.

"Dan, wait!" Sterferep called him back. "She was an assassin! She was here to kill the chief researcher, scholar Lorca!"

"What?"

"Dwarpal is taking Lorca to get some medical aid. We must take this woman to the dungeons."

"Right away, Lance." Dan adjusted his grip as he held the unconscious woman vertically in his arms and followed after Sterferep.

"How could you not have questioned her?" Sterferep demanded. "I am astonished!"

"I beg your pardon, Lance. Every day she would come here to the deliver breakfast. Never has there been an issue," clarified Dan innocently.

Sterferep had Dan stop. He turned towards the woman and removed the mask from her face. She was beautiful. She must have been in her mid-twenties. Fair-skinned, perfectly-shaped lips like rose petals, and the same stunningly-long eyelashes he had seen in the room. Though the side of her face was bruised and a stream of dried blood sat frozen on the side of her lips, Sterferep could not stop staring at her.

"Such beauty…what a shame! Take her to the dungeons and I will come with you."

Both started to walk towards to dungeons. Knowing the murderous intent of the woman, Dan was frightened to carry her, but his burden was lessened with Sterferep at his side. They reached the dungeons and placed the unconscious assailant in the darkest cell and locked her away.

CHAPTER 3

DYMONDO

Meanwhile Dymondo and Kor made their way to the royal court. The court at Gammafor was marvellous and was attended by many of the island's noblemen. There the King would hear the pleas of the people and would generally assent to their requests if he deemed them appropriate. He would also get a daily update from his advisers on the educational and economic status of the kingdom. He liked to know about the state of Gammafor's fertile farms, its soil, orchards and reservoirs. Any decline in the quality of these resources he addressed immediately. Then he would ask the physicians to inform him on the sanitary facilities of the country, and discussions would take place on improvements. Once the necessary tasks were completed, the King would then hear any criminal cases. Usually there were few because most people in the kingdom were educated and moral, but on the odd occasion a case came before him, he would listen closely and aim to be just in his decision.

When Dymondo entered the court, everyone stood at attention.

"Relax, no need for that. Please let us proceed with today's hearings," said Dymondo as he strode in and sat on his beautiful, golden throne encrusted with blue, purple and yellow gems. The armrests of the throne were in the shape of two golden lions. Dymondo, himself, wore a mixture of silver and golden armour with light-blue, silky fabrics.

The flag that fluttered atop the royal castle at Fourtfor was comprised of a golden lion lying on a field of half-purple and half-royal-blue cloth, the national colours of Landsfor during King Balathaar's reign. When Gammafor was formed, Dymondo ensured the traditional blue colour of his father's kingdom remained a part of his own flag and crest. Therefore, the crest for the Rains of Gammafor was a golden battle lion stitched on a royal-blue, shield-shaped fabric. The flag was the same with a gleaming yellow lion sewn onto a royal blue background.

"Education Minister Olivious!" roared Dymondo.

"My King," responded Olivious meekly.

"News has reached my ears that some fathers in the nation are preventing their young girls from attending school when the law clearly states education is compulsory up to the age of eighteen…for all! Is that true?"

No answer came from the frightened Olivious.

"Education Minister Olivious!"

"Yes, my King, that is true."

"Disgusting! Within the next three days I want every child attending school irrespective of what their stupid fathers say, and I want every head tutor in the schools to ensure the children are attending. Strict and prompt action is to be taken on this. Let this be a warning! All those parents and guardians who prevent their children from attending school shall face my wrath! I assure you, Minister Olivious, if this law is not obeyed, then I shall be very harsh in serving my punishment! Negligence will not be tolerated!" screamed Dymondo.

"It will be done as you command, my King." Olivious had his head down and his voice trembled.

Dymondo paused and lowered his voice. "Olivious, you are a great politician and a great minister. I am astonished that you could leave this grave matter of education unattended this long. As I understand it, this breach in policy has continued for ten days, yet you are absent of action. You disappoint me, Minister."

"Forgive me, my King, for I shall from now on be vigilant in matters of education."

"Indeed, you must. You are the education minister, and education is very important! Right, I have said enough and you have heard enough on this matter. Just concentrate on executing my order."

"Of course, my King."

"Right…let the other proceedings begin!"

After this heated opening, the courtiers and the King got down to the daily discussions and hearings resolving problems and completing tasks in a much calmer manner.

"Attention all, Queen Ohio enters!"

15

"Mother!" Dymondo spoke. He stood up from his throne. He was surprised by the announcement.

Everyone in court got up. They bowed to the gracious Queen as she entered.

"Hail Queen Ohio! Hail Queen Ohio!" Everyone shouted.

Dymondo walked up to her, kissed her hand and then embraced her.

"What a great surprise. You honour us, mother."

"Gratitude, my son. How do you fare?"

"Well! I am so pleased to see you…and slightly surprised. You should have sent word; I would have come to receive you myself at the shore."

"It is meant to be a surprise."

"Well received, mother. Most definitely, well received. Other than that-"

"Other than that I wanted to see my son. After all I too must see how my son fares his kingdom," she laughed.

Dymondo's smile weakened as she said that. Ohio was fast to notice Dymondo's hesitance.

"I but jest, I am here on holiday. I'd like to spend more time with you," she then said.

A portion of Dymondo's smile returned. "Come! Sit at the throne," said Dymondo as he put his arm around her and gestured to his seat.

"No, No. I do not wish to interfere. I come here to visit you. Not get involved in political matters. I am very tired from my journey and seek rest. I will retire to the royal guest chamber. Let the court proceedings go on."

Dymondo nodded and gestured towards his servants to come forth.

"Take Queen Ohio to the royal guest chamber," he ordered them. "Mother, shed your fatigue and rest well. I shall come to visit you soon."

Ohio smiled and as she left with servants and guards, everyone bowed again.

After the ministers and courtiers had finished presenting the necessary business of the day, Dymondo called for music and encouraged everyone to dance. The royal musicians arrived and soon the court was filled with the sounds of the lute, banjo and soft violin. As the music played, everyone at court performed the traditional Landsforian courtroom dance and enjoyed a tipple of the finest sweet red wine. At times the King would remain at the party till late, but sometimes he would retire to his chamber early and let the revellers go on without him. On this particular day, he remained, smiling at the enjoyment of the others.

Dymondo brought a balanced approach to his work. He would always give great thought to a given situation and circumstance prior to making his decision. He treated all equally and took his role seriously, repeatedly making attempts to improve on his actions the next time round. The welfare of his people was paramount. He was thoughtful, clever and sharp and in many ways difficult to pin down. He made some decisions with an emotional heart and some through pure pragmatism. He was neither greatly loved nor greatly feared, but he was respected by all his people. He made most all of his governing decisions himself with hardly any aid from his political advisors, ministers and courtiers. He was a natural and just leader.

Dymondo was not brutish like his eldest brother, but he had a fine body of medium height, toned to perfection. He had dark, medium-length hair and a tanned complexion. Highly skilled in hand-to-hand combat and the art of weaponry, and a musical maestro, he not only enjoyed listening to music, but composed many fine musical pieces himself, some of which were played at his court for the enjoyment of his dancing courtiers.

The evening was coming to an end, and the King had announced his retirement for the day. Dymondo kept an eye around the court for Sterferep, who had not yet returned from seeing Lorca. Little did the King know that Sterferep was dealing with an assassination attempt.

Little by little, the noblemen began to take the King's leave and disperse. The King himself stood from the throne and paid his respects to the departing courtiers.

Chief Minister Puyol, walked out with education minister Olivious and waited until they were away from court to speak to him.

"That must have been tough for you, Olivious," Puyol said.

"Yes, but we all know the King is strict about these matters. I should have used more initiative."

"It is good he is strict about education…is it not?"

"Of course. We are fortunate to have him as King."

"He is yet young, Olivious. What he has achieved so far is commendable."

"Indeed, but…"

"There is much room for improvement. I know."

"He only needs to take a step back and consider situations before charging at them with full speed."

Puyol did not reply.

"Do you not agree?" asked Olivious.

Creases formed on Puyol's forehead. "Today he was right to act quickly."

"Yes, I am not complaining about today, Chief Minister."

"Overall? Yes…the man can at times act like a boy. But he will only get better. At least it seems he's headed in that direction."

"I hope so…I do hope so!"

The two ministers continued walking until Sterferep hurriedly ran past them heading straight for the court.

"Apologies, Ministers!" he shouted as he ran by.

"What could that be?" asked Olivious.

Puyol shrugged his shoulders. "I do not know."

"Shall we follow?"

"Not sure, Olivious. I'll linger at the senate for an hour or two just in case the King summons anyone. But you head off home." Both nodded and went their separate ways.

Sterferep rushed into the court and went straight over to Dymondo.

"My King, I bring urgent and distressing news!"

"What is it Sterferep?"

"If the King would be so kind to step aside?"

"Of course," said Dymondo and went away with him.

"My King, Scholar Lorca has been poisoned," whispered Sterferep.

"Preposterous! Who dares invite death by assassinating Lorca?"

"Lorca yet draws breath…just barely. He currently is with the royal physician and the apothecary and the assailant has been seized."

"Who is this man?"

"A woman; she brought him his food along with a scorpion of the desert. The creature stung his finger."

"Scorpion of the desert? Their sting can be lethal! Outrageous! Does the assailant talk?"

"She has been taken to the dungeons. We have yet to commence interrogation. To restrain her, I had to raise my hand. She is yet unconscious. I came straight to you after having thrown her in the dungeons and after seeing that Lorca is in good care."

"After a strike from you…yes… I can imagine she will be out of her senses for a while."

Sterferep tightened his lips and shrugged his shoulders.

"Could you have not raised your hand?"

"It happened so fast, and she was attempting escape. I know I shouldn't have—"

"This assassination attempt is a breach Sterferep; it must not be taken lightly. How many people are aware of this?"

"Yourself, my King, along with the guards, Dan and Dwarpal, the dungeon master, the apothecary and the royal physician."

"No more must know for now, for the welfare of the society. I am appalled by the negligence of the guards outside Lorca's chamber. I shall certainly not be merciful in announcing their punishments!" said the King and began to walk away.

"A request, if the King would entertain," said Sterferep, causing the King to stop.

"Dan and Dwarpal are to be blamed, I agree. But I request that you show mercy towards them. Dan is young and soon to become Lance, and

18

Dwarpal—no matter how much I abhor the man's arrogance—he too is competent, loyal and a true servant. It is their first mistake and a genuine one. Please be kind."

"I cannot promise anything, Lance, for I am disappointed!"

"Dy—"

"No! Do not "Dy" me right now Sterferep! You know Lorca was doing an important investigation. If he dies, then we would have waited for nothing! We will have to start all over! I shall return to my chamber now, and you will accompany me! I would like to meet this…assailant!"

"Would it not be beneficial for the King to allow the dungeon master to interrogate her?"

"Perhaps," Dymondo said as he began to march out of the hall. His mind was too clouded with anger to ask about the nature of the interrogation. If he had asked, he would have learned that the dungeon master was an utterly unmerciful person.

As the King stomped off in anger, Sterferep followed close behind. Kor noticed their departure and promptly joined them.

"Where are those guards right now?" asked Dymondo.

"They should be back at their posts."

"Back guarding an empty chamber?"

"The chamber contains Lorca's scrolls and findings. But I have locked it, so no one could have entered in our absence."

Dymondo shook his head and continued marching forward, now towards Lorca's office. They all reached Lorca's office and found Dwarpal and Dan standing outside with their heads lowered. At the sight of their monarch, Dan and Dwarpal went down on one knee. Dymondo walked up to them and stood over the two with his hands on his waist. "How could you…?" Dymondo started to shout, but saw other guards and Lances walking down the corridor towards them. He paused and waited for them to pass. The passing guards and Lances bowed to the King and continued to walk on.

"Sterferep, please ensure that this chamber is sealed! You two come with me." Dymondo began marching back towards his own chamber. Kor followed behind and gestured to Dan and Dwarpal to follow. Sterferep checked Lorca's chamber, and once he was sure it was locked and the key was fastened tightly to his waist; he too followed Dan and Dwarpal.

When Dymondo reached his own chamber, Lance Tamaris Putyn, another one of Dymondo's trusted men, was standing outside. He was tall and slim but built. He had a thin face and long light-brown hair.

"Greetings, my King," Tamaris said with a bow.

"Greetings!"

Tamaris noted the King's mood and said nothing further as he opened the door. Dymondo stormed in followed by Kor who winked at Tamaris who responded with a cheeky grin. Kor then followed the King into his chamber with a straight face, followed by an intense and apprehensive looking Dan and Dwarpal.

The ever serious Sterferep entered last. "Shut the door," he said to Tamaris as he passed. Tamaris obeyed and quickly closed the chamber door after Sterferep.

The sudden entry of the five men into the chamber startled Mysteria, the royal chambermaid, who stopped what she was arranging and moved to stand in a corner. Dymondo went over and sat down on his large chair and stared outside the window at his kingdom, then looked over at the demure girl standing quietly in the corner.

"My lady, are you the new royal chambermaid?" he asked.

"Yes, sire," said Mysteria in a melodious voice. She was a pretty little flower with curly, black hair and soft, dark skin. Her flat, oval face suited her golden eyes.

Dymondo was very angry, but he did not want to crumple her spirit. "Please my lady, would you be so kind to step outside for a few moments whilst I speak with these men?"

"As you wish, my King," she said and walked outside to wait with Tamaris Putyn.

Dymondo waited for the door, then turned to the others.

"So, our chief researcher, scholar Lorca has been poisoned by a woman that brought him his food every day and our two competent, as you describe them, Sterferep, guards let her in without having carried out a thorough search…am I, right?" asked the King, looking at the two guards who still had their heads down.

"That is correct, my King. We should have been more vigilant and taken more caution and care," explained Dwarpal.

"We apologise for our incompetence, my King," added Dan.

"Lift your heads and look at me!" barked the King.

The two did as they were told.

"No man makes errors on purpose, that I know. But scholar Lorca was working on something very important! This is not just an attack on him. It is a conspiracy against our kingdom! Whoever did this was aware of Lorca's research and was doing what they could to stop it. Clearly they don't want me to discover the truth. So your mistake was more severe than you know."

"My King, may I speak?" asked Sterferep.

"Go on!" Dymondo said waving his hand furiously in the air.

"Dan and Dwarpal work very hard day and night and are true and loyal servants. I request my King show mercy and kindness when announcing their punishment."

Dwarpal looked up in astonishment at Sterferep's kindness in trying to defend them both. Dan too looked up but was not as stunned as Dwarpal.

"I understand, Sterferep. These two are under your tutelage, are they not?"

"Lance Kor fundamentally oversees the Lance training, but these two I have selected to train myself, that is correct."

"Sterferep, just look at their mistake! They were meant to inspect the food and question the woman who served it, every day. But they were negligent and now look at the consequences! What if Lorca dies? Who will be responsible?"

"My King, we accept any punishment you announce!" said Dwarpal.

Dymondo shook his head and looked outside his window again.

"My King, please show mercy," Sterferep persisted. "Scholar Lorca is in safe hands and I am sure the royal physician and the apothecary will mend him soon."

Dymondo shook his head again and did not know what punishment to serve. After long consideration, he at last spoke.

"Both of you will be assigned to a harder training regime. You will start at the crack of dawn and will not rest until dark! I cannot have any of my guards, soldiers or Lances behave so imprecisely. If Lorca's health deteriorates or he dies, further punishment will be announced. Now, out of my sight!" roared Dymondo and waved his hand in the air again and turned away from them.

Sterferep gestured to the two young men to leave. They bowed and knelt before Dymondo and left immediately.

"Dy—"

"No, Ster, now is not the time for this!" replied Dymondo and continued to stare out the window. "I wish to be alone. Send in the new royal chambermaid and leave me."

Sterferep knew it wasn't the time but he had to say some words before he left.

"Forgive me if I just say this before I leave. At the banquet, I saw King Grygerious's head turn towards you and Lorca as he spoke to you at the table, and when Lorca took you away to a corner to discuss it further, King Grygerious's eyes followed you both around the banquet hall and his smile vanished." Dymondo looked over at the tall Lance but did not say anything in return. After saying this, Sterferep and Kor, both bowed and left the chamber.

Mysteria quietly re-entered and stood in the farthest corner with her head down once again.

"You may continue with your work, my lady."

Mysteria curtsied. "As you wish, my King," she said in her soft voice and continued to work.

"What is your name?"

"Mysteria, my King."

"Mysterious name," smiled Dymondo. Her beauty was a cool spring that washed away his anger. "Does that mean Lady Mergonagie has left the royal chambermaid position?"

"Yes, sire. She retired from her position yesterday. Her old age would no longer allow her to work."

"Yes, I can imagine. Great lady, though. Always kind and caring towards me. I just hope she gets to spend more time with her grandchildren now. She often spoke of them at length."

"Oh, she loves them, sire. Yes, and I hope so too."

Dymondo smiled.

"I also hope that I can be a good royal chambermaid to you," she smiled.

"I'm sure you will be."

"…In every way," she added hesitantly and lowered her eyes.

"Why do you say it like that? Have I come across as abrupt? Apologies if I have, dear Mysteria."

"No, no. My King has been kind. It's just…."

"Say it, Mysteria. You need not be afraid."

"I am twenty-five years old, my King. Lady Mergonagie was elderly. The other chambermaids were whispering in the servant quarters that generally a young royal chambermaid is also expected to fulfil duties of a…"

"Of a?"

"…a mistress…. which is fine, but I just hope I can fulfil that part of my duty as well."

Dymondo stood up, shocked.

"Why do you believe you won't be able to perform that duty well?"

"I have never been with a man, my King."

Dymondo shook his head. "I am not one of those Kings, Mysteria. I do not consider my royal chambermaids as my mistresses or any of my helpers. Everyone is free here. You know that, don't you?"

"Yes, but what I have heard—"

"Forget that rubbish! I, the King, am saying this to you. For me, you are the royal chambermaid. That is all. Apart from your chambermaid services, no other service will be required of you. You need not worry. You have my word," smiled Dymondo. She looked at him with immense relief and satisfaction and smiled back and nodded. Dymondo turned to remove his cloak, walked over and handed it to her.

"My King…" Mysteria spoke as she took it from him.

"Yes?"

"Please do not for one moment think that I said what I said because you are not handsome. You are the most handsome man I have ever seen. It is just that I do not believe in the notion of mistresses, hence, the reason I said what I said."

"You need not explain yourself, my lady. I don't believe in mistresses myself." Dymondo removed his royal jacket and handed that to her as well, which she also took.

"And same goes for you, Mysteria. Do not for one moment believe I said what I said because I don't find you attractive. I find you very attractive," smiled Dymondo.

Mysteria smiled back. "You are cunning with words, my King."

"I only speak the truth."

Mysteria turned towards the wardrobe to hang his garments. She bit her lower lip and narrowed her eyes mischievously. She desired him. She did not want him to notice her dilating pupils or the fact that her nipples had now become visible through her dress.

CHAPTER 4

FRAIL SOVEREIGNTY

Grygerious was a lustful man. He was married to the beautiful Gilgenia, whom he never cared for. He did not have time for her feelings or her thoughts and choices. He rarely visited her chamber at night, and when he did, he only sought to fulfil his lustful desires. Many of these encounters took place without the consent of his wife. But when Grygerious had a thirst, it had to be quenched. At first, he enjoyed forcing himself upon Gilgenia, but after a while, he began to find her frustrating and ultimately unsatisfying. At times, after an unpleasant session, he would strike her across her beautiful face.

He resorted to taking mistresses, which served to satiate his desire and give him variety. He would lay his prying eyes on these women during court sessions and make it his prime aim to bed them, which he eventually did. And if by chance, he saw a beautiful young woman in his kingdom on the streets, he would invite her to court. But there was a price. To be a beautiful young woman at the Doosran court was to become a target of Grygerious's filthy character.

Grygerious was a well-groomed but vain man—an unfit King driven only by his selfish desires for liquor and women. He was at once cunning, cowardly, conniving, feeble, lazy and treacherous. He paid little attention to political affairs or matters of state, and he possessed neither an ounce of strength nor any knowledge of warfare. His only arts were deception and conspiracy. He was frail, soft and amiable, and he made his decisions based on emotion and not practicality. He generally preferred short-term gains over long-term profits. He brought a relaxed approach to his work, which often fell into indolence. His subjects liked him, but like Shilathaar, he was not respected. His people knew they were safe; not because their King was powerful, but because he had powerful kin.

Grygerious was of average height, with soft clean skin, a slim frame and silky, blonde hair. He was a pretty man of thirty, but unlike his older brother, he looked younger than his age. He loved musical instruments, though he could play none himself, and adored his maidservants singing to him. He mostly loved to be in the company of women, enjoying all the attention they gave him despite most of it being pretentious. He frequently took mistresses and was a womaniser, but he had no sense for politics and no knowledge on how to rule a kingdom. As such, he regularly needed his politicians, ministers and courtiers to advise him on matters of state. The people of Doosranfor became accustomed to their King's relaxed approach to governance and enjoyed life. Meanwhile, all those who loathed the languid life moved to Dymondo's island. Although the emigration numbers were significant, Grygerious still had enough subjects who adored him and his outlook as they themselves had, too, become lethargic. Nevertheless, his people constantly suspected that behind Grygerious's clean façade, there lurked a sinister man.

Doosranfor was known as the warmest island in the realm with a good climate all year round. Before the division, citizens of Gammafor and Fourtfor would come to visit the warm island for vacation. As such, the royal court sat in a large open-air courtyard with guards dressed in cream and white clothing and surrounded by dancing courtesans. Semi-nude young women bathed in the many shallow pools of water and danced for the entertainment of the men. Throughout the space, stood white pillars draped with gorgeous, silky sky-blue and white fabrics that billowed in the cool, morning breeze. The pillars were of smooth, white marble, contrasting with Grygerious's throne of gold.

Grygerious entered swiftly, skipping more than walking. He was late for court by at least an hour as he was every day, much to the continued frustration of Chief Minister Karnigol Aparata and Chief Courtier Gray Sylon, who were more concerned with running the kingdom. Grygerious wore silk linen and two diamond studs in each ear. As usual, he was clean shaven and let his long, silky, blonde hair hang loose. He took to the throne and all others sat before him. Both male and female musicians stood in the corners playing harps and other instruments, but not loud enough to drown out their King's voice.

"The latest, please, Chief Minister," said Grygerious.

"All is well, my King…"

"But how can that be," the King retorted, "when my father, may the Gods give him a place in heaven, decided my younger brother Dymondo should be the King of two islands?!"

The court fell silent. Just like Shilathaar, Grygerious repeated his complaint about his father's decision every day at court.

"I am not in the position to comment on this, my King," said Chief Minister Karnigol.

"Correct, you are not!" said the King and stood up with everyone following suit. He walked down from his throne with his head high and arms behind his back and stopped when he got to the centre of the court. He glanced over to the male servant carrying a tray of sweet wine and beckoned him over with his skinny finger. The servant walked over head down, and Grygerious took a silver goblet of wine from the golden tray, drained it, and grabbed another.

"This court has as much talent for politics as it has for music, dance and the performing arts," said Grygerious as he walked over to the one of the shallow pools and began leering at the semi-nude dancer frolicking in the water, who winked and smiled back at the shameless King. Grygerious took another gulp of his wine. He had to conclude matters of court urgently as now was his play time.

"I want each of you to come up with a solution. You all have three days starting from now," said the pretty King.

"Solution for what, my King?" asked Courtier Gray. He had a very mellow and soothing voice and spoke slowly as though he was intoxicated. He was in his late thirties.

"Solution for how I can become King of all four islands!" he proclaimed. "That is all for today's session. All ministers may disperse and get on with the task. All the lovely ladies and harp players follow me!"

With that, he left the court, followed by his cortege. He walked through his palace and directly towards the open-air baths. All ministers gradually left the court muttering amongst themselves; all but Karnigol and Gray.

"Hah!" sighed Gray in relief once everyone had left. "Another three days of no work at all."

"No work? He has asked us to come up with solutions on how we can improve his economy," replied Karnigol.

"Correction, my lord, he asked everyone to come up with a solution on how he—that halfwit—can become the ruler of the four islands; surpassing the mighty Shilathaar!"

"You are forgetting Dymondo, dear Gray."

"I do not know much about him and his valour, but I do know of Shilathaar. He is the greatest!"

"He is a tyrant," clarified Karnigol in an old voice. Older than Gray, Karnigol was a man of dignity, unlike his King.

"Even so, our King is no match for him in battle," replied Gray.

"Grygerious does not wish to fight. He but conspires…" whispered Karnigol.

Karnigol was right. The beautiful, young women who usually sat around Grygerious in the baths would incite him into believing he should slay his two brothers and seize the realm, not by strength, but by treachery. They would tell him, if he did not do this, then his frailty and vulnerability would one day be his downfall.

"What a demon! He has no honour or shame," whispered Gray. "Do you have a strategy for him?"

"I do… but I have not yet presented it to him."

"You must tell me!" implored Gray.

"No, I cannot tell anyone other than the King himself. I am not proud of this plan, dear Gray. It is deceptive and evil. But I shall tell it to him on the fourth day."

"On the fourth day, he won't even remember what task he set before us."

"Come on Gray, we must do our duty."

"I came up with a solution the first time he tasked his ministers with something. It was not as a grand of a task as this, but I still gave it my labour. I have yet to present that solution to him, and I know for sure he will never ask for it because he has forgotten all about it. I am sure all the other ministers know this, too."

"Gray."

"Chief Minister Karnigol, he has now asked us to do this particular task seventeen times. I remember the first time he set us to it. After four days, he failed to ask his ministers for their solutions. The second time, he failed to even present himself at court. After a few glasses of red wine and an hour in the baths, he will not remember a word of his own instructions."

Karnigol had no reply but to stare at the beautiful marble ground before him. Gray was right; Grygerious was useless at following up on his own instructions. The two ministers many times would make important decisions on his behalf without his knowledge—a great risk they frequently took out of necessity. All other ministers were too afraid to take any actions without first hearing a decision from the King. But Grygerious never decided on anything. Even when ministers sought his permission before the implementation of a new initiative, he would say to them he would return with a decision in two days and then be away from court for the next six. To move everything forward, Chief Minister Karnigol, with Courtier Gray's help, made most of the decisions.

"I am going home to my wife and have some long-overdue coitus," Gray said. "The children are at school, so it's a good opportunity, and my wife will be pleased."

"Oh Gray, have some shame, young man," laughed the wise old Karnigol. "I see Kalaria as my daughter!"

"The King has no shame. He is openly sinking his face between the breasts of his countless mistresses during his daily baths. Why should I be ashamed of having sex with my own wife in my own house?" jested Gray.

"Away with you, Gray. I will see you in court tomorrow," smiled Karnigol.

"I say, Chief Minister, you too should head home. Only you are to be found in the senate after court, scribbling away on your scroll and carving your slates. Go home and spend some pleasurable time with your wife," Gray continued to joke.

"Err...now that will not be necessary. I am quite alright."

"Suit yourself. I'll see you tomorrow at court, old man...and don't work too hard," said Gray as he started to walk off.

"Someone has to... we cannot all walk away from our duties."

"Hah! Duties? What duties?" Gray proclaimed, holding his arms out as he continued walking backwards. "Everything is how it should be. Life continues. No improvements required."

"Says who?"

"The ruler of this beautiful and musical land! The place where all men hold their cocks between there lazy soft legs... oh wait a minute... do they even have cocks?" laughed Gray spitefully.

Karnigol could sense his frustration. "Quiet, young man! Someone will hear!"

"No one will hear. The King is sitting in a hot bath surrounded by beautiful nymphs, sucking on their erect nipples whilst having his cock stroked. All the other ministers are home thrusting their seedless penises into their women's twats. And everyone else is either dancing, or playing the harp or enacting a scene from one of Maximillian Shoves-Word's many plays."

"Julius Breaksteer."

"Shoves-Word is better. Breaksteer is more famous in other lands," smiled Gray.

"You say men in this land have no cocks? Well...much thrusting is taking place all around, don't you think?"

"Fine, I will let you have that comment, but pit any of our guards up against one of the Lances from Gammafor—no, forget the Lances, pit them against a lowly Gamman guard—and I assure you, their cocks will shrivel up to nothing, and they will piss in their silky, white togas and break wet wind!"

Karnigol looked here and there to ensure no one was around. He then walked up to Gray and placed both his hands on his shoulders.

"Gray, calm yourself. Be quiet now. I know your frustration. You are a clever politician and diplomat, but this is our life. We must serve our King. He has no head for politics or diplomacy, true. He does not know how to run a kingdom," whispered Karnigol. "That is why we have the opportunity we have—to run this kingdom like a King should. This is a great learning experience for us and it will make us better scholars and politicians. Deep inside, both of us know that we are in charge and so far it is going well.

"Just well enough."

"Yes, I know. But as long as the King gets his women and wine, we can do anything we wish. And when I say anything, I mean anything."

"What are you implying, Karnigol?"

"I believe you understand what I mean," answered Karnigol with a subtle grin. "Does that not give you satisfaction?

"Running the Kingdom?... At first, but now it is getting monotonous— the same old excrement every day!"

"Ssh! Gray, I order you to keep your voice down! Not as Chief Minister, but as a person you respect. Please say no more."

"But I am not used to being so idle."

"Well then, think of the benefit such idle time gives you to learn what you have always wished to learn. My father made sure I kept away from blades and maces, but now I am learning how to wield a sword. You too should learn the gladius or the spear. It will do you good."

"Karnigol, you are like a father to me and my mentor. I cannot disrespect you and I am not disrespecting you now. I am just so fucked off by this entire situation. It feels like my head is going to explode. Sometimes I cannot bear it!"

Karnigol hugged Gray. "You must remain strong, Son. Good days will come. Learn the sword."

"Aye, aye! No need to get emotional with me now old man," smiled Gray as he gently pulled back from his mentor's embrace. "The only other respectable person in this kingdom apart from yourself is perhaps Queen Gilgenia. Damn, I feel so sorry for her. She is one of the most beautiful women in Doosranfor, and our King does not even look at her."

"Gray, that is not your place. We must not involve ourselves with the matters of the royal family."

"True, but what I say is not wrong."

"Right, head home and do not let your mind be clouded with such thoughts."

"Too right. I mean just imagine me thinking about politics whilst I bang my woman! Hah! That would indeed be inappropriate."

"All the Gods, please put some sense into this boy's head!" prayed Karnigol.

"Impossible. There is no space, ha-ha!"

"Go," smiled Karnigol, "and I too shall head home for the first time ever before midday."

"That's more like it, old man! Now you have joined the celebrations. Oh and… from whom can I learn the gladius?"

"Try the old cobbler on Bargyle Path. He lives in an old green hut. You will see it."

They both smiled and left the court in different directions.

As Karnigol walked home, he thought of Gray's comment regarding Gilgenia, Grygerious's wife. This alliance had never been her choice. She and the King had been forced into it, and as such, she continuously suffered insults and disrespect as her husband chose to spend more time with his mistresses than with her. Still, the Queen remained honourable and faithful despite her husband's atrocities. She always dressed elegantly in decent dresses that covered her shoulders and upper arms, setting herself apart from the half-naked courtesans preferred by Grygerious.

Meanwhile, Grygerious sat in his fresh-water bath, filled with a combination of sensual aromas, as perfumes and cleansing oils were poured in to make the water irresistible. The sun shone brightly in the sky, warming the water. It was a glorious day in Doosranfor with blue skies and hardly any clouds. Around the large pool stood servants holding golden platters of savoury foods, succulent fruits and containers of sweet wine and liquor. Inside the bath sat the King himself surrounded by many beautiful young women—all maidservants and all nude. Some scrubbed his shoulders, some his arms and others his feet. Grygerious held a golden goblet of wine in one hand and with the other gently touched the ladies as they came close. One magnificently beautiful young woman in her early twenties sat nearest to him. She too was holding a golden goblet with wine in one hand and a bunch of black grapes in the other. She fed her King the grapes and giggled as he touched and caressed her naked body.

"The Gods truly bless us with great sun and breeze this afternoon," Grygerious said. "It is a perfect day to just relax after a tiring day at court."

All the girls giggled and smiled at Grygerious's comment. The young woman next to him came closer and sat on his lap.

"A tiring day, was it my King?" she asked. She giggled as she put the goblet to his lips for him to drink and then placed the bunch of grapes above his head for him to pluck with his tongue and lips. He tugged the grape from the bunch and held it in his front teeth, then brought his lips closer to hers for her to bite half. Their lips collided and they both laughed as the girl playfully leaned away.

"Tiring! Of course, my lady! Every day is tiring! It is not easy being King!"

"Of course, my King, you work very hard!" agreed the girl as she came close again to his face and the two kissed. When the kiss finished, he placed his hand over her wet breast and began rubbing his thumb over her tight nipple.

"What worries my King? Why is sire not enjoying his bath this afternoon?"

"Many thoughts occupy me, Cresenia! The most pressing is how I can become King of all four islands!"

"Is that what the King desires?"

"Above all! However, I do not believe in bloodshed and war! So how can I remove my brothers from power? This thought occupies my mind every day!"

"Hmm... a rather precarious situation! Wars are not only won on battlefields, my King... there are other ways!"

"What other ways?"

"Their mention is forbidden!" she giggled.

"I wish to hear them, my lady," said Grygerious as he grabbed her entire right bosom tightly. Cresenia groaned.

"It is a conversation to be had in private," she purred.

She had Grygerious's full attention.

"Tell me!" he commanded.

"Not here, my King; for there are too many ears. I shall tell you of it when it is just you....and I..." she said, bringing her lips to his ear "...in the royal chamber." She gently bit his ear and chuckled.

Grygerious was not a patient man. "Disperse! All of you!" he shouted and all the servant men and women left the bath and surrounding area, leaving just Cresenia and the King alone in the steaming pool.

"Now...there is no one else but us!"

She rubbed herself against his manhood and they gently began intercourse as she started to tell him: "Have you heard of poison damsels, my King?"

"Poison damsels?"

"Yes, my King, a poison damsel is a mysterious, but greatly seductive woman!"

"Like you?" laughed Grygerious and thrusted faster.

"Oh!" she groaned and continued to explain. "No jest! Listen carefully. She is a woman whose charms would ensnare her lover in her insurmountable beauty."

"Go on."

"But this is not a normal woman… oh no!" groaned Cresenia.

"Then what is she?"

"A poison damsel! And he who indulges in sexual intercourse with her shall perish from the poison that flows inside her. Some men have perished by just the exchange of saliva from a kiss. Those who are very weak."

"Nonsense! How can a woman be poisonous? Would the poison not kill her?"

"No. These practices still exist, but they are not known nor available to the common man. A young girl who is orphaned gets kidnapped and is made to consume poison at an early age, bit by bit every day."

"And does that not kill her?"

"Yes, many die even by exposing them to a low-intensity of the poison. But there are those who do not and develop a tolerance. They are then continuously fed this poison…gradually becoming stronger and ever more immune to it. As the poison gets stronger, and they become immune, they become more lethal. This continues until the girls become adults. Then these women are sent to entrap men. If a man ends up having any sexual contact with them, he will meet his end!"

Grygerious had no words. He stopped thrusting and withdrew.

"Oh, my King, why stop?!"

"Where are these women?"

"I am surprised this means so much to you, my King. Every Chief Minister would know how to locate them. Poison damsels are at times sent to remove men who cause hindrances and concerns to Kings. Now…may we continue?"

Grygerious was no longer interested in coitus and stood up.

"Marvellous!" he said. "Come with me right now, for I shall summon Karnigol to discuss this further!"

"The time for that shall soon come, my King. Everyone has retired for the day."

"When will that time come?"

"Soon, my King!" There was a slight frustration in her voice, yet her smile remained intact. Cresenia put her arms around him and dragged him into the water playfully

"Tell me Cresenia…these damsels…what do they look like?"

Cresenia let out a sigh of dissatisfaction. "They are beautiful young women, my King. Incalculably beautiful."

"Tell me more."

"Well…they do have one distinguishing feature, though it is not definite. A majority of these women have striking blue eyes."

"Blue eyes eh? Ha-ha! Sounds slightly absurd!"

"Whatever the King wishes to call it; now where were we?"

"Show me your eyes, Cresenia."

"The King suspects me?" she smiled. "See…my eyes are not blue." She widened her pretty light brown eyes as she brought her face close to his.

"Ha-ha I but jest with you!" he smiled and both went back to making love in the bath.

CHAPTER 5

THE TYRANT AND HIS WIFE

As he walked, the ground beneath his feet trembled. Everyone in the court stood at attention and bowed as he marched up to the shining silver throne, situated ten steps off the ground. As he reached his seat, he stopped and turned to face his court, his heavy cloak swinging behind him. He stood tall and broad; wearing black fur boots and a black fur tunic which went down below his knees. Over the tunic, he wore heavy, golden body armour with shoulder plates that covered his chest. Attached to the armour were golden chain tassels that hung from his shoulders down to his elbows. Placed on his thick head of dark, wavy hair sat a golden crown made of sapphires and rubies. His chin supported a thick, groomed beard, and his golden groin support, he wore as a belt around his waist. He was King Shilathaar of Forprimiera.

Under his rule, the island of Forprimiera was now much restricted. Shilathaar loved the control and the power he had over his people, and he was both ruthless and reckless in his decisions. It would be correct to say he was a dictator, feared but not respected as he was driven by arrogance. The atmosphere in the city and villages was hostile and tense. He had no space for delicate objects in his life.

To Shilathaar, his sword and his mace were all that mattered. He was skilled in warfare and an effective commander of armies. In past battles against Blee and Orakray, he had led many men into battle under his father's banner and captained several winning legions. He did not face any intrusions since no one in the land was a match for such a warrior.

When he made his decisions, no one dared to question them, regardless of them being reasonable or not. During his reign, no person was permitted to leave the island to see what life was like elsewhere. His subjects constantly looked upset and gloomy, yet they lacked nothing; hence, they did not complain about their fate. This was how Shilathaar ran his island.

***

"Sit," he commanded in his deep voice as he sat on his throne. On one side of him, rested his fierce golden mace with its singular spike at the top and on the other his glimmering sword.

All of the courtiers followed their King's command, and once settled, the chief courtier, Orpictus Rali, stood and bowed to get the King's attention. The King permitted him to speak, and the chief courtier unrolled his scroll.

"My King, you will be pleased to know that the country is prospering. Food is plenty, farms are full of vegetables, and crime has decreased as more men have taken up noble professions to earn a living. Children are studying well and are becoming knowledgeable, and the overall health of the subjects is good."

No reply from the King. Not even a nod of acknowledgement.

"Does that not please my King?" asked the chief courtier hesitantly.

The King looked at him; "Hmm…" he grunted. He was clearly not satisfied.

"What else does my King want?" Orpictus asked.

Shilathaar glared at his chief courtier. "You know what I want! I want to be the lone King of the four lands that make up our kingdom. I am the eldest son of King Balathaar. I am the rightful heir and ruler. So why am I only the King of Forprimiera?!" he shouted.

Orpictus kept mum as the King's anger was boiling.

"Don't tell me all is well, Chief Courtier Orpictus. All is not well."

Silence lingered over the court.

"What else?!" roared Shilathaar.

"My King, we have a criminal to present to you," said Orpictus.

"Criminal? Who dares commit a crime in my kingdom?"

"Call him in!" shouted the bald Orpictus. Though he had joined the court of Forprimiera with a full head of hair, now the only hair remaining were the ones around his temples and the back of his head. Orpictus was the kind of person whose life hung by a thread. Any slip of the tongue before the King could result in him in having none. To survive, he learned to be clever and patient.

Two soldiers brought in a man dressed in a dirty, tattered, white tunic and bound in heavy, iron chains. The man had soulful eyes.

"What has he done?" growled Shilathaar.

"My King, this man is a local bread merchant. He sells bread to the people. A thief attempted to steal his bread, so he gave chase until the thief ran into an alley with no exit. The thief was trapped and drew a small knife from his pocket to steer this bread merchant away. Undeterred by the blade, the bread merchant fought the thief and managed to take back his bread, but during the brawl, the thief got wounded by his own knife and expired."

"He murdered a man! That's a grave sin!" exclaimed Shilathaar.

"My King, the man he killed was a thief, a menace to society. I assure you his death was unintentional. This vendor earns his living respectfully."

"Very well... we shall give him a painless death!"

"No, my King, no, please have mercy!" shouted the bread vendor.

"My King, I truly recommend you show this man mercy for all he was attempting to do was rescue his merchandise from a thief. Punishment is in order but not death, my King," said Orpictus assertively.

Shilathaar realised he had decided recklessly, but he could not go back on his words now, and he could most definitely not have a mere courtier speak to him in such a way.

"Silence! I shall hear no further argument, Orpictus! Killing someone is wrong; therefore, it is punishable!"

"Yet the intent was not there..."

"...Orpictus! Quiet!" roared Shilathaar.

Orpictus lowered his head and said no more. Shilathaar stared at his chief courtier's bald head, his red eyes boiling with anger. He thought for a while. The thief was in the wrong to carry weapons and to steal. The vendor genuinely had been trying to rescue his bread.

"Very well!" Shilathaar said. "I will spare his life purely because he did not have murderous intent. But imprisonment for the man is in order! I sentence him to seven years!"

Orpictus was surprised yet relieved. Generally, Shilathaar could not be moved after ordering an execution. Still, this was a horrendous decision in its own right.

"Take him away!" shouted Shilathaar.

The vendor wailed and begged to be set free, but no one listened. As the man was led out, the courtiers looked over at him with sympathetic eyes but could do nothing at all.

"That shall be all!" announced Shilathaar smashing his hands against his thighs as he rose from his throne. Every courtier stood immediately as he rose and held their breath as he walked down the steps from his throne and out of court.

Everyone sighed in relief as he left. All the courtiers began gathering their items and headed for the door, murmuring. The old Prime Minister walked over to Orpictus.

"It is never a simple day for you is it, Orpictus."

"No," replied Orpictus wiping the cold sweat from his bald head. "But we can think of today as simple. It could have been a lot worse."

"I suppose. I remember the times when he would refuse to go back on his words once he had uttered them. Perhaps things are changing."

"I wouldn't be too pleased and perceive this as an improvement. Much more is yet required. Pardon me, Prime Minister, but I must head home, for I do not wish to stay here any longer than I need to."

The Prime Minister nodded. "Neither do I, Orpictus …neither do I." Orpictus nodded back and swiftly headed for the exit but stopped and turned.

"Was there something in particular, Prime Minister?"

"No, no Orpictus head off home; I was just casually exchanging words with you."

"I appreciate that. You too should head home. Doesn't this place frighten you?"

The old man pondered for a while. "Sure it does! The entire city frightens me, though. Whom does it not frighten? Shilathaar's anger erupts like lava. Only you have the courage to stand in its path."

"If the coin hadn't been so good, then I would have never found the courage to do so. I would've happily risked my head in attempting to escape to Gammafor. Living in fear every day is just outrageous! I kiss my wife goodbye every day as if it's going to be my last because I fear, one of these days, I may not return."

"Everyone is frightened, Orpictus, not only you."

"And you say he's changing? Nothing will change around here. If anything, it is likely to get worse. I must go, Prime Minister, forgive me."

"Off you go, Orpictus! May the Gods go with you."

"And may they go with you, too," Orpictus said and headed home.

The Prime Minister took another deep breath and looked up to the marvellous, handcrafted, marble ceiling overhead. He was the only one left in the great hall. He placed his hands behind his back and let his head drop. A salty tear dropped upon his tongue and his lips shook as he wiped the rest of his tears away.

Shilathaar headed for the training ground after court. Generally he would spar with Gladiators, but today he would spar with a recently acquired elephant as the animal required taming. The elephant stood like a God upon the sands with ten ropes around its neck and ten strong guards standing at the end of each one, doing their utmost to keep the beast under control.

Shilathaar looked at the beast, and he gestured to the guards to unleash the animal upon him. The guards did as commanded and moved back into the corners of the compound. Queen Silvenia had wandered over and was now in the viewing gallery to witness her King train with this out-of-control creature.

"Bring me the grapes!" she ordered one of the maidservants as she reclined on the couch.

Shilathaar put up an awesome display charging toward the elephant and positioning himself to climb atop the beast to control it, but the animal was adamant and avoided every attempt. The elephant would swing its trunk preventing the King from getting near. Shilathaar eventually noticed his wife in the gallery. Both exchanged cunning smiles. She placed the bunch of grapes back onto the silver plate before putting her hand between her legs. Shilathaar took note and wiped the sweat from underneath his nose. He gained a sudden boost of energy, knowing his beloved wife was watching him from above.

The elephant trumpeted, raising its two front feet and its trunk in the air only to smash its feet back down onto the sand. It swung its trunk with vigour, only just missing Shilathaar. Shilathaar yelled at the beast—a roar that was more than equal to the elephant's trumpet. Shilathaar's body gleamed in the sun as he sped toward the elephant and ran up the trunk but misplaced his footing and just missed the elephant's forehead. The elephant took advantage of the slip and threw the King off onto the coarse sand. Silvenia placed her hand upon her chest, though she did not flinch at her husband's rough landing. Not a crease of tension shown on her forehead, only a lustful smile.

Blood began to flow from Shilathaar's lips. He tasted it and his eyes turned red. He wiped the sand from his face. The sand felt wet from the sweat and blood. The elephant's onslaught had not finished. Shilathaar turned to see the beast charging at him with great speed, but he got up and moved out of the path of the stampeding animal, and just as the elephant rushed past, Shilathaar struck his iron like fist upon its tough tusk with tremendous force. The tusk snapped off and fell to the ground.

Silvenia began to vigorously pleasure herself at the sight of her man breaking off the elephant's thick tusk with one blow.

Shilathaar's anger grew. He had had enough. He ran towards the elephant, which lifted its foot to crush the King, but Shilathaar reached up and grabbed the foot with his bare hands. The beast could not put its foot down as Shilathaar's powerful hold was immeasurably strong.

Silvenia's hand moved faster as Shilathaar threw the foot to one side, causing the elephant to lose its balance. Then Shilathaar again ran up the trunk, this time getting the footing correct and sat upon the animal. Silvenia was at her threshold of climax as the elephant attempted everything to throw the King off.

"Hook!" Shilathaar ordered. One of the guards threw the bull hook to him, so he could tame the elephant. Shilathaar caught it with precision and placed it hard upon the elephant's head.

"Calm!" he ordered the beast. His voice boomed in the elephant's ear, striking fear into every part of the animal. The elephant was no longer out of control. The now-tamed animal settled. Silvenia too was satisfied.

"Calm!" Shilathaar repeated his command. The elephant sat down as Shilathaar sat upon it victorious. He threw the bull hook back to the guard and sat on the animal with his hand placed on his hips looking up to his wife in the gallery. She raised her head high and stood and leaned upon the bannister rail and smiled and nodded at him. Shilathaar smiled back.

She was heading to baths and beckoned him to follow her with her index finger; winking at him as she left the balcony. Shilathaar jumped off the elephant, patted his new obedient animal and handed it over to the guards. The guards were now able to control the elephant with the bull hook. Shilathaar brushed off the dirt from his biceps and hands and marched across the training ground toward the baths.

CHAPTER 6

LANDSFOR

Prior to the division of Landsfor, it was a united kingdom, comprised of four islands, ruled by the powerful King Balathaar Rain and blessed by the Lord of Water, God Aquinious. Outside Landsfor, lay the Outer Islands. On the two northern outer islands were the kingdoms of Blee and Orakray, while to the south lay the single island kingdom of Haask. Many times, the northern Kings attempted to conquer Landsfor, but each time failed miserably. To put an end to all the futile fighting, a peace treaty was enacted between the Outer Islands and Landsfor; however only the two northern Outer Islands of Blee and Orakray signed the treaty, and as time went on, the nations became allies and eventually relatives.

Only the kingdom of Haask, the southern Outer Island, decided to remain impartial as it always had. Before the treaty was signed, if any of the northern Outer Island kingdoms attacked Landsfor, Haask would decline to help Landsfor or any of the invaders. For that matter, Haask never tried to occupy any other land, and for anyone who dared attack Haask, they suffered a gruesome fate. As such, the name of Haask was uttered with utmost respect throughout the realm.

Landsfor was profoundly influenced by historical invasions long before the reign of King Balathaar and his father, King Komodothaar Rain. The invaders brought with them lifestyle changes, rules and laws, and though they always left, their laws, influence, and archaeology remained. They had much influence on the people, and grandparents told many heroic stories of ancient heroes to their grandchildren, inspiring them to become just as valiant. Due to these influences, the people of Landsfor wore a mixture of attire, some influenced by their own history and some by the invaders. They were polytheists, worshipping multiple Gods and deities, just like their invading forefathers. Though Doosranfor enjoyed warm sun through the year, generally, the rains poured down onto all the lands and there was never a drought. As such, the soil on all four islands was rich and fertile. A large variety of vegetables and fruits grew and the people were blessed by the Goddess of Wind Fizha for the fresh air they breathed, often enjoying the sight of pure white clouds gently gliding over green forests and plains and brushing against sturdy mountain peaks.

There were many learned men and women on all four islands as education in Landsfor was of the highest standard. Those with wealth, lived in large houses constructed after the style of villas and staffed by house servants. Keeping servants or slaves was a controversial matter on Gammafor and Fourtfor, but under Shilathaar's and Grygerious's rule, masters owned slaves with impunity. Dymondo disagreed with this notion deeply, and for years engaged in debates over the topic with his politicians and ministers. He wished slavery to be abolished as he believed every person had a right to freedom; however, he understood the realities of tradition and economics. Thus he conceded that people would be allowed to keep house servants or 'helpers,' as he liked to call them, instead of slaves, but the master must not own the person. However, as the matter had not yet been settled and the law codified, the people continued to purchase and sell slaves and treat them as they saw fit. But Dymondo, himself, followed what he believed in. He had many servants and chambermaids, but he treated them well and like free people. They had homes to go to after their day's work, and for those who did not have homes, he had servant rooms built, so if the servant wished, he or she could stay in the castle.

Before King Balathaar died, he astutely had his eldest son married to princess Silvenia of Orakray purely for allegiance with King Orayus. Orayus Laaris was a powerful ruler, yet King Balathaar and Shilathaar had won many battles against him before the treaty was signed and their alliance was formed. After the treaty and the subsequent marriage, King Balathaar and Orayus kept good relations. Silvenia was only a year younger than Shilathaar, and as it turned out, Orakray was conveniently situated closer to Forprimiera, the island of which Shilathaar became the ruler.

When Shilathaar was growing up, he was not a sociable person. He adored his weapons and wrestling much more. After a full day's training, hunting and wrestling he would take his wine, an evening bath and would generally take one of the maids to his bed. As it turned out, this made him and Silvenia a great pair. She was eccentric and had a dirty mind. Although it was not public knowledge, she would on occasion ask her maidservants to summon one of the gladiators from the ludus into her own chamber to engage in coitus with them. Shilathaar knew of her activities with the gladiators and she knew of his with the maidservants, but this did not sour their lustful relationship in anyway. She knew the passage to his heart, and that was to keep adding fuel to his one and only desire, to become King of all the islands. She would constantly prompt him to build strength and allies. This pleased, and to a certain extent, aroused Shilathaar as he saw that his wife was not a gentle flower—that the same maliciousness lingered inside his spouse that lay within himself. In return she delighted in her husband exerting his power and control, whether it was over his subjects or over her in bed.

Seeing the benefit of the marriage alliance with Orakray, King Balathaar had his second son Grygerious married to Gilgenia from Blee, the island nation to the north of Doosranfor. She was a year younger than Grygerious, and after their own peace treaty was signed, she would come to visit Fourtfor with her parents when The King of Blee, Pharose Godsay, now a good friend of King Balathaar, would come to visit Fourtfor for holidays. The feud between Blee and Landsfor had existed when both King Balathaar's and Pharose's fathers were on the throne. Due to the old feud, King Balathaar was cautious of Pharose, but he could not overlook Pharose's effort to establish a friendship with him, so he cunningly decided to put an end to his worries and suggested the alliance of their families through marriage. Unfortunately, the betrothed were wed against their wills.

Oddly, it was Gilgenia and Dymondo who became great friends. When Gilgenia would visit Landsfor with her parents before she was betrothed to Grygerious, she and her younger sister, Rubiana, who was two years younger than Gilgenia, would spend much of their time with Dymondo, riding their horses down to the island shores, laughing all the way. Gilgenia and Dymondo soon became the best of friends and she began to love him as she spent more time with him. When Rubiana, did not join them on their adventures, it gave Gilgenia and Dymondo time to grow much closer. Dymondo, however, only saw Gilgenia as a friend and nothing more.

Grygerious was closer to Helemanen, Gilgenia's elder brother. Grygerious and Helemanen were very much alike in age and personality. Both were lecherous and desired nothing but wine and women. When Helemanen would visit, both he and Grygerious would disguise themselves as men of lesser station and sneak into underground brothels and ale houses, often not returning until the early hours of the morning.

When the engagement was set, Grygerious refused as he was not interested in getting married and wanted to continue enjoying his sweet wine and mistresses. Gilgenia refused as she knew what a slimy personality Grygerious had. She knew that, like her brother, he was nothing more than a sex fiend and a dirty-minded person. But Balathaar and Pharose, more concerned with their alliance, insisted that the marriage go forward. Gilgenia hoped for Dymondo to intervene and offer to take her hand in marriage, but he remained silent. Gilgenia gathered all her courage and expressed her love to him, but he kindly refused. She tried harder, forcefully kissing him, but he withdrew from the gesture as kindly as he could.

Dymondo felt bad for refusing Gilgenia's love, and most of all felt terrible that she had to marry his womanising brother. But his mind was set, and his refusal broke Gilgenia's heart. Nothing was left for her now. When it came to the thought of love, she became a stone. All her dreams, desires and wishes had perished, and all that remained was to do her duty. Thus Grygerious and Gilgenia were tied in wedlock.

Meanwhile, the kingdom of Haask lay to the south, situated near Gammafor. Haask was a powerful nation with high walls surrounding its border. As such, very few could enter, and only after much deliberation. This included rulers and Kings of the neighbouring lands. Haask was an independent and impartial kingdom with no friends and no enemies, and they wished to keep it that way. Haask was a rich land that did not require any resources from any other kingdoms. It was a kingdom of great might, and anyone who attacked perished in the attempt. For those that extended hands of friendship, such proposals were kindly rejected. Haask lived in harmony and caused no harm or concern to anyone, and in return they expected not to be disturbed.

People whispered that King Balathaar once sent a message to the King of Haask asking for one of his daughter's hand in marriage for his own son, Dymondo, but the King of Haask politely refused, adding that he was the father of four sons and had no daughters to give. King Balathaar buried all expectations of any counter proposal that may arrive from Haask regarding his daughter, Nilharia, but he would regularly send seasonal and festive greeting scrolls to the King of Haask. Haask never reciprocated the gesture.

There was a small island north of Haask and south of Gammafor. Haask never claimed it as their territory; therefore, the island was assumed to be part of Gammafor, and Dymondo used it to banish criminals from his kingdom. Rumours said a vicious tribe resided deep in the forest, but other than the criminals Dymondo sent, nobody ventured to the island to find out. It was not forbidden for Fourtans and Gammans to travel to the island, but hardly anyone did, and no man from the island ever visited the mainland either. However, Dymondo had a tall fort built on Gammafor's southern shore and had guards situated atop it to keep a close eye on the island for any activity.

CHAPTER 7

NILHARIA AND VELVIA

Next day, when the time arrived for singing and dancing to begin, at Gammafor court, the attractive young sister of the King, Nilharia Rain, and her beautiful friend and lady in waiting, Velvia Dweller, took to the floor first. Nilharia was a jovial young woman. She was nearly four years younger than Dymondo and a striking beauty. She had amazing green eyes and long, wavy blonde locks which crashed down to her soft shoulders. Around her forehead, she supported a braided Goddess look. Her figure seemed moulded by the creator himself. Any man would find it hard to restrain fixing his gaze on that marvel. Her jewels, pins and chains were made from gold and generally encrusted with crystals and diamonds. She loved the colours light blue and white and would habitually choose to wear dresses of these colours. On rare occasions, she would dress in a light summery yellow. Her friend, Velvia, often told her, when she wore yellow, events took an inauspicious turn. But she ignored her friend's advice and did as she wished.

She lived in the royal palace at Gammafor, choosing not live with her mother at Fourtfor as Queen Ohio would generally ask her to constrain her ebullient and zestful nature. The princess was fickle and capricious and she despised her mother's continuous restrictions and scolding. Her mother

44

would teach her to sit straight and be elegant like a princess, but Nilharia would not listen. Instead, she decided to go live with her brother in the royal palace and the royal castle at Gammafor. Her brother couldn't be happier with the arrangement. He adored her. She was the apple of his eye, and he always saw her as his daughter rather than his younger sister. The people loved the jovial princess as her innocence and exuberant behaviour would bring a smile to everyone's face.

Velvia her best friend and lady in waiting had been orphaned at an early age. She came from a poor family. Her father made cider from the apples that grew on a tree in their back garden and sold it to the local alehouse. One dark night, some drunken men, to whom the alehouse keeper had refused more ale, knocked on the cider maker's door. The men caused a ruckus, demanding more drink. When the poor cider maker refused, one of the drunken men in a rage ran a knife through his stomach causing the poor man to collapse to the ground and die instantly. Velvia's mother screamed and shouted as she came rushing to the door and called upon her neighbours for help. By the time the neighbours arrived, they found the cider maker's wife had suffered the same fate and were only able to save the little girl. Thus little Velvia, was orphaned.

The case went to the King's court and after Velvia identified the murderous men, King Balathaar sentenced them to be hung, then drawn and quartered. During the trial, Queen Ohio took compassion on the young, timid and frightened girl and decided to become her guardian. Velvia grew up in an orphanage, but one with all the top facilities to support orphan children. The Queen also insisted Velvia study till the age of eighteen, and once Velvia had completed her studies at the age of nineteen, she became Queen Ohio's lady in waiting. When Princess Nilharia turned nineteen, Velvia was appointed *her* lady in waiting at the age of twenty-two. Velvia was mature for her age partly because what she had witnessed, and Velvia and Nilharia soon became friends. Nilharia adored Velvia and Velvia in turn cherished Nilharia.

When Nilharia moved to Gammafor, she asked her brother Dymondo to give her a chamber near Nilharia's. When Dymondo met Velvia, he was struck by her beauty, and instantly agreed to Nilharia's request. Though Velvia did not notice at first, Dymondo had instantly fallen in love with her but he restrained himself from expressing it. Over time, though, she started to realise that Dymondo had feelings for her.

Velvia had straight dark red hair; dark brown eyes, fair skin, and a nice smile. She would usually be seen in either soft, red cotton dresses or thick, brown ankle-length tunics with a cream stola. She did not wear much jewellery and used silver trinkets to hold her clothes in place. Velvia had a sarcastic nature and was happy to speak her mind but knew when not to as well. On occasion, she would point out flaws in people and in their plans which was not well received by many. With others, she came across as dry, blunt and honest. But not with Queen Ohio or Nilharia. With them she was a different person smiling, talking freely and relaxing in their company.

Most men would find Velvia attractive and would make advances, but she would refuse straight away. The personality she put across to people was generally uninviting. Most men at court admired her beauty and elegance but were dissuaded by her unforthcoming attitude. The King however, was in love with her and over-looked all her crudeness. He was a good judge of character and felt that there was more to this woman than she was revealing. He wanted to become friends with her and wanted her to smile and laugh in his company just like she did in Nilharia's and the Queen's. So far this had not been achieved. Up till then, he had only tasted the bitter strong outer shell of her public nature and not an ounce of benevolence. One element he found to be strange in her personality was that she would be highly protective of Nilharia. This was good in a way, as Velvia was her lady in waiting, but by doing this, she would at times also move aside the elements that could be beneficial to Nilharia.

As Nilharia started dancing, all cheered the princess. Velvia joined her on the floor and everybody enjoyed their dance and applauded once they had finished. One by one all the noblemen in the land asked the women at the court to dance and all merrily danced together.

***

After court, Nilharia skipped down the corridor towards her chamber, while Dan stood guard outside. Dan admired Nilharia, finding her to be very pleasant.

"Princess Nilharia," he greeted, as she reached the door.

"Dan, how do you fare?" she responded.

"Very well, my Princess," he responded, "Lady Velvia waits for you in your chamber," he further informed her.

"Is that so?" Nilharia said standing there looking excited. She squinted her eyes and gave Dan a big smile.

"Yes, I allowed her into your chamber. I hope that is fine with you?"

"Yes, of course, that's fine," replied Nilharia. "I can always trust you, Dan. You will be taking your Lance test soon, am I correct?"

"I must wait until the Lorca has recovered, my lady," Dan said, opening the door.

"Oh, yes…I heard…about that," Nilharia said regretfully.

Dan lowered his eyes in shame.

She placed her hand upon his wrist and rubbed it gently. "Don't worry, dear Dan. All shall be well. Lorca will recover and you shall get to sit your exam." Nilharia comforted him.

"Gratitude, my lady."

"Not at all. Thank you, Dan." She smiled at him again as she entered. Dan shut the chamber door and sighed.

Once inside, Nilharia found Velvia standing by the desk near the window.

"Lady Velvia," jested Nilharia, "How do you fare?"

"Oh, leave it now will you!" said Velvia sounding disgusted.

"What is the matter with you?" asked Nilharia as she walked up to her and softly held her hand.

"Urgh!" she gestured, "I just despise court. I do not know why you ask me to accompany you."

"Because I have to be present. I am the princess, and as you know very well yourself, it can be very boring. So, I need you by my side. You are a dear friend to me, Velvia."

"Kind words, Nilharia, but I have just about had enough of your brother making advances towards me."

"Come now, Velvia. The King himself admires you. He has a kind heart, he is the kind of King who doesn't take mistresses," said Nilharia in a mischievous manner. "So, if he is interested in you, then that is a good sign. Who knows, one day you may end up being Queen!" mocked Nilharia.

"Nilharia, seriously I am not in the mood for mocking."

"Oh, dear we *are* upset, aren't we? Perhaps this will cheer you up," said Nilharia as she removed her beautiful silk dress and stood before her unclothed. Velvia smiled and walked over to her and stood very close. She gently placed her hands behind her lower back, around her hip and held her gently and lovingly. The other hand she placed on her fair face and ran her fingers gently up and down Nilharia's cheek.

"You know, Nilharia, this always brings a smile on my face," replied Velvia.

The two kissed and laughed at the same time and slowly the kiss became passionate and Velvia too removed her dress and both embraced each other unclothed. The kiss continued as they moved towards the bed and got under the sheets and began caressing each other's bodies tenderly.

Everything got interrupted by a knock at the door. It was Dan.

"Princess Nilharia! The King approaches!"

Nilharia and Velvia stopped and looked at each other in shock and horror.

"Quick, compose yourself!" Velvia said jumping out of bed to grab Nilharia's dress and throwing it at her. "Hurry!"

"Yes, I am doing that!" Nilharia snapped.

"Your hair!

Nilharia hurriedly combed her hair with her fingers as Velvia too got dressed and did the same.

There was another knock at the door from Dan. "Princess!"

"Yes Dan!" Nilharia yelled. "I heard you the first time round." she added under her breath.

Dymondo walked up to the door without noticing that Dan had been speaking to the door. Lance Sterferep strode behind him.

"Good day Dan!" Dymondo said.

"Good afternoon my King," replied Dan as he bowed and knelt.

"Is Princess Nilharia in her chambers?"

"Err... yes my King, she is. I saw you walking down and I have already informed her of your arrival."

"Is that so, Dan?" laughed Dymondo.

"Just in case she was asleep, my King."

"Thoughtful of you, Dan. Was she sleeping?"

"No, my King, but still it gives her time to compose herself in case she was."

"Thoughtful. You do care for her a lot."

"My King," said Lance Sterferep, "Dan is ready for his test."

"Lance Dan!" announced Dymondo. "Soon that will be your title."

"One of the finest fighters we have!" smiled Sterferep. "The King can be very proud of him."

"Excellent, Dan, a pleasure to know you are ready."

"My King is kind and so is Lance Sterferep," said Dan.

"It's praise well deserved," said Dymondo. Everyone stood silent for a moment as Dan lowered his eyes.

"Do not let past transgressions cloud your mind, Dan. I have heard that Lorca is on the mend. Once he is back on his feet, I shall get Lance Kor to test you." Dan nodded and his eyes expressed gratitude.

"A knock at the door would be appropriate, wouldn't it, Dan?" laughed Dymondo.

"Of course," Dan knocked on the door and Dymondo called for his sister, "Nilharia!"

"Lady Velvia is currently visiting the princess, my King," spoke Dan. Dymondo's eyes widened and a slight smile crossed his face. "Is that so? Well, it would be great to see her too!"

"Yes brother, do enter!" called Nilharia in her sweet voice from inside. Dan opened the chamber door and let the King in. Dymondo expressed his gratitude with a small nod. Lance Sterferep waited outside with Dan.

"Nilharia, my sister, how are you? How do you fare?" Dymondo asked as he entered. He sounded excited and was very pleased to see his younger sister.

Nilharia ran up to him and hugged her brother. Her head reached his chest and he placed his loving hand on her head and kissed her forehead.

"What has my sister been up to?"

"I beg your pardon brother?" Nilharia asked, somewhat in shock. She knew her dress was creased and her hair was messy. *Could he tell?* But no, Dymondo was just asking. He did not notice her ruffled clothes. The only thing noticed was the unmade sheets on the bed but he chose not to say anything.

He looked over at Velvia and greeted her.

"Lady Velvia, how do you fare?"

"Very well, my King." She was not happy with the interruption nor to see him. As much as she tried, she could not hide her feelings well. She at times answered back with monosyllabic answers or abrupt responses full of scorn. Dymondo did not like this but he always ignored it, being too taken by her beauty. She knew this and it meant she could get away with saying anything to him.

Dymondo looked back at his sister and smiled. He held her arm softly and walked her over to the desk near the window. "Come sister, let us talk."

Lady Velvia looked on in envy as he held Nilharia's arm.

"Lady Velvia," said Dymondo as he sat down at the desk, "why don't you also bring a chair across and join us?"

"I am fine, my King."

Dymondo stared at her and his smile faded from his face as now he had to command her. "Lady Velvia, would you please be so kind to join us?" He said it quietly yet assertively. Velvia did as commanded and joined them at the table.

"Nilharia, it is so good to see you. Apologies for not being able to visit sooner. I know we meet every day at court, but that is no meeting. But you know what duties are required of a King and what is expected of him."

Nilharia smiled and they both laughed.

"How are your studies? They must be coming to an end now? Am I correct?"

"Yes, brother! You are right, I am nearly finished."

"Of course, of course. Well… as soon as you're finished, I'd like you to prepare you for the next step in life. Marriage! You are twenty-five-years-old now!" Nilharia smiled and looked away.

"You too, Brother! You too should marry soon!"

"Ha-ha! As soon as I find the right woman, I will," said Dymondo looking at Velvia. Nilharia did not like his look, but she hid her feelings.

"Would you be kind enough to accompany me to the kingdom of Haask once your education has finished?" asked Dymondo.

"Haask?!" Nilharia and Velvia's faces showed horror.

"Yes, Haask. I believe you and the Prince of Haask will make a great match! The prince is strong, worthy and handsome...so I have heard. I have not seen him."

"But Brother...Haask?"

"Yes, yes I know. I will rekindle the attempt father made with them years ago; I must try!"

Nilharia giggled and pretended to be shy. Velvia sat there listening to the two while staring out of the window, feeling disgusted inside.

"Lady Velvia, you too. Would you like to accompany us to Haask?" requested Dymondo as he turned to her. "I insist."

Upon hearing this, Velvia was pleased—happy to know that Nilharia would not be going alone.

"Gratitude, my King. Yes, that's very kind of you to ask me along. I am sure the princess would like my company."

"Wouldn't we all?!" laughed Dymondo staring at Velvia. "If Nilharia takes a liking to him, then the prince of Haask will most likely be spending more time with her as they will be getting to know one another. That will leave just the two of us. Perhaps we too can spend some time together." He smiled at Velvia, and she hesitantly smiled back.

"But there is time until my studies finish. There are many lessons still," said Nilharia. She did not like what Dymondo had just said to Velvia.

"Of course," said Dymondo and rose from the table. "Right I must be on my way. I'll leave you to your private conversations."

They all stood up, smiled and paused to look at one another awkwardly. Dymondo felt unwanted. He could tell the ladies wanted him to leave. Dymondo was not too concerned, but as he left, he looked at the bed again and decided to comment on it.

"What on earth have you been up to? Just look at the state of that bed!" he mocked.

The two looked at each other in horror, their jaws dropped, and their smiles vanished.

Dymondo laughed and looked back at the girls, but before he could see their faces, Nilharia and Velvia both put back on their false smiles.

"We were jumping," Nilharia covered and started laughing.

Dymondo threw his head back and laughed out loud, as did Nilharia and Velvia. Dymondo then hugged his sister and turned for the chamber door.

Nilharia followed him to the door feeling impatient for him to leave. Nilharia loved her brother. She always felt protected and cared for when he was around, and generally she enjoyed his company, but today her mind was elsewhere. Today she just wanted to be with Velvia.

As Dymondo left, Nilharia watched as he and Lance Sterferep walked down the corridor. Then she looked at Dan, gave him a sweet smile and thanked him for making her aware of the King's arrival.

Dan knew the smile was genuine. He admired Nilharia and, since Lorca had been taken ill, he had taken great pleasure in standing guard outside her chamber and had quickly become loyal to her. However, he was completely ignorant about her relationship with Velvia. Like everyone in the kingdom, Dan thought Nilharia and Velvia were just good friends. But Nilharia had no concern that Dan would find out. Though almost a Lance, he was innocent and kind. She knew she could trust him. For his part, Dan was falling in love with her, but he knew all too well that Nilharia was a princess and that nothing would ever materialise between them. Nevertheless, his heart beat for her. As she stood in the doorway, Nilharia noticed the love in his eyes, but she chose to ignore it. She closed the door and took a deep breath.

"That was close. Anything could have happened there," she smiled.

"To be perfectly honest I couldn't care less!" Velvia grumbled.

"Velvia, he is our King and my brother. You must respect him and stop being abrupt with him. He only tolerates you because he has taken a liking to you."

"Oh please, save the talk!" said Velvia. "So he plans to take you to Haask?"

"Yes, and I must go and choose a prince for myself," giggled Nilharia.

"That's not funny, Nilharia! It is about time your brother found out about us."

"Are you mad?! That can never happen."

"He will have you married off to a prince from Haask! Is that what you want? What will you do when this prince demands that his beautiful, loving wife perform for him in bed? What will his reaction be when he finds out his wife's thighs do not moisten for him? Or for any man?"

"Velvia I do not want to discuss this right now," responded Nilharia. She wanted to remain blissfully ignorant and did not like the conversation of "what will happen when the secret is disclosed?"

"I shall deal with the problem when I have to face it," she said.

"That is no solution. Your brother again makes an advance, and he will continue to do so. He forever tries to woo me. Yes, any other woman would be delighted and find it flattering, blessed with the notion that one day she could become Queen. I know Dymondo, he is a good man, a good King. And yes, I feel safe in his kingdom. But there have been many times where I have rejected his advances, and still he continues."

"But Velvia—"

"I understand his advances are sincere and he would never force himself upon any woman. I truly admire Dymondo for this, but it is all moot. My thighs will never moisten for him. It is not him. I just don't like men, in that way," smiled Velvia. "And neither do you, Nilharia, so you should stop giving Dymondo false hope about Haask and stop smiling at that poor guard outside."

"What can I do? I cannot do anything right now, so please let us not discuss this any further. I do not know what will happen when he finds out about us, and I don't want to deal with it right now. He has too much on his mind already."

"So you think it will not go down well?"

"No, it will not go down well at all. Just imagine if I uttered to him; 'I, Nilharia, your lovely sister, is in love with Velvia, whom happens to be the very same woman you are in love with and she loves me back and not you!'"

"No perhaps not, Nilharia." Velvia was quiet.

Both remained silent for a moment and avoided eye contact with one another and looked at the cold ground and did not know what to say. However, Velvia realised it was Nilharia who made the first attempt to console her last time, and that she should try to console her this time.

"Right, so where were we?" smiled Velvia.

Nilharia's beautiful face lit up with a huge smile.

"Take off your clothes!" she commanded.

Velvia smiled back and raised her eyebrows. She was impressed by the dominance of her lover. It turned her on. Velvia removed her clothes and displayed her perfect curves.

"What about you, madam? You still stand before me clothed?" asked Velvia.

"Come over here!" Nilharia was still in command mode. She made Velvia walk over to her slowly and untied her silk dress and let it drop to the ground. Nilharia smiled and giggled. They both bit their lower lips gently and began kissing one other whilst still giggling. Soon the passion returned and both ran their hands through each other's hair and fell on to the bed enraptured.

"I love you, Velvia!" gasped Nilharia when the kiss ended.

Velvia's eyes said as much or more in return.

CHAPTER 8

APPROACH

The next day, the Gammafor court was a marvel. The King was in a jovial mood and all pressing concerns were dealt with speedily. After that, abundant amounts food and wine were served and there was lots of music and dancing.

Education Minister Olivious went back to discussing matters of state with other courtiers but was heavily under the influence of the sweet wine, and could not string together a proper sentence. He became a spectacle.

Nilharia as usual was dancing with Velvia, as Dan looked on with a furtive eye. He stood with Lance Kor, and many unmarried young women of court would come up to Kor and converse whilst they sipped on their wine. He would allow for a few charming words and humour, igniting the fire of desire within their hearts. Dan chuckled at some of his remarks whilst watching the beautiful Nilharia dance. Sterferep walked around accompanied with Dwarpal to ensure all was in order. At times, he would walk by the lovely ladies flirting with Kor and drop a joking insult at him, making the women laugh.

"Right, we shall get more wine, shall we not?" said one of the ladies standing with Kor.

"Quite right, that we shall," said the other.

"Shall I have the maidservant come over to you, my lady?" proposed Kor.

"No, we shall be fine. You stay right here, Lance, we shall return presently," giggled the third, and all walked away to get more wine.

Dan moved closer to Lance Kor. "You and your women," he whispered.

"Quietly now, Dan; these are women of status. Ill must not be spoken of them."

"Do you love any of them?"

"I love all of them, but I have not yet met such a woman that could sweep me from my stance."

"Yet you decide not to wait?"

"In my opinion, waiting is wrong. I but enjoy what life hurls at me."

"Or what this court hurls at you," laughed Dan.

Both laughed quietly. "Focus on your training, Dan, and careful with your words as I will be testing you," laughed Kor. Dan smiled and continued to watch Nilharia.

Across the room Sterferep and Dwarpal spoke of other matters.

"We need to fetch more flagons of wine."

"I already sent some maidservants down to fetch more flagons; they should be here by now."

"See to it then," instructed Sterferep.

"I shall, Lance," sighed Dwarpal. "But all is well, so why be concerned? The servants are looking after the courtiers very well."

Dymondo had drank a challis or two more than usual. He finished his drink and rose from the throne. All dancing and music stopped. Everyone looked at him.

"Do continue. I shall join the dance!" All cheered and applauded the King as he took to the floor. He bowed to Lady Velvia and invited her to dance with him. She accepted his invitation, and everyone applauded the King and Velvia as they danced. Nilharia pulled Dan onto the dance floor.

The King and Velvia danced quietly for a while just staring deep into each other's eyes.

"Lady Velvia," spoke the King gently amidst all the music and noise.

"My King,"

"You look beautiful!"

"The King is gracious. Gratitude."

"My lady, I would like to make a proposition, if you'd entertain?"

"Of course, my King," she replied. She would have liked to tell him to go away, but she knew it would be difficult for her now to refuse anything he asked for.

"Would you care to have dinner with me tonight?"

She paused and just smiled, and they carried on dancing. "I await an answer, my lady," he persisted.

"My King, I am flattered. But I am not worthy."

"I decide that, my lady, and you are in every way worthy to wine and dine with me this evening."

"The King is again kind, but I…"

"…I but request, my lady."

"My King I do not know what to say…"

"…say yes!"

She paused and he kept looking at her with smiling, hopeful eyes. She wanted to refuse for she knew after dinner, more wine would follow. Eventually, there would be an invitation to visit the King's chamber. But she could not refuse the King. Dymondo had gathered much courage to ask this and the consumption of extra goblets of wine was only making him more bold.

"Yes, my King, I would love that," she said masquerading her feelings. Dymondo's eyes sparkled yet he kept calm and elegantly continued to dance.

Nilharia continued dancing with Dan but kept a close eye on Velvia and Dymondo. She was extremely jealous. For Dan it was a dream come true, and he wanted this moment to never end. Still he could never have imagined what came next. After a few steps, Nilharia said the most unexpected words to him.

She brought her mouth near to his ear and said, "Put your hand on my arse."

Dan looked at her in surprise, as though he had seen a ghost. He was baffled. He looked around and gently moved his hand down and then moved it away again.

"Put it back!" she whispered.

"My lady, the King will have my head!" Dan whispered back.

Nilharia looked around to make sure no one was looking in their direction. Then she pulled him into a nook just outside the court. It was a small confined area and there was hardly any room, definitely not enough for two people.

"Dan, I want to you to do exactly as I say and not say a word," instructed Nilharia.

"Princess, I…" Dan was terrified.

"Ssh! Just do what I say! I shall explain later."

"No Princess, please excuse me!" Dan began to move past so he could leave.

"Dan! Listen to me," she growled under her breath as she pulled him back. "I cannot trust anyone but you with this. You must promise not to tell anyone."

Dan stopped and spoke under his breath. "I promise…"

"My thighs do not moisten for men, but for women, says lady Velvia."

Dan did not know what to say.

"I have been sleeping with lady Velvia."

Again, Dan did not know what to say.

"But…"

"…But what?"

"But I think I moisten for both men and women…I know I do for women…I just don't know whether I do for men. Help me." Dan struck himself across his face with his hand.

"Am I dreaming? I am startled…"

"Just shut up, Dan, and…kiss me!"

"Princess!"

"Kiss me, you idiot!"

He made the most of the opportunity and kissed her as passionately as he could, as though the realm was facing the apocalypse. Nilharia groaned in pleasure.

"That was good. Now feel me." She put his hand between her legs. Dan could not believe what was happening.

"Am I moist?" She was panting.

"You are!" He too was panting.

"I knew it! Now suck my breast!"

"What!"

"Do it Dan!"

"But…"

"Oh!" She quickly released her left breast from the clutches of her dress. Dan hesitated. She licked his lips with her tongue. He then caressed, kissed and sucked her breast as he was ordered to.

"Great! Now drop your kilt!"

"What?"

She did not respond and untied his belt in a hurry and his kilt went crashing to the ground along with his blade. She beheld and grabbed his manhood hard in her hands. Dan could still not believe what was happening. She got carried away in emotion and kissed him again. He kissed her back. They kissed deeply and for a long time.

"Now…fuck me, Dan!"

Without responding, he heeded her command. The session was intimate due to the lack of space. It was fast, furious and rather short. But it was the best moment of Dan's life. When he had finished, Nilharia quickly composed herself and pulled her summery yellow dress back down over her legs.

"Dan listen to me, you must not speak a word of this to anyone!"

"I do not wish to die early, princess Nilharia, so you need not worry." He was still panting.

"Good. I am sorry to put you in a situation like this, but I know you wanted me," she winked. "And I think you're cute too. So, you were my first choice. I know this is bad of me, but please try to forget this incident as nothing can ever become of us. I just needed to know. I love Velvia. It was wrong of me to do this to her, but I knew of no other way. Forgive me."

"I'll say nothing more of it, Princess. Now go back to court!"

She sneaked out of the nook and hurried back to court. A few moments later, he too came back. Fortunately, no one had been around to witness anything. Everyone was too jolly and intoxicated. Nilharia started dancing with Dan again. At first, they found it awkward but soon they both started mischievously smiling at one another.

***

Across the court, Sterferep still stood by Dwarpal. A long silence ensued between the men until eventually Dwarpal spoke the most unexpected words to Sterferep.

"Lance…I never got the opportunity to express my gratitude for the support you displayed for Dan and I when we stood before the King."

Sterferep looked over at him. "None required," he said, keeping a straight face despite wanting to be more effusive in his response.

"It is required. I have much respect for you, Lance Sterferep."

"That's kind."

"Dan and I will forever be in your debt. Can you forgive my past audacities towards you and consider it a result of my adolescence?"

Sterferep now had to smile. He placed his hand on Dwarpal's shoulder. Both gladly welcomed the beginning of a new friendship.

The music came to an end and everyone bowed to bring the dance to a gradual halt. They all applauded.

"Very well, I expect you at dusk in the royal dining hall," said Dymondo to Velvia quietly as he moved back from the floor. She curtsied to the King and stepped back.

"All at court!" Dymondo announced as the music stopped. "I retire to my chambers, but please continue the music!" Everyone cheered and applauded as the King left. Velvia moved aside to get more sweet wine and stood in the corner wistfully. Nilharia finished her dance with Dan and walked straight over to Velvia.

"So, what did my brother say," she giggled.

"Your brother invites me to dinner."

Nilharia's smile faded immediately.

57

"But surely…"

"…Oh, leave it, everything is an act of witticism for you," snapped Velvia under her breath. She placed the chalice of wine on a table nearby and sneaked out of court with Nilharia following behind her.

"Velvia, wait," called Nilharia as she followed her out of the court and into a passageway. For a moment, she thought Velvia knew of her and Dan.

"Did you accept?" asked Nilharia.

"Did I have a choice?"

"But surely…" Nilharia stopped as two guards walked by bowing and to her. Nilharia waited for them to pass.

"Come…" she took Velvia by the hand and into a room nearby where the clay pots were kept. She shut the door behind them firmly, so they could speak.

"But surely this merely means a dinner and nothing more?"

"Nilharia are you in slumber? Wake up! Your brother is in love with me. I understand he is a good man. But what he does not know, is I am yours!"

"Yes, you are! You are mine!" spoke Nilharia as she kissed her.

"All futile!" replied Velvia as she withdrew from her kiss.

"Velvia!"

"Nilharia, we have to tell him! There is no other reason as to why I would refuse the King! I cannot refuse him!"

Nilharia did not know what to do.

"He cannot find out! No! He cannot!"

"Then I must dine with him this evening, have wine with him and…fuck him if he desires it!"

"No!" Nilharia began to weep.

"Yes, Nilharia! Yes! And if I am to live, I must adhere! I do not wish to spread my legs to him anymore than you wish for me to, but I must and if I fail to present ample reason for not doing so, then I can be removed from his palace and castle!"

"Oh Gods! What are we to do?"

"Simple. You have to tell him."

"No, I cannot! And you must not either!"

"We cannot remain silent. We must tell him. Or he will have me tonight!"

"No! Tell him… tell him you love someone else, another man! He will not force himself upon you!"

"If he demands a name, then what name should I give him? Should I let an innocent suffer because you cannot be honest with your brother?"

"He will not do that!"

"He is kind hearted. He might not. But people fail to see right from wrong when they're in love. If Dymondo does not understand, then there will be innocent blood on both our hands! Do you wish that?"

"No!"

"No, No, No! Nilharia, do but say anything else?"

Nilharia began to cry.

"Nilharia, you have taken our relationship as a mere lark all this time. You deserve this. Many times, I warned you; there will be a time when this day will arrive, but you ignored it every time!"

"I didn't know what to do!" she screamed.

"Ssh! Someone will hear!"

"I don't care right now!" Nilharia shouted.

Velvia slapped Nilharia hard across the face. "Have you lost wits?! You risk discovery!"

"How dare you?"

"Quiet, you childish woman! And gather your senses!" whispered Velvia.

Nilharia stopped crying and wiped her tears.

"Forgive me, Nilharia, for I had no other choice but to calm you down." Velvia placed her hand on Nilharia's face. Nilharia removed it.

"Please Nilharia, show me the path for I have no solution."

"I don't know! I cannot fathom a path! All I know is that you must not lay with him tonight. Do whatever it takes!" Nilharia said as she wiped away her tears and began to walk out of the room.

"Where are you going?"

"To my chamber. I'll see you tomorrow. Remember my words," snapped Nilharia.

"So that's it?!" Velvia responded. "You are so stupid, Nilharia! You just like to run away from situations! You do nothing about them!"

"You know what Velvia, you can fuck him! I don't care! At least we'll be even!"

"What do you mean?" Now Velvia was angry.

"You said I only liked women and not men…well that's not true!"

"What are you saying?"

"I needed to find out, Velvia. And there was only one way to do so."

"I don't understand."

"Don't get me wrong, Velvia, I love you and only you. But I needed to find out. I felt bad for doing it, but not anymore, not after you struck me across the face."

"What did you do?"

"That cute guard, Dan, I fucked him in a nook!"

With that, Nilharia quietly left the room and headed towards her chamber. Fortunately, no one witnessed Nilharia's tears or anguish, or her confession. Velvia, though, was left standing in anger and shock. She stood in the room pondering for a long while. Her hands were balling into fists.

Soon after, she too left the room feeling completely helpless. Nilharia's childishness had ruined everything. Velvia was truly on her own.

CHAPTER 9

FINE WINE AND DINE

Before Velvia knew it, evening was upon her. As the sun went down, the tension between Velvia and Nilharia evolved to utter acrimony. Nilharia had wept all day in her chamber and had no other plan for the night than to remain under her bedsheets and cry more. Velvia for her part was in utter grief. She could not think of a way to avoid this dinner. She did not love the King. However, her refusal could leave her banished, and being apart from Nilharia was not an option. So she swallowed her pride and headed to her chamber and dressed in her best outfit. Despite her heart being elsewhere, she still had to appear presentable for the royal dining hall and for the meal with the monarch. She wore her favourite colours and trinkets and looked absolutely dazzling.

For Dymondo, it was the night he had been waiting for. He dressed in his finest, groomed his hair, shaved close, and donned his best royal clothes. Mysteria's heart pounded hard as she watched how Dymondo intricately groomed himself and tended to every small crease on his jacket and robe. She remained quiet throughout the entire time he got ready. He left the chamber with a simple goodbye and headed into the dining hall.

Velvia had not arrived yet, so he eagerly waited until she walked in. When he saw her, it was if a celestial being from the heavens had descended and brightened his hall. He walked over to her and went down on one knee and took her hand and kissed it softly and told her how beautiful she looked. She smiled as the gesture was kind. He took her by the hand and sat her beside him and they sat down to eat. He occasionally asked her if the food was good and whether she needed more wine, but other than those pleasantries, no other talk took place. He was nervous and she was not interested. After the dinner finished, Dymondo called in for the sweet and delicious fruits. Velvia wanted to say what was in her heart, but she could not, and his silence did not aid her in her struggle. Eventually, after the fruit was consumed, Dymondo broke the deadly silence.

"Lady Velvia."

"Yes, my King?"

"Would you like to rest now and sit more comfortably?"

"That would be nice. Forgive me, my King but I do not belong to an affluent family, hence, I do not know how to behave or compose myself at dinners. I hope I made no mistake?"

"Please, my lady. You worry without reason. Let us retire to my chamber, where we can talk more freely, away from the shackles of formality."

At those words, sweat began to form on Velvia's forehead and palms. Her nightmare was about to begin. She quickly and discreetly wiped her hand on the side of her dress before Dymondo took hold of it and started walking her towards his chamber. Lance Tamaris stood guard and let the King and Velvia in. Once inside, Dymondo saw that Mysteria had gone home, but the chamber looked miraculous.

"The royal chamber is beautiful, my King," Velvia complemented.

"Please, my lady, do feel at home. Take a seat."

He offered her a large soft chair and took the one next to her for himself. Velvia hesitantly smiled at him, and Dymondo could not believe he was finally sitting beside her inside his own chamber; away from the world and away from everybody. For him it was a dream. He took hold of her hand, but when she looked away, his smile faded.

"My lady, may ask a question?"

"Of course, you may."

"Are you happy?"

She paused and very nearly spoke her heart but managed to gather herself and gave him half a smile. "Yes, I am."

"You do not seem to be."

She kept quiet.

"Velvia, let me put you at ease. You are free to say whatever you wish. Say what is in your heart."

"My heart?" she laughed.

"Yes."

"No, my King, it your desires I am here to fulfil."

Dymondo withdrew his hand and sat back in his seat.

"I did not command you to fulfil anything, Velvia. I merely asked…"

"…Yes, you are King, your wish is a command. Is it not? Who has the courage to refuse your requests?"

"No one Velvia. But I do not wish for any lady to be in my company when she herself does not desire it. Is it true, you do not desire to be in my company?"

She looked away and rolled her upper lip underneath her bottom lip.

"Is it true?" Dymondo snapped.

Velvia jumped and saw the agitation on Dymondo's face—a reaction she was not expecting. "Yes, I do not wish to be here with you, my King," she said assertively, yet in a low voice.

For Dymondo, the ground cracked beneath him, and he felt he was falling into a deep, dark chasm with no end. His dreams were shattered and his sudden frustration impaired his ability to think rationally.

"Then why are you here?" he asked her sternly.

"To please you, my King. I cannot refuse the King!" Velvia now had a softer tone.

Dymondo stood up and walked around in haste with his hand on his hips.

"Velvia I love you! With all my heart!" He was pleading with her, but his voice was still aggressive.

"I am sorry, my King. You are a very kind man, but I do not love you."

Velvia stood up and went over to him. He turned from her in anger. He was furious.

"Fine then, leave, lady Velvia!" he growled.

But she felt empathetic towards his broken heart and stayed to console him. She went around to face him, and for the first time touched him of her own accord. She placed her hand on his cheek. "Look at me," she said.

Dymondo looked at her with his gloomy, sad and expressive eyes.

"I am truly blessed by the Gods, that you love me. I too love you, but as a friend, but we can never be lovers."

"Am I not worthy?"

"No, Dymondo, you are the best person, the best man and the best King I have ever known."

"Then why?" asked Dymondo removing her hand vehemently.

Velvia upon seeing her loving gesture rejected folded her arms and stood back and answered him directly. "I am in love with someone else."

Dymondo further moved back and eventually fell into his seat with his head drooped low. Velvia again tried softer words with him, but he was like a volcano on the cusp of eruption.

"I sympathise with your situation Dymondo," she said, "but we can never control love. Whom we will fall in love with and when…we just don't know."

Dymondo gathered himself, but he was still frustrated and infuriated. "Right, I won't hold you back anymore. You are free to leave, my lady. But…"

Velvia got scared. The punishment she feared was surely to follow.

"Who is he?" Dymondo's blood was boiling now.

"That I cannot tell…"

"Oh, Velvia have some mercy at least! Tell me something!" shouted Dymondo.

Velvia jumped. She wanted to be as far away as possible from him, but the courageous young woman stood her ground.

"No, my King. That is not necessary for you to know."

His eyes turned red in rage and he clenched his fist tight and shook it in the air. "Tell me, Velvia!"

"Why, so you can have that person banished or even killed?"

"I command you to tell me or prepare to suffer the consequences," Dymondo had lost all control now. His manners and etiquette had evaporated and he had become like a child who had just had his favourite toy snatched away.

"My King, you are frightening me. Calm down, I beg of you," said Velvia.

"Calm?!" he snarled and stomped over to her, taking hold of both of her arms, and shaking her. "Listen to me once and for all!" he seethed. His teeth were clenched together so tight, his face trembled. Shivers went down Velvia's spine. "I waited years for us to have an evening together! You ruined everything for me! My heart is broken and my dreams are shattered! If I wanted to, I could have had you whenever I wanted to, Velvia Dweller! But no! I have been kind and gentle, and this is what I get? Do not for once take me for granted, woman!"

Velvia struggled in his grip. "You have been kind and gentle only to hurt me, like you are now!" His hold tightened on her and her pain began to show on her face.

"Tell me his name, and then you can go!"

A tear emerged from her eye. "Never!" she snapped at him. "I will never tell you that!"

Dymondo was no longer Dymondo. He had transformed into an outraged beast.

He pushed her down on the bed. She was terrified and did not know what to do. His senses had shut down and all righteousness had dispersed. He picked her up again and held her by the arms again but this time even tighter. He brought his lips up to hers, leaving only a small gap between her lips and his. She turned her face from right to left to avoid contact.

"I can take you right now and no power in the world can stop me," he growled. She felt his breath upon her face. Velvia's anger had now reached its zenith. Her eyes filled with tears and wrath. She looked at him with hatred and repugnance then violently pressed her lips against his, but this was not a kiss. This shocked Dymondo and he tried to withdraw from the collision, but she held the back of his head against her face tightly and spoke as she held his lips against hers.

"There you go. What are you waiting for?! Go ahead! Fulfil your lust! There is no one here to stop you! Do whatever you wish with this body of mine! But I vow to you, I shall lay still just like a corpse! Because this is what I am to you now! I do not love you!"

Dymondo struggled to pull away, but as he turned his head, she followed.

"What stops the great King Dymondo Rain? Do it!" she screamed.

Dymondo managed to struggle himself free and turned his face away from her. She was burning in the fire of her fury. She turned him around so that he faced her again, then she tore off her dress.

"There! Take me! For I am yours to do as you wish!"

Dymondo turned away again.

"Why do you look away now, my King?! This is what you were dreaming of! There! Now you know what a look like without any clothes!"

She walked in front him again and he tried to avoid her with his eyes.

"No! You look now! This is what you want, isn't it?" She took his hand and placed it between her legs. He tried to remove his hand but her grip was now tight. He could not.

"Am I wet? Answer me? Am I wet?"

Dymondo lowered his eyes whilst fighting her to take away his hand.

"Am I wet?!" she roared.

"No."

She shrugged away his hand.

"Right. Because I do not love you! I don't want you! Understand? I love someone else. I will never have that love for you! Never!" She shook her head as she yelled at him.

Dymondo felt disgusted with himself. How could he have let his anger control him like this? How could he stoop to such a level? He walked over to his wardrobe and extracted a large cloak and put it around Velvia.

Velvia threw it to the ground.

"Fuck your gesture!"

"Velvia, please! Cover yourself!" He had his voice back. He again took the cloak and covered her. This time she took it.

"I am ashamed of myself, Velvia."

Velvia was crying but silently. The sight of him disgusted her.

"Please…forgive me for what just happened."

"Never! Fuck your apologies!"

"Velvia, I thank the Gods, for granting me back my senses in good time, for they had abandoned me, and I mistreated you in anger."

"Fuck…your…apologies! Have me executed if you wish, but you are nothing but shit to me now! I shall never forgive you. You may not have taken me forcefully, but you hurt me, Dymondo Rain." Velvia spoke lowly now, crunching her words.

Dymondo folded his hands before her and apologised to her again, but she just stood there weeping and shaking her head.

"I will call Lance Tamaris and he will take you to your chamber." Dymondo was utterly disappointed with himself. As Velvia wiped her tears, Dymondo gathered her trinkets which had dropped all over the ground. He picked up her ruined dress from the ground and carefully folded what remained of it and placed the trinkets on top and handed it to her. She covered herself appropriately with the cloak and took from him her dress and jewellery. He opened the chamber doors and looked outside. Fortunately, Lance Tamaris had placed himself away from the door, so he had not heard. Dymondo called upon him and asked him to escort Velvia back safely. Tamaris noticed the look of distress on Velvia's face, but dared not ask or say anything.

CHAPTER 10

MYSTERIA

She knew Velvia had visited Dymondo's chamber the night before and assumed she may have left in the early morning hours. So the next morning, Mysteria quietly and cautiously knocked on the royal chamber door where Lance Tamaris stood guard outside.

"What is it?" asked Dymondo, curtly.

"It is I, my King, Mysteria," she answered in her gentle soothing voice.

"Enter."

She entered slowly and hesitantly.

He was sitting on his large armchair, which was usually placed away from the window, but today was placed opposite. There, the King sat, slouching and staring emptily outside.

"Good morning, my King," she said.

"Morning, Mysteria," came the deflated response.

"How do you fare this morning?" she asked again whilst re-arranging the bedsheets.

"Well, thank you." Another punctured response. But soon Dymondo remembered his manners. "And you?" he finally asked in return.

"Good, my King. The King is not ready for court today?"

"I will be absent from court today."

There was a long silence whilst she got on with her chores around his chamber. She was eager to ask him more about the night but could not muster up the courage to do so. She eventually got around to cleaning the armchair. His eyes remained fixed outside, but she could see his eyes were red and had dark circles underneath them. It was clear he had not slept a wink. His face was expressionless, but his eyes looked sad. She had to say something.

"My King…"

"Hmmm…?"

"May I ask a question?"

He turned towards her with his empty face. "Yes, but one which I can answer monosyllabically."

"Mono… what my King?" she asked innocently.

Dymondo rolled his eyes and said, "Yes, you can ask me Mysteria, but only one question and be quick please."

"What happened last night?"

Dymondo took a deep breath and stared at her. She stared back at him with unblinking, piercing eyes. Her long lashes looked beautiful. She had eyes in which any man could get lost. They were deeper than the ocean and full of mystery. They both stared at one another for a while and eventually both broke into a smile. "Mysteria… that my dear is not a quick question to answer, is it?"

She continued to stand there and just smile back. She looked pretty when she smiled with her pearly, white teeth.

"Come here, and sit beside me," said Dymondo, gesturing to the bed. She walked up to the side of the bed and sat, bringing her feet onto the bed and resting her chin on her knees. He stood and turned the armchair so that it was facing her and sat back down. Her ankles were entwined and her knees were slightly apart and she had wrapped her arms around her legs near her feet. Her feet were clean and cute. The skin seemed soft and she had short shiny toenails.

"So, come on… tell me…" she had a hint of jealousy in her words.

Dymondo noticed the resentment and smiled once again. "Lady Velvia came to visit last night."

"I know… proceed, my King."

"I made my feelings known to her, but she does not have the same feelings for me…she does not have *any* feelings for me. Upon hearing this… I got angry and I grabbed her by her arms with force and sternly asked her why. Mysteria, I am ashamed of my behaviour."

"Did you…?"

"No! No! Thank the Gods no…! I realised in good time. I did however misuse my powers as a King."

"How?" she asked. She was not impressed and had now placed the side of her face onto her knees looking away.

"I commanded her to tell me who she loved. She refused to say and I grew angrier. I threatened her by saying I could do anything I wanted with her."

"Then?" Mysteria asked nervously rubbing her fingers together and staring at her nails.

"She got angry and removed her clothes and prompted me to do what I was threatening."

"Then?"

"She was as cold as stone and said to me her body was mine for the taking, but that I would never receive her love, passion or respect. In anger, she brought her frigid lips against mine and placed my hands upon her body. I withdrew. My senses came back and I felt ashamed for my actions and words. I put my cloak around her and begged for her forgiveness."

"Naked?" She turned to him, looking at him with more disgust.

"She was, yes. I was clothed but she was not. Oh… it was terrible… she told me to…take her. But that is not what I wanted. I tried to impress her, I tried to be gentle, I tried to be caring, I tried everything!"

"And after that you resorted to force?"

Dymondo had no response. He lowered his head in shame.

"By doing that, you believe a woman would love you?"

"Of course not, Mysteria; I am not justifying anything. I merely held her tightly and spoke to her in a loud voice. I know what is right and wrong! My mind got clouded and I stooped to this act under frustration and defeat! But as I said, I am not justifying anything. The act was wrong."

"What happened after that?"

"As I said I realised all this was wrong. I put my cloak around her and commanded Tamaris to escort her home. She left. I apologised countless times for my indecent behaviour."

"Then…?"

"Tamaris heeded the command. I said that I was deeply sorry for what I had done. It was wrong."

"What did she say to that?"

"She said she will never forgive me."

"And now you cannot forgive yourself."

"Yes."

Mysteria sighed and rose from the bed. She walked over to him and held up his lowered head and placed it against her navel. He was still sitting down and he accepted the gesture and put his arms around her waist and dug the side of his face into her soft slim stomach. They both held that position for a while.

She slowly went down on her knees and her face was now at the same level. She held his face in her soft hands and made him look at her.

"You realised in good time, my King. Yes, it was wrong, but it could have been worse. You could have bedded her with force and then realised much too late, which would have been disastrous. But you realised before that, so please try to forgive yourself."

He nodded in agreement.

"You apologised to her, and there is not much more you can do."

"But she should forgive me, should she not?"

"No, my King. What you did was hurtful and only time can heal such a wound. Just as the dust of time gradually clouds a mirror, these memories will take time to become opaque. But all will be well, you'll see."

"You're right."

"Now rise, my King… you have a kingdom to run! It is midday and you are still in your nightgown." She smiled at him and stood up and went back to her chores.

"Mysteria…"

"Yes?"

"Do you forgive me?"

She stopped working and turned to him and smiled. "My King, I am your royal chamber maid. It should not matter what I think. You are my King, and you pay me well for the work I do. You treat all your workers kindly, and you do not believe in slavery. I cannot ask for more. I have my own life and dignity and respect. If I was living in Doosranfor or even Forprimiera, I would have been a toy for the Kings of those lands. I would have sucked Grygerious's cock dry by now or been bruised by Shilathaar a thousand times. I probably would not even have been alive. And here I am sitting on the royal bed with my feet up, on the fine silk bedding and talking to you as an equal! That is more than enough for a mere chamber maid like me."

"Mysteria, please! There is no need for…"

"…And you are also concerned about what I think of you! My King, you are far too kind!"

"Spare the praise for someone who is worthy. I clearly am not worthy after last night. Do you forgive me?"

She smiled and it brought tears of joy to her eyes. "My King, you are just great…"

"Mysteria!" He was serious. "Do you forgive me, after what I did last night? I want the truth! I do not like giving commands."

She toughened up and wiped the water from her eyes. "If you ask me as your worker, then of course my King! The King is great! But if you ask me as your friend and well-wisher, dare I call myself your friend…"

"…you are!"

"then…No!"

His eyes dropped and his head lowered again.

"May I ask something, my King? Will you not ask me the reason?"

"For what? Why you won't forgive me? It is clear. You think I have erred and cannot forgive me for it just yet."

"True... but there is more..."

"What?"

"Every young woman has a dream that one day she will find a man that loves her more than anything on this realm. I do not have such a man in my life. But you are the only man I know who cares for me and respects me the most. I had placed you upon a plinth. This is the man I would like the love of my life to be—how every man should be. And you did this!?" she started to cry. He rose from the armchair to hold Mysteria in his arms and she began to cry even more.

"Mysteria...I have fallen from your plinth. That hurts me. But I did not know you held me in such high regard! I thank you for doing so." Now he held her lovely face in his strong hands. She looked at him in anger as he wiped her tears with his fingers. She looked even prettier when she was angry. In truth, she was jealous. She did not want any woman near him. She did not like Velvia because Dymondo had feelings for her. But this was a young innocent woman who knew her place, but did not know that she had fallen for the King.

"I apologise to you, too, Mysteria," he said and backed off. "Please continue with your work. But work around me. I'd rather lay in my bed for a while.

"What of court?"

"The time for court is over now. I am sure the ministers can handle one day without me. After all, have I ever taken a holiday?" he smiled and removed his night gown. He was wearing his pyjama bottoms, but not his top. He walked over bare-chested to Mysteria and handed her his gown. She could not take her eyes off his muscular physique.

"Stop staring," he laughed.

"Oh!" she groaned, "How can a woman not!?"

"Mysteria... the chores please..." he again said and smiled. He lay in his bed.

She too smiled back and just as she was about to say something, there was a knock at the door.

"Yes?" said Dymondo from the bed.

Sterferep entered. "Pardon me, my King, but all at court noticed your absence."

"Ah, yes, Sterferep. Was all handled, though?"

"Yes, my King, all is well for today, but I was concerned for your wellbeing."

"Yes, all is well, Sterferep. Thank you for your concern."

"My King."

"I am taking today as a rest day. I shall return to court tomorrow. Please could you let everyone know?"

"Right away, my King," said Sterferep and left immediately.

Mysteria watched the door, then turned to look at Dymondo as he again closed his eyes. She bit her lip.

"My King?" she asked in a soft voice.

"Yes?"

"Did you like it when I held you close? Did you feel relaxed?"

"Of course, and I thank you."

"Would you like me to hold you close to me as you rest...?"

He sat up in his bed to look at her, and she looked back with passionate eyes.

"Mysteria... it might...not be...entirely correct to do so..."

"That's fine, my King."

She looked at him no more and continued working. But eventually she finished, and when she did, she walked over near his head where he lay with his eyes closed. He was awake. She knew.

"I take your leave now, my King," she said softly. She did this purposely.

"Mysteria..."

"Yes, my King?"

He opened his eyes and held out his hand to her. She smiled and took his hand and he pulled her closer.

"I thought someone said something about holding me close?"

"I thought someone said it might not be right?"

"The person who said that is juggling with many rights and wrongs in his head."

"And that is why this other person offered... to eradicate those disturbing thoughts."

"Does that person still offer?"

"If the punter accepts."

Dymondo smiled and she smiled back. She let go of his hand and walked around the bed to the other side to get in. She got under the silky, white sheet and lay beside him, bringing Dymondo's head slowly to her bosom. She placed his face in her cleavage and he took a deep sigh of relief and groaned as he pressed his face further into her breasts. They both withdrew and looked at each other. Then she looked down and slowly untied the white ribbon lying across her cleavage. She slowly untied the next one down and then the final one. She then placed his head back into her breasts, only this time there were no restrictions, and the dress came apart.

There, the King took refuge in her naked breasts.

He kissed them and placed his mouth around her lovely erect nipples as she moaned in enjoyment and excitement. His soft lips drove her crazy. She gently bit into his strong shoulder as they held each other tight. He was tired after the restless night and she from her morning full of chores, and now they had become relaxed in each other's arms. But after a few passionate embraces and mischievous gestures, the two became truly passionate, got carried away in the moment and made love before falling into a deep slumber.

CHAPTER 11

THE MORNING AFTER

Dymondo's slumber ended, and he discovered his face in Mysteria's breasts, his head clasped gently and lovingly against her heart by her soft arms. She was asleep and she looked gorgeous. It was already the next day. They had both slept through the previous afternoon, till the next morning. And what a beautiful morning? There was a steady, clean, fresh breeze in its air. It flew into the chamber through the window bringing the morning sun. Despite being slightly cold, the wind had a fresh fragrance to it.

Dymondo had his own arms around Mysteria's attractive firm waist. He gently moved his arms and lifted his face from her chest. She moved slightly as he did, but remained asleep. He admired her beauty and gently brushed away a lock of hair from her face and stroked her soft cheek. He smiled and kissed her on her forehead and slowly moved out of bed and searched for his clothes. He picked up his pyjama bottoms from the floor; put them on and walked up to the window. As he breathed in the northern gusts, he reminisced about the events of the previous night. He began to feel ashamed of letting his lust take control and tread all over his principles. Dymondo firmly believed in love. He believed, one must only bed a woman when he is deeply in love with her. He loved Mysteria, but just as a friend. She admired him more than a friend. He had managed to gauge that from her countless jealous expressions when he was getting ready to meet Velvia.

He continued to feel bad. He could not marry this woman as he did not love her but it would be wrong to purely use her for bodily needs. She had given him what she had not given to any man before. Dymondo knew it was her first time, therefore, the burden was much greater and he could not ignore this. Still, strangely he felt that last night was special and there was a sense of comfort on both sides. Perhaps it was because they knew each other and she was more of a friend to him than a royal chamber maid. He always admired her beauty and rather enjoyed the unexpected coitus.

Dymondo walked up to her slowly, going around to the other side of the bed. She lay there on her front with her bare back facing the King. He gently stroked her hair and she moved onto her back. Her breasts were uncovered but she was still asleep. Dymondo smiled and gently lowered his head to kiss her tranquil lips.

This broke her slumber and Mysteria realised she was in the King's bed. She suddenly sat up. With one hand, she grabbed the white sheet to cover her breasts.

"I apologise, my King," she spoke hurriedly, "I should have woken up before you and… Oh dear… Look at the room!"

She tried to get out of the bed, but Dymondo softly held her back.

"Mysteria…it's fine. Please relax."

"No, my King, I overslept!" She was still anxious and worried about waking up so late.

Dymondo held her face in his hands and said, "Look at me."

She relaxed and stopped fretting. Dymondo brought his lips near to hers and kissed her gently. "Remain where you are," he said and removed his clothes and got back into bed. He brought her head very close to his bare chest and held her softly in his strong arms. She had never experienced so much care before. She released a large sigh and brought herself closer to him and he too held her tight.

"Mysteria, you can agree that we both deserved some relaxation?"

"My King is too kind," she said meekly.

"No Mysteria… you are kind. Last night all my worries vanished."

"I am glad, my King. Forgive me, if I forgot my place and overstepped the mark, but I could not see you linger alone in anguish."

"You are a wonderful woman, Mysteria, and there is no need for an apology."

"I felt that you needed an embrace," she smiled.

"Ha-Ha, I needed a lot more than that it seems," laughed Dymondo.

"I must get dressed and clean the chamber my King," she said.

"Mysteria… I make the decisions around here," smiled Dymondo.

"Forgive me… do I have your permission, my King?"

"No, you do not! I will now give you your last command."

"Last!" She sat up and placed her hand on her mouth. "Oh, my gosh I have erred!"

"No! No! You misunderstand. When I said "last," I meant…from now onwards; I shall only request you to do things for me," smiled Dymondo.

"My King!" gasped Mysteria. "You bestow so much favour on me!"

"Enough! Your command is to remain exactly in the position where you are most comfortable at this moment."

"That would be here in your arms."

"Then remain so. From today onwards Mysteria, you are my friend! Do I have the honour of your friendship?"

"My King, why do you say this? You have the right to everything!"

"No Mysteria, all my servants are my workers. They merely work for me; I do not own them."

"That is why you are the finest man in Landsfor!" she spoke with pride and watered eyes.

"No one calls it that anymore…"

"…I do…You do…?"

He sighed: "Yes Mysteria…You are correct… I would like everyone to call it Landsfor again. Why do we speak of other things when I wish to talk about something else?"

"Then talk to me," she said and moved her hand from his waist to his chest and began gently circling her soft finger around his nipple.

"Mysteria…I truly respect you and love you as a friend."

"You are kind."

"You are aware, that I am in love with another woman?"

"I know, you are in love with Velvia Dweller."

"I strongly feel that one must only bed the woman whom he truly loves."

"It is a very noble thought, my King."

"But I have erred."

"No, you have not…if you feel you have erred by bedding me, then do not, because you love me."

"But Mysteria, I am not in love with you…for which, my lady, I sincerely seek your forgiveness."

"My King, you love me as a friend…as you have just said."

"Oh, very much so!"

"Then you needn't ponder over last night. We are friends as you say. And you have given me certain rights over you as I am no longer obedient to your commands…correct?"

"Very much so."

"Then, my King, please do not worry about last night. It is something which we both desired. You required a woman's touch, and I am

76

completely in love with you. I desire you… And when you were in my arms I could not resist you. Therefore, my King, stop worrying," she smiled.

Dymondo kissed her and she held his face in her hands and then grabbed a hold of his hair just above the back of his neck. She placed her lips so close that when she spoke, they brushed against his.

"I will always be there for you. I love you, Dymondo Rain. I do not wish for anything in return, be it status, gold, jewels, your explanation or your justification. I only want the never ending right to love you unconditionally for the rest of my life—even if last night ends up being our first and last fuck. Do not ever ask me to stop loving you and do not ask me to bed or wed another man!"

She let go of his hair and he glared into her eyes. She was serious. She looked directly at him.

"I do not want you to provide me with a position or any wealth. Do not force yourself to love me. Even if you wish me to be your Queen, please only ask me when you too have fallen in love with me. I shall wait forever for you. That's all I request…my King."

Dymondo again held her in his arms.

"I do not know where this relationship will go, Mysteria, but I will certainly grant your request. I shall continue to love you as a friend. I from now on, will not command you. You will not be asked to bed or wed any other man. The only wealth you shall receive is for the tasks you do in my chamber. I am not in love with you; therefore, I will not force myself to either, but…"

"…but what?"

He gently placed his hands in hers and pinned her down on her back onto the bed and lay on top of her. She groaned in pleasure as he did.

"…but I will certainly continue to love you as my dearest friend and if I fall in love with you…I expect that you will bestow upon me the honour of being your lover."

She raised her head to kiss him. He kissed her back and the kiss turned zealous. Both now aroused, they looked at one another and gave each other cheeky smiles and embarked into another steamy session of intercourse. It was completely opposite to the one the night before. Where last night was tender, respectful, and caring, this was rough, raunchy, and erotic.

At climax, they fell in each other's arms. Mysteria kissed him, got out of the sheets, gathered her clothes and began to dress.

"I request you to lay with me for a while longer, my lady!" said Dymondo.

"If only you had been so polite with Lady Velvia last evening, my King," taunted Mysteria.

Dymondo sat up in his bed and stared at her. She got dressed and turned to face him and looked him seriously in the eye.

"My Lady, I...I..."

"Yes, I know, you would like to ask why I brought this up. My King, and forgive me for believing I have the right to speak to you in this manner, but you owe Lady Velvia an apology." She began to gather items around the royal chamber while the King sat in his bed staring at the bed sheets.

"I apologised many times that night."

"Yes, my King, but you must apologise again."

Dymondo nodded. "You speak the truth, my Lady Mysteria. I most definitely shall apologise to Lady Velvia again."

Mysteria smiled and came over to him and ran her soft scented hands through his thick hair with love and kissed him again on his lips.

"Rise! Seize the day! Go to court, my noble King!"

CHAPTER 12

APOLOGY

ysteria's words drummed in Dymondo's ears as he prepared himself for court. Dymondo was baffled by her. How could her words have so much effect on him? He chose to not ponder on it too much as Lance Sterferep and Lance Kor fetched him from his chamber. Mysteria had already cleared the chamber before their arrival, so that nothing was out of place. They all left together and headed towards court.

"Court may begin!" he announced, once they arrived.

"Hail the King of Gammafor and Fourtfor!" spoke Majesma as he stood up to speak. "All in the kingdom is well my King. I would like to introduce to the court a new minister who has joined our political team, with your majesty's permission of course."

"You may."

"Noblemen and women of this land, I hereby announce the appointment of Defence Minister Urayu Dero. He is learned politician and a fine economist. A true philosopher from the great educational institution in Fourtfor, the Grand Dominuscus. He will take care of all matters relating to border security and defence," announced Majesma.

Dymondo nodded at Majesma and Urayu and both bowed in return.

"Defence Minister Urayu, I welcome you. I believe we all are expecting great things from you in the coming years."

"I will do my utmost best, my King!" spoke Urayu. The court

proceedings went on and eventually came to an end.

"Now bring the musicians and let the dancing begin!" announced Dymondo. Everybody took to the dance floor. Nilharia would usually be the first person on the floor, but this day, she looked very glum. Dymondo feared that Velvia may have told her of the incident. He gathered his courage and walked up to Lady Velvia, whom was surprisingly not standing beside Nilharia.

"Lady Velvia, I would like to have a word with you in private if I may?"

Velvia gave a repulsed look to Dymondo but bowed her head and curtsied. He endured the sight and led her out of the room, as the musicians and dancers filled the court and the entertainment began.

Nilharia took a goblet of wine as she watched Velvia follow Dymondo out. Velvia had not come to Nilharia's chamber after that evening, nor the next day. In fact, Nilharia had not spoken with Velvia since their encounter in the clay pot room. Nilharia guzzled down her wine and took another and gulped that down too. After which she stomped out of court towards her chamber, grabbing Dan's hand on her way out, dragging him along with her.

Meanwhile, Lance Sterferep followed his King with Lance Kor just behind. With his Lances catching up in the distance, Dymondo stomped down the corridors with Velvia in his wake and went up to his chamber.

"Come in, Lady Velvia," he said when they arrived at his door.

Velvia, struggled to contain her anger, but followed him in. As far as she knew, this could be a repeat of the previous night. Seeing the monarch marched in with Lady Velvia behind him, Mysteria gathered herself up and stood in service.

"Sterferep and Kor… please remain outside," requested Dymondo. They both nodded and took guard at the door. When the door closed, Dymondo yanked his cloak off and threw it onto the bed, startling Velvia. He walked in a circle punching his fist into his other hand and then walked swiftly over to Velvia. This made her jump and Mysteria gasped.

"My Lady, I sincerely apologise for my inhuman behaviour the other night," Mysteria breathed out as did Velvia, but soon Velvia gathered her confidence and crossed her arms.

"You should! You should be ashamed! But, really, I apologise to you. You're King. You can do whatever you wish! And when you had the opportunity, you did nothing! Hah!"

"Velvia…please…" Dymondo said compassionately.

"No!" Velvia shouted.

"Ssh!" Mysteria intervened.

"Shut up, you stupid bitch! You're a chamber maid. Know your place! I am the lady in waiting to Princess Nilharia!" Velvia had long forgotten her own history. Mysteria looked at Dymondo and her eyes began to fill with water. Dymondo looked over in despair.

"My Lady, it is a request. Do not speak to Mysteria in that manner."

"I say it to you…O King! Keep your apologies to yourself for I do not require them. I shall never forgive you! You can beg as much as you like."

"Velvia please!"

"No!"

"I beg for your forgiveness. It was wrong for me to…"

"…to do what you did! Yes! I wonder what Nilharia will think of it. She does not know yet."

"Velvia have mercy. Nilharia will never forgive me. Please, you cannot tell her!"

"Oh, I will…King!"

"Please I beg of you. I am prepared to give you anything in return."

Velvia paused and thought. "Anything?"

"Anything!"

"Fine then…" she stood back and a vicious grin appeared on her face. "Remove your clothes!"

"Clothes?"

"I will take your leave my King," spoke Mysteria.

"No, bitch! Stand right there!" exclaimed Velvia.

"Do it King! Or else I shall not be as merciful, and I will ask you do it in front of your Lances! Shall I ask them to come in?"

"No! No! I shall do it," spoke Dymondo as his head dropped in shame. He removed all his clothes until he stood stark naked before her. Mysteria lowered her eyes. It was shameful.

"Keep your eye fixed on him, bitch! I want you to watch!" Velvia walked up to him and grasped his privates hard by her hand. Dymondo endured the discomfort but stood stern. Velvia loved this. She loved this control over him. She enjoyed humiliating him. She wanted revenge.

"Hah! Helpless, pathetic bastard!" Velvia walked up behind him and whispered in his ear. Dymondo's was now angry. He was King after all. Dymondo eyes showed his fury and her clasp tightened even more until he finally released a grunt.

Mysteria placed both her hands over her mouth as tears rolled down her soft cheeks. Upon hearing this, Velvia let go and stood back again. Dymondo caught his breath and became relaxed.

"Place your hands in between your legs from the back and lower you head so you can grab your ears! Do this and I shall not tell Nilharia or anyone," demanded Velvia. Dymondo looked at her in disbelief. "Velvia…"

"Do it!" He did as he was told.

"Hold the position…."

Dymondo did so with ease.

"Now say you're sorry."

"Lady Velvia, I sincerely apologise for my behaviour last night. Please forgive me. It shall never happen again," spoke Dymondo with his head between his legs.

"Damn right it won't! Good! Now get up and put some clothes on…my King," she taunted. "I have seen enough of your disgusting body," she said and turned her back. Dymondo grabbed his trousers and slid them on straight away. Velvia turned to face him. Her eyes were red and she ground out her words.

"Don't you ever come near me again, Dymondo Rain, let alone touch me! I will spare you the embarrassment and not tell anyone anything, but I shall never forgive you!"

"Lady Velvia!" Mysteria intervened.

"Didn't I say quiet, bitch?!"

"No! You listen to me now, bitch!" spoke Mysteria wiping her tears and marching up to her. "This man is truly repenting for his actions. Repentance is penance! And you now have had your vengeance too, so why the attitude? He did not force himself upon you. Yes, what he did was very bad, but the least you can do is show some kindness to the countless apologies he has made!"

"You dare speak to me this way, whore? Oh, you don't know what you have stirred! I can have your tongue removed. One click of my finger and Princess Nilharia will have you put in the dungeons."

"One click of my finger can have any decision made by your princess overturned within moments, you arrogant condescending filth! You forget you too are just a servant like me. Lady in waiting for the princess! Well call me whatever you wish but I have the King's ear!"

Velvia had no answer.

"You can go tell whomever you wish, bitch, because no one will believe a word from your stinking mouth! So, don't you stand in my King's chamber and threaten him of exposure. And if people do believe you, then so what! A King took a mistress! Ha-ha! There is nothing eyebrow-raising about that! Consider yourself fortunate this man is fighting to abolish slavery! If it were not for him, you would have been an object, not a person, and your feelings would not have mattered in the slightest! You yourself said the King can do whatever he wishes. He could have done whatever he wished with you and no one would have batted an eyelid, you whore!"

Velvia had finally met her match in Mysteria. She had Velvia cornered from every angle.

"Don't ever…threaten the King again, or I shall tear your vicious tongue out myself with my bare hands! Now get out!"

Velvia, embarrassed, looked at Dymondo for some support, but after what she had done to him, he evaded eye contact. Velvia left the chamber completely humiliated. Dymondo's heart was shattered as he fell to ground with just his trousers on. Mysteria came rushing over and knelt on the cold floor and placed his head against her bosom. Dymondo was furious and heartbroken. He did not cry, but this incident left a hole in his heart. Mysteria did not say a thing and neither did he, for a long while.

"You did right. You apologised and she took her revenge. But you let it go too far. Your penance is complete," she said gently.

Dymondo held her tight with both hands.

***

Dymondo failed to sleep the following night. He had allowed Velvia too much freedom and deeply regretted it. He was utterly quiet when Lance Sterferep and Lance Kor came to his chamber in the morning with Lance Tamaris, Dan and Dwarpal with them. Dymondo walked fast, nearly stomping to court, his cloak floating in the air behind him.

The assembly noticed him late, and the honourable acknowledgements were also late, along with the announcement of the King's arrival. Courtiers failed to stand up in time as he entered. Dymondo swung his cloak around and turned and sat down swiftly. The people did not turn for him.

"What is this?" Dymondo addressed his courtiers.

"Apologies my King," some of the courtiers said as they realised he was there.

"Do you have no respect anymore?" shouted Dymondo.

Everyone bowed their heads and knelt on the ground. Dymondo looked around and saw everyone in that pose.

"Alright, alright! Rise!" Everyone stood up and took their seats and positions. Lance Sterferep and Lance Kor took their positions beside the King, whilst the other three stood among the courtiers.

Nilharia remained away from Velvia. Dan walked up to her and stood beside her. Both exchanged smiles. Nilharia acknowledged that Velvia noticed this and gave Velvia a malicious look.

By the end of the day Dymondo's heart was content. Since morning he had just been trying to forget what had happened.

CHAPTER 13

INTERROGATION

D ays after the attack, Dymondo decided to finally visit the dungeons. He marched down the dank corridor, flanked on either side by Kor and Sterferep. The dungeon master, a large, fat man, clothed only from the waist down and holding a spear, opened the door and bowed to the King.

"Where is she?" the King asked sternly.

"This way, my King," the man said in a coarse voice. He led the way through the dark, narrow, stone corridors. Wall lamps were lit and the ground was covered in hay. The stench was bad, but compared to other dungeons in the realm, Gamman and Fourtan dungeons were the cleanest.

The man stopped in front of a large wooden door. "She's inside there."

"What has she said so far?

"Not a word, my King."

"What have we done to make her speak?"

"We filled her cell with large spiders. She screamed and ran around the cell the entire day. We tied her hands to a large ceiling beam, forcing her to stand for days. We did not let her sleep. We gave her strong doses of wine to loosen her tongue. But no use. If she does not speak now, then we will try slowly dripping cold water on her forehead."

"Hmmm…"

"She is a woman, my King—a young woman. After this, we shall have no choice but to revert to physical torture. I am aware it is not policy, but she is a tough nut, sire. Do we have your permission to break protocol and torture her?"

"No, not yet," said Dymondo promptly. "Her crime is grave, but I do not like torturing women. I shall try to reason with her."

"She has a foul mouth on her, my King."

Dymondo looked at Sterferep and Kor.

"Does she still hang from the ceiling frame?"

"Yes."

"Open the door."

"My King…err…"

"What is it?"

"She hangs naked, my King."

"Naked? Why?" asked Dymondo sternly.

"Forgive me, my King, but this was a process. She has been that way for hours."

Dymondo was furious. "Why? With whose permission did you disrobe this woman?"

"My King, it was a decision I was hesitant to make, but I wanted her to speak without me having to inflict any physical injury. Hence *I* made the decision."

"Why do the Gods put in me such situations?" Dymondo was heartbroken and lowered his head.

"My King, do not let your emotions enter into this," said Sterferep, placing a hand on the King's shoulder. "She is a criminal. She attempted to take a life. I suggest you show less empathy."

"Ster, I—"

"No, my King, she is a criminal. She did wrong. Unrighteous women are not exempt from punishment."

"Did you violate her sexually?" Dymondo asked the dungeon master.

"Never, my King!" the dungeon master honestly replied.

"Very well. Go inside and cover her."

The dungeon master did as he was told.

"You may enter, my King."

Dymondo, Sterferep and Kor entered the humid chamber. The woman's head hung downwards with her soiled arms and hands tied to a thick ceiling beam and her feet just about touching the ground. Her long, thick, black hair covered her face completely. The dungeon master had put a large shawl over her body covering her nakedness. Only her fair arms and her dirty feet and calves were on display. She was unconscious and excrement ran down her legs onto the hay below. She smelled terrible. Dymondo covered his nose.

The dungeon master lit the lamps, then, with a big shovel, swept her waste into a large straw pail along with some hay, and took it out. This disgusted Dymondo and Kor. Sterferep was unmoved. The dungeon master returned promptly with a large bucket of cold water and splashed her face violently with it. She gasped as she gained consciousness.

"Up! The King is here!" barked the dungeon master. He went up to her and moved the wet hair away, revealing a fair, yet dirt-grimed and sweat-filled face. The woman blinked continuously to get the water out of her eyes. When some water entered her mouth, she spurted it out and opened her eyes. They were ridiculously blue. She was stunning—the kind of woman who could entrap any man in her beauty.

"Speak, young woman! Who are you?"

She levelled her angry eyes at the monarch. If she could slay someone with a look, Dymondo would have been dead. She spat on the ground in response. Dymondo grew angrier.

"I am not here to waste my time! I am here to speak to you!"

"Speak? If you wished to speak to me, then you would have come on the first day. Not waited days on end. I have been locked in this chamber with spiders, piss and shit, being nothing but a naked spectacle for your dungeon master and his stooges to behold!"

"Woman! You have erred! You made an attempt to take my chief researcher's life. I believe we have been kind up till now!"

"Then kill me and finish me off, you incompetent idiot!"

"Enough!" shouted Dymondo. "I will not tolerate a foul-mouthed woman! For that I can have your head! But I wish to know who you are and who sent you! And you will answer!" His voice echoed. Kor had never heard him sound so commanding before.

"I shall never talk, King Dymondo, for I have sworn to protect the secrets of my master. I will lay down my life but not utter a word!"

"You shall blue-eyed one, you shall!"

"I shall *not*! And what is this? This cloth you give me? Why now? The entire time I have been crawling around in this chamber naked in my own excrement with insects and spiders. I do not want your mercy now!" shouted the woman, vigorously shaking herself until the large cloth fell to the ground and she hung from her arms stark naked.

"My lady...!" spoke Dymondo and went to reach for the fallen cloth, but Sterferep held him back because she had begun to shake and scream even more.

"No! No! Don't you dare! Don't you dare cover an inch of my body, you heartless beast!"

"Believe me, my lady, I had no knowledge that your clothes were taken from you! I shall be stern with my dungeon master for this. Please accept the cloth."

"Fuck your cloth! I no longer need it. Why do you evade your eyes? Look at me. Look at my soiled bosom and the hairs around my cunt. Smell the stench of urine and shit between my legs! Behold my dirty thighs. See the hair growing under my arms and on my legs! What do I look like to you? A woman? No I am just a living corpse!" she cried, violently shaking her perfect figure as she hung. Her wrists were blue from the tight chains and had started to bleed from the vigorous tantrum. Sterferep and Kor both lowered their eyes. Dymondo turned his back.

"Look this way, O great King. Your dungeon stooge has sat in here and stared at my parts for hours on end! Why can't you do the same?" Look!"

Sterferep, still facing her, looked into Dymondo's eyes. The Lance shook his head, imploring Dymondo not to grow weak.

"My King, gather yourself," he whispered. "She is a criminal. Deal with her as such."

Dymondo gathered himself, straightened his face and turned.

"Silence!" he shouted. The voice echoed to the river Krool. She stopped screaming instantly.

"One more word from you, and I will have your head!"

"Then have it!"

"And I shall, once I have finished asking you some questions!"

"I shall not answer!" she screamed.

"What is your name?"

"Fuck you!"

"Who sent you?"

"Fuck you!"

"Dungeon master!"

"My lord,"

"Take her down at once!" Dymondo's eyes were red as lava.

The dungeon master rushed to lower her chains, and the woman crashed to the ground and groaned in pain from the impact. He then removed her chains uncaringly and stood her up.

She stood on wobbly, numb legs, breathing through her nose, with anger and tears in her eyes, staring straight at Dymondo.

"Dungeon master! Water! Much water!"

"Guards!" shouted the dungeon master. "Bring pails of water!"

"Do not let them in here. You take it from them," commanded Dymondo.

Sterferep and Kor looked at one another.

The dungeon master took the water pails from the guards. They tried to peep in to look at the unclad prisoner, but the dungeon master pushed them out and shut the door. He then placed the water buckets in front of the King. Dymondo knelt and checked the water with his hand.

"It is not too cold, warm in fact," he said. He removed his own cloak, belt and sword and gave it to Kor to hold. He grasped the bucket with both hands and lifted it and walked over to her. She seemed to calm down and eyed him strangely.

"Here," he said softly. "Here, my lady, the water is not too cold. Scrub yourself. I will not look and neither will these men," He held the bucket over her shoulders, turning toward the others so as not to see her.

"Dungeon master get her a clean cloth to dry with and some clothes to wear," he said.

The dungeon master ran out to get the ordered items.

Dymondo began to pour, but the woman pushed the bucket out his hands and most of the water spilled onto the hay. Sterferep unsheathed his sword and held it out in front of her with the tip only inches from her throat.

"No! Sterferep, it is alright," said Dymondo. "My lady, shall we try again?"

She started to sob.

"I am about to pour. Gentlemen please look away!" he ordered. Then Dymondo gently and slowly poured the lukewarm water over her again, trying very hard not to look at her as she cleaned away the dirt and muck. The water finished and Dymondo picked up another pail and began to pour again. By the time, the dungeon master arrived with a fresh piece of cloth for her to dry with and some clothes for her to wear, Dymondo had poured five pails over the woman to get her clean. He handed the cloth to her so she could dry herself.

"Everyone, look the other way as the lady dries herself!" commanded Dymondo not looking at her. The woman kept looking at Dymondo and suddenly felt regretful for having sworn at him for she could see he was a kind and caring person.

"I am done," she said softly, still staring at him.

"Dungeon master, give her the clothes!" ordered Dymondo, still looking away. Sterferep glanced up and saw her gaping at the King and rolled his eyes.

"Can we look now?" jested Kor.

"Kor," said Dymondo.

"Pardon me, my King."

She wrapped herself in a large cloth given to her by the dungeon master, who was now too looking down at the ground. She cinched the cloth tight around herself.

"You may look now…" she said again softly.

"That's better, is it not? Dungeon master!"

"My King."

"This is the first and last time. Do not take your torture to such lengths ever again. Women are to be treated with respect and care, even if they have committed a crime. Do not remove a woman's clothing ever again. If we capture any female criminals from now onwards, you shall inform me, and I will deal with it in my own way! Am I clear?"

"Of course, my King."

"Give the lady a new clean cell and clean this one right away."

"Of course, my King."

"Now, will you give me the name of the conspirator?"

"My King has been kind," she said. "Clothes, water and a clean cell are gestures well received. But what you seek weighs more in value."

"What else do you want?"

"My King, why are you negotiating with her?" interrupted Sterferep.

"There now, Sterferep. The lady has endured much pain."

"She is a criminal."

Dymondo ignored Sterferep and turned to her.

"What is it that you seek?"

"One of your guest chambers would be a good start."

"I cannot promise that. I need time to think."

"You can have time to think." She stared directly into his eyes.

"Do not worry," he said. "I shall return soon."

"My eyes will be searching for you," she said holding her look and placing her hand on his arm. Dymondo too was getting lost in her sapphire eyes.

"My King!" spoke Sterferep assertively. "Shall we go?"

Dymondo had no reply as he was still gazing at the beauty before him.

"My King!" shouted Sterferep.

"Yes?"

"Shall we?"

"Indeed." Dymondo gently removed her hand and walked toward the door, but before he left, he stopped and looked back at her once more. Her eyes were that mesmerising.

Dymondo marched out of the dungeons, trying to shake the image of her beauty from his mind. He was followed by Sterferep and Kor.

"I fail to comprehend, Dy. When will you stop wearing your heart on your sleeve?"

"Leave it, will you, Ster."

"No I shan't!" He strode in front of his King, turned and faced him.

"Ster, not now."

"Then when? This is not Lance Sterferep or King Dymondo talking now. We talk as friends. Do you not see what she is trying to do? She is playing with you!"

"Remember, she is a criminal, my King," added Kor.

Dymondo looked around. It was only the three of them in the corridor.

"I know! I know! I need someone that can guide me on this."

Sterferep placed his hand on his shoulder.

"Queen Ohio, your mother is currently on holiday here in Gammafor. Seek her advice and counsel."

Dymondo nodded. "I shall."

CHAPTER 14

COUNSEL

Amidst the division of Landsfor, poor Queen Ohio had suffered the most as she beheld her beautiful Kingdom torn to pieces. It was as though her heart had been cut into four. Dymondo understood her pain and would come to visit her regularly to pay his respects. They would sit together for hours talking about his childhood and what it was like when she left her father's home to come and live in the royal castle. Dymondo ensured his mother got all the comforts and luxuries she required to live happily, yet the Queen worried day and night about her other two sons, who hardly came to visit her, though she sometimes visited them. She was disheartened to know there was no love, just formality, left between the three brothers, but what could she expect after the peculiar and concealed nature of their births, a dark secret the sons did not know and which had been kept from them and the realm for years.

Every time Queen Ohio would visit Shilathaar and Grygerious and attempt to talk sense into them, her efforts were always in vain. Dymondo, however, respected his elder brothers and would frequently invite them to celebrations and triumphs, which they attended but only to display their false love and appreciation. Out of formality, they invited Dymondo to their own celebrations.

Dymondo was genuinely pleased at the achievements of his brothers, but Shilathaar and Grygerious had jealous hearts and resented Dymondo's achievements as they were far greater than their own. Thus, Shilathaar and Grygerious maintained their distance from Dymondo, often greeting his accomplishments with false praise and cynicism. Fortunately, Shilathaar and Grygerious did not do this to Dymondo's face, though they did display their shame from time to time at the celebrations and made a point to leave as soon as the festivities ended. They saw these celebrations as an act by Dymondo to salt their wounds and keep their envy and anger blazing within their hearts. But Dymondo's intentions were sincere. He was not holding these events to display wealth and prosperity. He was merely trying to bring the family closer together. Unfortunately his attempts too were in vain.

Dymondo knew his brothers did not love him, but when they came to his island, he still smiled and welcomed them and paid them the proper respect in their own land. As time went by, though, Dymondo made fewer attempts at rebuilding the relationship with his brothers as his efforts brought continual failure. His brothers just couldn't erase the hurtful memories of the past.

Shilathaar and Grygerious both were both unsatisfied that Dymondo had more land than them. Dymondo, however, was satisfied with what he had and the fact that he had won the respect of his father and proved himself a worthy ruler. Though he knew it was his father's wish for him to rule all four islands, he was content with what he had been given and did not seek to overthrow his brothers. After all, there were other lands in the world he could conquer if he ever decided to increase his holdings. Shilathaar and Grygerious, though, remained blinded by jealousy and wounded by failure, which enflamed their anger and prevented them from discerning right from wrong. Arrogance and fury killed their ability to think, and history shows that when this happens, destruction is not far away. Advancing human desires are omens of calamity and often bring nothing but devastation.

***

Queen Ohio had been staying with Dymondo for a while now, and that evening, after visiting the dungeons, Dymondo visited Queen Ohio and narrated to her the entire story of the attack.

"Why are you feeling pity for this young woman, Dy?" she asked after hearing what had happened.

"Mother. She's a woman. I thought you would understand her plight."

"She tried to murder your courtier, Dy. She is a criminal! Punish her. As King, you should know that sometimes you will have to make tough decisions. Generally this isn't a problem for you. Why is this so difficult, my son?"

"My dungeon master kept her in rough conditions to get her to speak. My heart torments me for what happened in my name."

"Tell me Dy, do you trust her enough to give her one of your guest chambers?"

Dymondo lowered his eyes. "No."

"Describe this young woman to me?"

"She is beautiful. Lovely eyes, fair skin."

"Ah! You are taken by her. What is it about her that makes you go against all your best judgment?" Ohio smiled.

"I do not know, Mother."

Ohio took a deep breath and placed her loving hand upon his cheek.

"Do not worry yourself. This woman has requested to be kept in a guest chamber. Very well. Trust your inner voice on this then, and do what you think is best. If it seems correct for you to keep her in a guest chamber, then do so. But remember, this woman is cunning. Never forget what she is capable of. So ensure the guest chamber is heavily guarded inside and out. I shall tell the royal blacksmith to mount iron bars against the windows. Have the servants and maids search the chamber for any sharp objects and remove them. She wants comfort, fine! But you must maintain tight security."

Dymondo nodded.

"Go now, and get some rest. If you wake up tomorrow and still feel you should move her to a guest chamber, then do it."

Dymondo embraced his mother and she kissed his forehead.

"Go get some sleep, Son. Remember as King you will have to take tougher decisions than this. This is nothing. In the future you will have to be strong. You cannot let yourself fall for every young, blue-eyed woman," she laughed.

Dymondo smiled and left.

***

The next morning, Dymondo took Sterferep and Kor with him to the dungeons. He met with the dungeon master and asked him to open the assailant's cell. They found her sitting there in the dark corner on the cold ground wearing the cloth she had been given the day before.

She stood up as soon as she saw him enter with Sterferep and Kor. Dymondo walked up to her and looked into her eyes again and she gaped back at him. Dymondo put his arms around her shoulders and walked her out of the dungeon. He held her head close to his chest, and she rested against him, grabbing his waist as they walked.

Sterferep and Kor walked out after him. Kor shrugged his shoulders, but Sterferep looked annoyed at this decision by his King.

Eventually, the woman stopped walking and looked at Dymondo with watery eyes and began to sob. He softly hugged her and rubbed her back. She cried for a long time, and Dymondo did not let her go.

"There, there," he consoled her. "Enough now, my lady." He stood her away from him and she stopped crying and looked to the ground.

"My lady, I do apologise for the treatment you had to suffer. I did not command it, believe me. But as King it is my responsibility to serve justice. You attempted to murder Lorca, did you not?"

She nodded.

"For that my lady, I must exact punishment, even if it is upon a delicate flower like yourself."

Sterferep rolled his eyes again.

"I must be just and fair. But if you co-operate and tell me where you are from, who you are and whom sent you, then I promise I will be kind when serving that punishment."

She nodded again.

"Will you co-operate with me?"

She did not respond.

"Dy, why show such courtesy? ...I mean—"

"Sterferep! Enough!"

There was silence.

"Kor," said Dymondo.

"Yes, my King."

"Take her to the maidservants' baths. Let her clean herself appropriately. Have all the maidservants keep a strict eye on her. Once she has bathed and the maids have her dressed appropriately, inform me. I shall meet with her immediately after to discuss matters further." She looked at him, he smiled, and she nodded back.

Dymondo then left with Sterferep as Kor approached the prisoner.

"Let's go my lady," said Kor.

She nodded and walked ahead of him.

"Tell me guard…"

"Lance, my lady!"

"Tell me, Lance… is he truly the King?"

"But of course, my lady. Why do you suspect…?"

"He is ever so kind and caring!"

"Yes, my lady, that he can be at times. But he can get rather angry as well!"

"Why doesn't he just kill me?"

"Well… I am not as learned as him, my lady, but I do know one thing. If you cannot win something through force, then you should try to win it with love. The King once told me that."

"Now that I know his tactic, why should I speak?" she smiled.

"Ha-ha! He knows you will speak."

"I will not," she said, turning to face Kor. Kor gently turned her around

94

again.

"We'll see."

"I'll admit, I am awe struck!"

"Yes, many women feel that way for King Dymondo. But he does not take mistresses."

"Rubbish!"

"My lady! Please let us get you to the baths," laughed Kor. "The King will not be pleased if he found out I am discussing such things with you."

Kor led the blue-eyed woman to the baths and clapped for the attendants. Twelve beautiful maidservants came running up to him, all smiling. They all wanted to be with Kor.

"Right, everyone! This is an important guest, someone of great concern to the King. I would have you all help her bathe and scrub and treat any wounds you may find. Have her then dressed in decent clothing and inform me straight away once she is ready. Am I clear?" All the maidservants nodded and smiled.

"Remember never to leave her out of your sight for even one second! I want all twelve of you to attend to her until she is ready!" They nodded and took the woman into the baths with Kor following them to the doorway.

"My lady, I shall wait outside," he said.

"Stay and keep watch, Lance, for nothing is hidden from you any longer," said the young prisoner. Kor raised his eyebrows and smiled, and she gave him a flirty smile back.

"No, my lady, for that would not please the King."

"I bet it would."

"My lady, you are clever, much more clever than I. He needs something from you...and to me, it looks as though you need something from him."

She turned back and came near to Kor. Her eyes were truly beautiful.

"I long for him," she whispered.

"I am not going to say more, my lady. Enjoy your bath," replied Kor.

CHAPTER 15

THE KING AND THE CRIMINAL

Tone twelve maidservants bathed her well. They scrubbed her hard and
cleansed her hair and nails with scented waters and oils. They treated
any bruises or cuts she had suffered and removed any unwanted
hairs. When done, they dried her with soft towels and cloths, then massaged
her with oils containing healing properties that moisturized her hard and
cracked skin. Her skin began to take on a healthy glow. They draped her in
a nice, cotton, royal blue dress and fastened it with blunt clips, and they
combed her luscious, long, black hair, which helped bring back some of the
shine it had lost during her time in the dungeons.

When they were finished, the maidservants brought the clean prisoner
out to Kor. She looked ravishing and sparkled like sapphire and blue topaz.

"Gracious my lady, you look gorgeous!"

"Gratitude, Lance."

"Bernarthia! Run to the King's chamber and inform him the lady is
ready for her audience, and that I am taking her to the discussion chamber!"
Bernarthia and another maidservant ran ahead to inform the King.

"Shall we, my lady?" The blue-eyed woman smiled and walked ahead of
Kor. The other maidservants at the baths giggled and waved to the
departing Lance. He smiled and winked back at them as he left.

"My! I cannot describe how beautiful you look," he complimented her
again.

"Gratitude again, Lance," she replied. "So, the King will see me now?"

"Well he already has," said Kor under his breath.

She shot him a look. "You have too," she said.

"Apologies, my lady. Yes, he will meet you now."

"No bother. After all, I must learn to jest about it."

"No, my lady, it was wrong of me to say that. We should be helping you forget about such things."

"Just like your King! Kind and sweet! You're a good man, Lance Kor."

They entered the discussion chamber, which was much smaller than even the discreet assembly room. It contained only a throne and two seats on either side.

"Sit my lady."

She sat down on one of the chairs and looked around at the silver decorations and blue drapes. Kor stood beside her, clutching his sword. Soon after, the King entered with Sterferep but stopped as he beheld the woman before him.

"My lady! You look wonderful!"

She stood up for the King and bowed. "It is your kindness, King Dymondo," she humbly replied.

"Sit," he said and walked over to his throne. Sterferep went and stood on the other side of her.

"Well, where do we begin, my lady? Shall we start again from the top?"

She nodded.

"My lady...what is your name?"

"Oromi, my King."

"And where do you hail from?"

She kept quiet.

"Listen, Oromi, as much as I hate to say it, you are in a lot of trouble and wrong answers can and will lead to severe punishments. You do understand, don't you?"

She nodded.

"I need to know who attacked Lorca. If you tell me...then I shall spare your life." Sterferep looked firmly at Dymondo. Dymondo did not look back at him.

"You shall spare my life? Do you give me your word?"

"Yes..." he replied hesitantly, "...my word. Where do you hail from?"

"I come from Fourtfor my King?"

"Fourtfor?! My kingdom?!...You were sent here?"

She nodded.

"By whom?! Who would commit such treason?!"

She remained mum.

"Oromi! I need answers!"

"My King, it seems as though you need something from me?"

"I do! Answers!"

"Well it so happens that I too wish for something in return."

Kor sniffed and Dymondo glared at him. Kor smiled and shrugged his shoulders. Dymondo sighed deeply and continued.

"In return, I shall spare your life. No more."

"That and something else."

Dymondo sighed. "What then?"

"First you promise you shall grant it."

"I need to know what it is first."

"Oh please! Is this some fruit market?" shouted Sterferep.

"Ster!"

"No, Dy! I can't stand by and watch you barter with this trash!"

"Sterferep, please, calm!"

Sterferep shook his head and looked to the ceiling. Dymondo gave Kor another annoyed gaze. Kor looked elsewhere.

"Do I have your word?" asked Dymondo.

"About what?" asked Oromi.

"If I grant your desire, then you shall tell me who sent you and why," Dymondo said.

"Yes, you have my word."

"Tell me your desire, then."

"I desire that you take me as your mistress."

"Mistress?!" Sterferep drew his sword. Kor's jaw dropped.

"Ster!"

Sterferep lowered his sword.

"My lady that is not possible! I cannot!"

"Why not?" shouted Oromi and stood up only to have to Sterferep's sword raised in front of her once more.

"Ster, put that away!" yelled Dymondo. "Listen, my lady… I cannot…"

"Yes, I heard that, but why not?"

"Because…"

"Because what?"

"My lady, you are an assailant and need to be punished for your crimes. I cannot take a criminal to bed!"

"You misunderstand me, my King. I do not seek to be consort or Queen. All I ask, my King, is for one entire day in your bed and in your arms. Then lock me away forever in your dungeons or have me banished. My only desire is you, just the once."

"Ah Ha! She's a poison damsel!" shouted Sterferep. Dymondo put his hand on his head. Kor moved away from her. "Tell me, Oromi, who plots this against the King?" accused Sterferep.

"Oh please! Spare me the ridicule! Me? A poison damsel? Why would I put a scorpion in your chief researcher's food, when I could have just kissed him blue?"

"She's got a point, Ster," muttered Kor.

"Shut up, Kor! Do you really think the King should be entertaining this farce? A week's more of physical torture would have had her talking! But now look, we are negotiating with criminals!"

Everyone went silent.

"My King, do not be reckless. She may have done what she did to Lorca just to get to you. You cannot bed this woman for she may be poisonous!"

"I am not! I swear to you, my King, I am not!" Oromi began to weep.

"Oh, that's rich! Tears to melt the heart of the King! My King, do not accept—!"

"Enough!" the King shouted. "You're both being ridiculous! There's no proof that poison damsels even exist! And it doesn't matter! I cannot sleep with her anyway!"

"Why not?!" Sterferep asked, surprising the others and himself.

"Mysteria will kill me!" spurted Dymondo. Oromi gave him a striking gaze.

"Dy!" shouted Sterferep.

"Ha! You *do* have a mistress!" shouted Oromi.

"Please do not call her that! Mysteria came to comfort and balm my wounded heart. I cannot betray her."

"Wounded heart?! Over whom?"

"Velvia. She rejected me."

"Velvia?! Was she your mistress before Mysteria?" asked Sterferep.

"No. She's in love with someone else and I don't know who. But she does not love me... Anyway, I was in despair."

"A woman refused you?" Oromi was shocked. "That cannot be. She must like other women then. What woman could refuse my King?" Dymondo ignored her.

Sterferep put away his sword and looked stunned. "You did not even tell me about Velvia!" he said to his friend.

"Or me!" added Kor.

Oromi could not understand why the King was explaining his actions to his Lances. But at the moment, he was not King nor were they Lances. They were old friends.

"Ok, listen, the both of you. It was a strange situation. We had dinner. I then took her to my chamber after dinner and I—"

"You placed your face in her tits!" completed Kor.

"No!" Dymondo turned to his other friend. "I mean, I wanted to, yes! But..."

"Ha-ha!" Kor could not stop laughing. Sterferep, despite his irritation, erupted into laughter, too.

"Please the both of you!"

"How long did this go on?"

"I loved her for a long time, but now that's all over."

"Why did you keep it from us? Who stood guard that night?"

"Tamaris, but he was standing far away from the door!"

"Tamaris knows!" Sterferep turned to Kor. Kor shook his head and laughed even more.

"Not in any detail. Listen, I apologise for not telling you."

Sterferep and Kor looked at each other and both nodded.

"Well it worked out in the end," said Sterferep. "Mysteria is much nicer than Velvia!"

"You're right, Ster, she is. That's why I love her," said Dymondo and turned back to Oromi. "And that, young lady, is why I cannot grant you your second request. I cannot bed you, for I love someone else," explained the King.

"Not my concern, O great kind King. You fulfil your promise and I shall fulfil mine! I will tell you who sent me to put an end to your chief researcher's stupid investigation, the one into your history and lineage. They sent me to kill him to stop it. There I have fulfilled half of my promise."

"Who sent you?! Tell me?!"

"No, my King. Get this friend of yours to swing off my head, but no names until you put your cock inside me!"

"How about if I put my cock inside you instead, would that help?" suggested Kor.

"Good suggestion!" she said, keeping her eyes on the King, "I *would* fuck you, Kor. I was nearly persuaded, but not right now. I desire the King! He will need to fuck me for an entire day and night if he wants to hear that name!"

After the inconclusive meeting, Oromi returned to the guest chamber where Sterferep made sure it was heavily guarded by no less than ten Lances on the outside and ten maidservants on the inside. All the security arrangements suggested by Queen Ohio were put into action.

CHAPTER 16

OROMI'S CONDITION

D ymondo was left in a quandary. To find out who sent the assailant, he would have to bed this woman, though Sterferep and Kor both cautioned him against that course of action. They feared she might make an attempt on his life during intercourse and recommended he continue to torture her to find out the secret. But Dymondo knew the beautiful young woman was adamant and displayed no fear of death. Because of this, he did not fear her. His only concern was for Mysteria and her feelings. He loved her immensely now and did not want to hurt her. Sterferep was right that he was better off with her than Velvia.

Oromi's mention of Velvia's preference for women had Dymondo thinking as well. Why would she say that? Was there any truth to it? Is that why he had been rejected?

All these thoughts made him unsettled and deeply worried.

That evening he asked Mysteria to join him in the royal bath chamber, and she accepted. The chamber was lit with assorted candles and colourful waxes surrounded the pool. Clothed maidservants held fresh, white, cotton cloths and sweet wine decanters. Dymondo removed his clothes and entered the fragrant pool while Mysteria too removed her dress and followed him in.

Dymondo dunked down in the water and placed his head on the edge. A maidservant quickly placed a soft cloth underneath him. Mysteria swam up to him and gently sat on his thighs. As she did, he lifted his head and smiled at her and she smiled back. He then brought his face forward and gave her a soft, slow, loving kiss. The kiss lasted for many moments and Mysteria had never kissed him for so long before. She did not want it to end nor did he. There was so much care, passion, tenderness and love in the kiss. When it did finally cease, he rubbed her cheek gently with his right thumb and placed his head on her pretty clavicle burrowing his face into the side of her soft neck. She stroked his wet hair and gently stroked his neck.

"What is the matter, my King? I hope all is well," she said and he hugged her tighter.

"Clearly something is worrying you. Tell me, as it will lift the burden from your chest."

"I do not know what to do, Mysteria. I'm confused."

"Look at me," she said.

He lifted his head to look at her. She held his face in her hands, and as she did, her elbows pressed her stunning breasts together. He stared into her eyes with a tentative glare.

"Now tell me."

He held her by the waist and spoke.

"As you know, an attempt was made on Lorca's life by a young woman. She tried to poison him. She was kept in the dungeon and tortured for several days but did not speak a word of why she was sent and by whom. I went myself to interrogate her. I found her tortured beyond reason. I commanded the maidservants to bathe and clothe her and present her to me in a decent manner so that I could hear her words."

"Clothed? Was she kept unclad?" asked Mysteria. She took her hands away from his face and placed them on her chest.

"Yes, my lady. Unfortunate as it may sound, that is the truth. I have strictly ordered the dungeon master not to do this from now onwards. Kor had her clothed and bathed."

"Kor!" scoffed Mysteria. "I am sure he enjoyed that!"

"Well, in fact, twelve maidservants carried out the deed; he merely supervised, staying outside," defended Dymondo.

"And after she was bathed?"

"Sterferep and Kor brought her to me and after much debate and deliberation, she disclosed some details. But the true culprit, the one who sent her, remains unidentified."

"So it was a fruitless effort."

"Not entirely…"

"How come…?"

"…She said she would disclose the name, upon one condition."

"Condition? She is a captive! A criminal! Is she not grateful for the King's mercy? You took her out from a rotting prison cell and gave her food, clothes and a hot bath."

"She is grateful, my love. But it is this mercy which landed me in a grand dilemma!"

"How is that, my King?"

"She mentioned that she had never seen such a kind and caring King before."

"That is rather true, my King. You are utterly generous," smiled Mysteria.

"Perhaps too generous for my own good."

"Why so?"

"She will only mention the name of her master and the true purpose behind the attack if I…"

"If you…?"

"Lay with her."

Mysteria's face fell, tears began to form in her eyes and her mouth went dry. She attempted to conceal her dread and gloom, but Dymondo could see it. She took a deep breath and gathered the courage to speak.

"So, what is the dilemma, my King?" A tear ran down from her eye as she spoke. Dymondo gathered it before it fell into the bath water and wiped her cheek.

"The perplexity is that…"

"…is what?"

"Is that I cannot do this to you, Mysteria."

Her face gained confidence from his answer. She knew now that he loved her with all his heart. For him to care for her in this way meant much to her.

"My King, I am your chambermaid, whom you have given much honour and affection to. Please do not worry about me and what I think. You must do what is required for the safety and prosperity of the realm."

"Yes, I agree with that. I must fulfil any task that is for the welfare of this land. But I cannot crush the hearts of those I most deeply care for along the way. I cannot do this without hesitation." Her heart lifted further from his unexpected verses.

"Those you care for, my King?" she pondered.

"You, Mysteria. I love you!"

There was silence. Mysteria closed her eyes and began to cry.

"O, my King, I love you too!" She kissed him again and again and he let her express her happiness. "O the Gods! Feel how fast my heart beats!" she said and grabbed his hand placing it on her chest.

"You are my future Queen!"

"But many Kings marry and take Queens, and they take mistresses even after marriage. But you are different. You just love me and that makes me feel special."

"Because you are! I don't need to take mistresses. I love you."

She hugged him.

"What of this dilemma?" he asked. "I cannot hurt you and I will not!"

"My King, the fact that you refuse to carry out such a task in consideration of my happiness is more than enough for me. I now truly know that you, my King, will always return to my arms, my bed and my house after your duties are finished; for I, have you now, forever!"

"That you do. No other woman in this world can turn me away from you!"

"And I am aware of this. Yes, it will pain me, but I can also understand that it is important for us to discover who sent her. Therefore, it is your duty as King to unravel this mystery and do what is required!"

"Spoken like a true Queen!"

"O, my King, I merely wish to be with you as your friend, lover and companion."

"That you are! But don't you wish to become my wife?"

"Oh, yes, most definitely, and I wish to have your children. I crave you. I do not want your treasure, your wealth, or this kingdom. I just want you. But, as your wife, I shall do all within my power to maintain and safeguard my husband's assets for that is my duty too. And it is within my power to grant you permission as your future wife that you fuck this damn woman until she begs you to stop and the information flows out of her!"

Dymondo looked into his love's fiery, wet eyes and admired her courage. The trust she was bestowing upon him was remarkable. They both kissed for a long time until she brought it to a halt.

"Only on one condition, though, my King!"

"Command me!"

"Before you do anything with her…you will love me like there is no tomorrow!" commanded Mysteria.

"That, my lady, shall not be a problem."

The lovers retired to Dymondo's chamber and made love until dusk with no coyness or hesitation. Mysteria had attained what she wanted, Dymondo's heart. And Dymondo got what he had forever wished for, to fall in love with a magnificent woman. Mysteria was the woman who was prepared to do anything for him and sought nothing in return except his love. She had won him over completely. After an entire night of lovemaking, they both lay naked in each other's arms.

"One thing, my King.

"Yes, my love."

"You should take caution during intercourse with this woman for she may make attempt on your life."

"Yes, I shall be cautious. Sterferep and Kor have already warned me of this."

"Is she pretty?"

"She is attractive… but not as beautiful as you."

"You flatter me!… O the Gods! I must be the first woman to allow her love to lay with another woman!"

"You certainly are not the first, my lady, and most certainly will not be the last! But this chamber and this bed is yours alone. I shall visit her in the guest chamber. After which, neither of us will ever mention this again."

"Correct. I agree."

"What will you do once you have found out the truth?"

"I do not know, my lady. I do not have the courage to be harsh with her."

"She is a criminal. She must be thrown back into the dungeons!"

"I may banish her to the outer shores of Fourtfor or to an island, where she can live out the rest of her life and never return to Gammafor or Fourtfor again. There are ten maidservants in her chamber right now. I shall have them keep watch during coitus. Ten Lances will remain outside."

Mysteria nodded. "You will visit her this evening?"

"No… after a few days. But I shall send word today."

They spoke no more after that. They just continued to lay there for a while, caressing each other's bodies. After a while, Mysteria got up and put on her dress. Dymondo too rose from the royal bed to gather his clothes. Mysteria gave him a fresh set of clothes as he once again headed to the baths. She told him that she was heading home for the next seven days and another chambermaid would be in service for that time. Dymondo did not question her, and they did not embrace or kiss as he departed for the baths. After watching him go, Mysteria steeled herself, took a heavy stroll away from the chamber, down the corridor and out the palace gate. Once on the street, she began to silently weep.

When Dymondo returned from the baths to his chamber, Mysteria had gone. Dymondo clenched his fist in anger. This powerlessness made him feel like a coward. Still he sent word to Oromi that he would visit her chamber in the next few days.

The next two days were quiet at court. All the tasks were dealt with promptly. The banjo did not twang and the harp remained unplucked. Sterferep and Kor remained silent and did not question the King, for they knew how torn his heart was.

CHAPTER 17

THE BLUE AND THE BLADE

On the third evening, Dymondo visited the ravishing captive in the guest chamber. He took along Sterferep and asked him to wait outside.

"My King!" exclaimed Oromi. She was wearing a royal blue dress that nearly matched her eyes.

"You are welcome!"

"I love this chamber," she said glancing around at the surrounding pillars where the maidservants watched and waited behind translucent veils.

"I have fulfilled my end of the bargain, now please, Oromi, tell me who has sent you?"

"Why are you always in a hurry, my King?"

"Oromi, I do not have time for games!"

"I have all the time for games. Games are fun! Do you not agree?"

"Oromi."

"Very well. To inform you my King, you have not kept your end of the bargain. You are meant to…" she stopped talking and walked up to him and whispered into his ear. "…fuck me! Is that what you are here to do now? I can assure you will not be disappointed!"

"Oromi, please!"

"I do not know why you hesitate. If you accept my condition, you will not only get to know your enemy but also my magnificent body. You hardly have anything to lose."

She moved closer to him and placed her bosom against his chest and grabbed his head from the back and kissed him. Dymondo did not push her away. She pressed harder and smiled against his lips.

"Kissing a woman who might be poisonous…may not be the best action to take," she said as she started to withdraw, but Dymondo grabbed her hair gently from the back and prevented her lips leaving his.

"You are not poisonous," he said and they both kissed passionately. Her breath smelt like roses and her lips tasted like sweet berries. She moaned as he caressed her breasts. Suddenly Mysteria came to his mind and he withdrew. Dymondo turned away from her and Oromi laughed.

"Well at least that is a start. You want me, don't you?"

"Tell me who sent you?" asked Dymondo with his back to her.

"You know the terms."

"That will never happen."

"By the look of you, I am now certain it will. So I shan't tell you….not yet."

Dymondo began to walk off.

"You cannot resist me, King Dymondo. I am irresistible!"

He stopped and turned.

She untied her gown, revealing her magnificent naked figure and, closing her eyes, she softly ran her fingers through her silky, black hair. Dymondo could not help but stare. But after a moment, he turned and headed out of the chamber.

***

It was long past midnight now, and Oromi was fast asleep in her bed when she was awoken by a discrete noise—a movement as though someone else was present in the room. She sat up and looked around. The ten maidservants that were meant to be standing guard were no longer there. *How could this be?* she wondered.

Still nude, she slid out from under the sheets, keeping a keen ear on the slow movement she could still hear. She kept vigilant as she moved towards her gown and swung it on to cover herself. She heard the sound again and tied the belt of the robe tight around her waist. She was certain she was not alone. *Where are the maidservants?* she thought. *How did this person get inside my chamber? Why weren't they stopped by the guards outside?* For a moment her heart fluttered. *Could it be the King playing games? Only he could get pass the guards. No,* she thought. *This is not him.* She noticed a dark shadow behind one of the pillars and took a fighting stance.

"Reveal yourself! I know you're there!" she exclaimed.

The figure emerged from behind the pillar. It was a slim figure dressed in all black, with a face mask. All else was covered from head to toe. Only red, devilish eyes were visible.

The masked intruder extracted a curved sword from its sheath and ran towards her at great speed. Oromi casually ducked the swing and with remarkable ease caught hold of the attacker's blade hand. She held on tight as the intruder strained to pull free from her grasp. At the first opportunity, she placed her leg between the intruder's legs, setting up a forward fall. As the attacker fell, Oromi pulled back hard on the hand she had in her grip. A tearing and breaking sound came from the attacker's hand and upon landing on the ground, the masked intruder wailed in agony, clutched the injured arm.

It was a man.

His arm was broken and hung lose from his body. Nevertheless the attacker made another attempt. He grabbed the sword with his other hand and ran at her again. Oromi, still in her battle stance, waited for the attacker to get near and at the correct moment made her move. Yet again she was able to smoothly dodge the blade. Showing mercy this time by not breaking his other arm, she managed to remove the sword from his hand and take it into her own. She flung the blade from one hand to the other swiping it through the air in a marvellous display of her own sword-wielding skills, then stopped and held the blade out.

"Stop! Who are you and why do you wish to kill me?"

The attacker had no answer.

Oromi moved forward and pitilessly sliced off his broken arm. The attacker cried out in pain as blood gushed onto the twitching limb below. He held onto the bleeding stump as he went down on his knees.

"It will be one body part at a time! The choice is yours! Will you tell me who sent you?"

"Never!" he replied as he stood up.

"Very well!" She turned and swung the sword again, this time through his right leg, just below the knee. The attacker tumbled over like a fallen tree and howled and screamed in agony. There was blood everywhere.

"I ask again!" Who…sent…you? Your pain can be over in one strike, but only if you tell me," she said, flicking fresh blood from the blade.

"I can't!" cried the attacker.

"As you wish," she said showing no mercy and parting his other arm from his body. The pain must have been unimaginable for him.

"It will be your other leg next and then I shall let you bleed for a while, before working on your other parts."

"No! Please finish me"

"Then tell me who sent you!"

"I cannot!"

"Fine! So be it," said Oromi and lifted the weapon in the air.

"No! Wait! Wait! I will tell you!"

She went close to him and grabbed him by chest. "Speak, you shit!"

Before the man could open his mouth, the room was filled with the King's guards and Lances. King Dymondo stormed in next, and Sterferep held him back and moved forward himself, running up to Oromi and taking the blood-stained weapon from her while Kor lifted her to her feet.

"What on Landsfor is happening here?" roared Dymondo.

"Speak! Speak! Who has sent you!" Oromi continued shouting at her assailant. The attacker did not respond. Oromi kicked his life-fleeing body vigorously as Kor pulled her back. Sterferep grabbed hold of whatever was left of the man by his chest.

"Who are you and who sent you?" he asked, grinding his teeth.

Dymondo walked up to Oromi and placed his hand upon her shoulder to calm her.

"Speak!" she shouted again.

"Fuck you all. I am finished!" responded the assailant.

"What on this realm is happening here?" Queen Ohio had now arrived. Oromi swiftly turned to Dymondo and pleaded with him.

"An attempt was made on my life. The same person that sent me to kill Lorca has probably now sent someone to kill me. My life is now in great danger, and the person behind all of this is someone in your own family!"

"Who?" demanded Dymondo, but before Oromi could answer, an infuriated Ohio intervened:

"Dymondo! What is happening here! You have forgotten how to command, boy?"

"Mother, I but…"

"Silence!"

"Lance Kor, shut that criminal up. Fasten her mouth and tie her hands immediately."

"No, wait Kor!" Dymondo objected.

"Lance Kor, your King himself said any order he gives can be revoked by my own! Do as you are told."

Kor's eyes apologised to Dymondo.

"No! No!" Stop! Listen to me…I need to tell you…" said Oromi before Kor pushed a cloth in her mouth and tied it across to prevent her from talking. He then used another cloth to tie her hands behind her back.

"Apologies, Oromi," he whispered loud enough for only Oromi to hear.

"Take her to the dungeon at once!" ordered Ohio.

Kor dragged her out of the chamber while Oromi struggled and made muffling sounds. Her eyes sought Dymondo's interference, but there was nothing Dymondo could do.

"Dy, this man is still alive," Queen Ohio said.

109

"Oromi said he tried to kill her!" Dymondo answered.

"You believe her? Looks as though she tried to kill *him*! There is no use keeping him alive. Even if we torture him more, he will not live long. Much blood has been lost. Look at this room. Pools of blood everywhere! Put this man out of his misery!"

"But, Mother, we can ask him questions!" said Dymondo.

"You can try, dear Dymondo, but his body has lost much blood and is losing more as we speak. We will not be able to keep him alive for long," she answered.

"Tell me, man!" Ohio turned to the masked attacker. "Who sent you?"

"I will not speak! No matter what!"

"Darn! Fine! Sterferep…"

Sterferep looked back at Dymondo. Dymondo gestured to him to put the man out of his misery. Sterferep did as told by running a knife along the intruder's throat.

"Take him away!" ordered Sterferep, and the guards took away the body.

"Wait! Show me his face," Dymondo commanded.

One of the guards unmasked the dead man's face.

"I have not seen this man anywhere before," said Sterferep.

Dymondo shook his head.

"Take him away, guards," ordered Ohio.

"Where are the maidservants?" Dymondo asked, registering the emptiness of the chamber for the first time. "Where were the Lances! Was there no one outside?"

"I do not know what happened, my King," replied Sterferep.

"Then find out! Who could have tried to kill her?"

"This person," replied Ohio.

"I know that! But someone must have sent him!"

"It was likely the same person that sent her," said Ohio. "That young woman is nothing but trouble! There is no need to show any more mercy towards her. You already have shown a great deal, and now this guest chamber looks like a battlefield. She is a snake. Either let her rot in the dungeon or banish her. Lances, get this chamber cleared immediately!"

"I want to know what happened to the Lances! What happened to the maidservants?" demanded Dymondo.

"Rest assured, my King, I shall investigate this attack!" said Sterferep. "I insist you and Queen Ohio return to your chambers immediately and rest. Tamaris! Please ensure that Queen Ohio gets safely to her chamber and stand outside it until the first ray of the sun. Dan and Dwarpal, you go with the King and make sure he reaches his chamber safely as well."

CHAPTER 18

BROTHERS OR NOT

The week past and Mysteria had returned from her home. Dymondo sat as his desk going through the scrolls in preparation for court, wearing his favourite royal-blue, velvet cloak and black shirt. Mysteria brought over some water in a beautiful silver container on a silver platter, along with a silver goblet.

"Gratitude Mysteria," he said with his attention on his scrolls.

"It is good to prepare, my King," remarked Mysteria sitting back down on the silky bedsheets.

"Hmm…" replied Dymondo.

"Will it all be ready by the time Sterferep arrives?"

"It will be, but for that my lovely, you will have to let me get on with it," he said and smiled at her.

"So, I am the one causing disturbance to the King? How will the King punish me?" she jested.

"Ah yes, punishment is most definitely due, my lady."

"And that would be?"

"If the lady would be so kind to come over to me, I can announce it."

She rose from the bed and strutted across to his table.

"Come beside me," he said grabbing her by the waist and sitting her on his lap. He kissed her and gently rubbed his nose against hers, and they both laughed.

"I think that is an apt punishment," he smiled and stood her up. She smiled and went back to sitting on the bed while he got back to his scrolls. Soon after, there was a knock at the door.

"Come in," said Dymondo.

"Good morning, my King. Are you ready for court?" asked Sterferep, sticking his head in.

"Ah yes, do enter, Sterferep. Carry some of these scrolls for me, please," said Dymondo.

"Of course," replied Sterferep, taking some from him. "Future Queen, Mysteria," he said bowing to her.

"Lance Sterferep," she bowed back and smiled.

Dymondo said his farewell to Mysteria and led Sterferep out of the chamber. Kor greeted the King and took some of the scrolls as they came out.

"My King," said Sterferep as Dymondo led them down the corridor.

"Yes, Sterferep."

"Forgive me, but if I may, I'd like to ask about future Queen Mysteria?"

"Yes, you may."

"You must now announce to the court whom she is to you."

"Not yet, Ster. I do not think it is yet time."

"But everyone will think she is your—"

"Sterferep. Please! Do not call her that!" Dymondo snapped. The King stopped walking as did his Lances. Dymondo turned to face Sterferep.

"Apologies, my King. Forgive my error. She most definitely is not....she is your love."

"Mysteria is a wonderful person, and you're correct, she is my love. Someone I call my friend. Whenever I felt utterly disheartened, she came forward and held me tight and embraced me. When she did, all my worries melted away."

"My King is gracious. It is through friendship I dared to make this suggestion."

"She has given me strength, Ster. I shared my heart's burden with her, and I trust her."

"Then why does the King delay his announcement? You love her, don't you?"

"Yes, yes, of course I do."

"Then why not propose to her in front of everyone in court and give her the rightful place she deserves?"

"No Ster...there is far too much going on right now. It would not be the right time."

"I understand, my King, but let me warn you: the people will form their own thoughts of her, until you tell them otherwise."

"I am aware. And we shall talk more about this later. Perhaps, when we sit down to share a glass of wine together, I will seek your advice further, but for now, we must head to court."

"Correct you are, my King," Sterferep said, and they all continued down the corridor.

Dymondo's entrance at court was announced by the doorman and all stood in attention and bowed and knelt in respect as he entered. Everyone sat down after he took his seat on the throne.

Scholar Lorca Loray was present in court after months, his life finally out of danger after the attack. Dymondo rose, smiled and addressed him directly. "Scholar Lorca!"

"My King," the old scholar replied in his old voice.

"I do not know what to say! It certainly is a pleasure to see you again after so long. I hope your health is now well?"

"My King, I bow before you and seek forgiveness for having returned so late to court."

"I am pleased to see you well and healthy again. For the time you took off whilst recovering, I have no qualms! That was understandable. But the time you took to complete the task..."

"My King has every right to be impatient at the task's delay. But forgive my insolence, my King, the task was so grand, it demanded solitude and my complete attention. As you know, the office became my abode."

"Yes, Lorca, Sterferep told me as much. You have been working hard, no doubt. You still look as though you require more nourishment, and your hair looks thinner and greyer than before."

"That is the least of my worries right now, my King. I wish to disclose to you my findings."

"Then speak, Lorca! For I wish to hear the outcome of your months of investigation," said Dymondo and sat back down. Everyone sat down except Lorca.

"I cannot say this in court, my King. My findings have grave implications, and I recommend the King hear them in confidence," said Lorca.

"Very well! Let other court proceedings commence, and I shall ask you to accompany me to my chamber after court. We can speak there in private."

Lorca bowed and returned to his seat.

The court proceedings began with reports from around the kingdom. Other issues were presented and resolved. Fines were given. Punishments served. After court, Dymondo commanded Lorca to follow him to his chamber. Dymondo led the way with Lorca following and Kor and Sterferep just behind. When they reached the King's chamber, they found

Mysteria sitting on the bed after having finished the cleaning. Mysteria took Dymondo's cloak, and the King placed himself in a large, comfortable armchair in the corner of the chamber. Mysteria then turned on the oil lamp, and Lorca entered and stood before the King with his hands folded and head down.

"Be seated, Lorca," Dymondo said, motioning to the chair near him.

"My King is gracious," the old man said as he sat down.

"Mysteria, my dear, would it be possible for you to ask Sterferep and Kor to step in as well?" he asked.

"Certainly, my King," said Mysteria humbly and privately pleased. He was now requesting her to do things instead of commanding her.

Lorca looked around, questioning the King's request to bring in the Lances. Mysteria brought them in and closed the door firmly behind them as they entered.

Lorca looked back at Dymondo, perplexed at the sudden look of irritation on the King's face.

"My King...?"

"Your length of absence angers me, Lorca! I set this task months ago, or has it been a year? Before the attack, I started to believe you had left the kingdom or were just too embarrassed to show your face. Did you not fear my wrath?"

"I give you my sincerest apologies, my King."

Dymondo held up his hand. He was not looking for apologies. "Leave it. Please now say what you must."

"My King is gracious and—"

"Leave aside the niceties, Lorca! Speak your words."

"Of course, my King, but I expected that we would not be in the presence of anyone. What about these three?"

"Caution, Lorca! Choose your words sensibly. *These three*, as you say, are my confidants; therefore, you need not be concerned."

Lorca lowered his chin into his grey beard. "Very well, my King. After my investigation, I have come to the following conclusion: King Shilathaar of Forprimiera and King Grygerious of Doosranfor may not be your blood brothers."

There was an awkward silence. Lorca sat up straight and anxiously waited for the King's lips to move. Sterferep and Kor glanced at each other, then straight ahead. Dymondo stared at the chief researcher and did not look pleased. He was in denial.

"Lorca, often months of confinement can cloud one's judgement. It looks as though the same has happened to you. I do not blame you for this. But I think I have tolerated enough of your nonsense."

"The King does not have faith in my words? I assure you I speak the

114

truth."

"Lorca, your statements include untoward claims about my mother and father. I will not allow such disrespect."

"And you must not, my King. Please listen to what I have to say, and if you disapprove, then I shall gladly place my neck on the block this very day."

From the look she gave, Mysteria did not enjoy that description.

"Speak!" demanded Dymondo.

"Your father was a good man, a good King. And your mother is a pious lady. I have all the respect for her. For the past months, I have been studying the scrolls and scripts on the history of the Rain dynasty. I went as far back as King Forothaar. Every son and daughter born is accounted for in those scrolls. I know of their birth time, whether they reigned or not, how long they lived, and whom they married. Everything. All scrolls are intact as the royal lineage ministers kept them immaculately. But…"

"…But what?"

"But there are no details, my King, of anyone beyond your father, King Balathaar. Every King must have the births of his children registered in these scrolls. There is no mention of any such births."

"And after spending months, you come up with the conclusion that we may not be blood brothers purely based on the fact there is no mention of it in the scrolls? Pathetic."

"These scrolls have been kept for years, my King. No Rain King has ever turned a lazy eye towards these scrolls."

"Still not enough evidence to conclude—"

"I will go further. It was rumoured that King Balathaar's seed was weak and unable to impregnate the Queen. I overheard the royal physician Ramos mention this to your uncle Marahud when I was a young economist. I did not mention this to anyone as I did not want my head to be parted."

"Hearsay! Neither Ramos or my uncle are here to testify to such a conversation. Move on!"

"You and your brothers were not born in the royal palace."

Dymondo sat up when Lorca said this. This was news to him, indeed. "Go on," he said.

"Your father and mother one day decided to go far from the kingdom to a beautiful yet remote place that only they knew of. Your uncle and the royal physician accompanied them. The holiday lasted nearly twelve months, and when they returned, the first-born, your eldest brother, Shilathaar, played in the arms of the Queen."

"They went away for an entire year? How inconsiderate!"

"Not so, my King. When the King and Queen returned to the palace with an heir, the citizens were overjoyed. They adored the new prince, but no one knew where he was born. After a year, the King and Queen returned to this place again with the royal physician and your uncle Marahud. They returned with their second son, Grygerious, after another twelve months, and a year after that, they went again and returned with you."

Dymondo kept quiet for a long while.

"It is the truth, my King," Lorca added.

"And what about Nilharia?" Dymondo was testing him now.

"My King, Princess Nilharia was born three or maybe four years after your birth. This was a natural birth. She was conceived and born in the royal palace. The King and Queen were astonished and overjoyed at her arrival."

"And you have evidence of this from your findings?"

"Indeed, my King. I can show you the scrolls now if you wish."

"No need just yet. First, tell me who else knows of this? Who else aided you?"

"Everyone knew of the King and Queen's holidays. But no one ever questioned it or looked into it until you asked me to look into the lineage. So only my son knows of this, my King. He aided me for a time in my research. As for the secret documents, they are in the chamber where I confined myself."

"But, Lorca, is this truly enough for you to come to such a conclusion?"

"No, my King, the evidence is not in stone, but think, why go on holiday to conceive a child, much less three of them?"

"It is common for a man and a woman to do so. It changes their surroundings."

"But why refrain from adding the details of the births of the princes and the princess in the royal scrolls?"

"Simply a slip of the mind. The King could have forgotten."

"Why does one brother have black hair, the other golden hair and the third brown?" Dymondo had no answer for that.

"Why do the brothers have different body frames and bear no resemblance to one another?" Again, no response from the King.

"Why is there no resemblance between the parents and any of their sons? And why does Princess Nilharia have Queen Ohio's eyes?" Dymondo had no answer to any of these questions.

"Lorca, see to it that no one hears of this. And I mean no one. Explain this to your son as well. Even your own wife is not to know. Is your son married?"

"No, my King, he's yet young."

"I forbid you and him to disclose this to anyone or you will be severely punished. Is that clear?"

"Crystal."

"Ample fine wine shall be sent to your home along with abundant coin for your hard work. Ensure the safeguarding of the documents, and bring them here to Mysteria. Go to your office now and bring them here at once. Sterferep and Kor shall accompany you."

"Indeed, my King, it shall be done. May I take your leave?"

"You may. And one other thing. Although I do not approve of such pleasures myself, if you wish to indulge in womanly company, you shall be given the key to the hall of pleasures for this evening or any evening of your choice."

"My King is gracious. Let me first ensure the documents are safe and then I shall let you know, my King," said Lorca with a smirk.

"Proceed."

Sterferep, Kor and Lorca left for the office.

"My, my, what a revelation!" said Mysteria.

"I know…but it explains the differences between me and my brothers."

"Gratitude for showing such faith in me, my King."

The King was lost in thought and did not respond.

"My King?"

"Oh yes…you are deserving of it," he smiled and moved to the bed still turning things over in his mind. Mysteria came over and removed his boots.

"Are you angry at Lorca for the news he has given you?"

"No, my love. Lorca was set a task to discover the great history of the Rain dynasty—to investigate every detail about every Rain King who had ever reigned. He was to investigate everything about the royal family and every member and highlight any suspicious realities. He did his job."

Shortly, Lorca returned with the documents with Sterferep and Kor behind him. He handed the documents to Mysteria, who gathered them and placed them on Dymondo's desk. As per her King's instructions, she would wait for everyone to leave before she secretly stored them away.

"Well done, Lorca. Take some time off. You have done well. I expect you back after seven days!" declared Dymondo.

"Gratitude, my King,"

"Gratitude, now you may go."

"Umm…my King…"

"Say it, Lorca."

"…The key, my King, Ha-ha."

Mysteria gave Lorca a demeaning look. The moment was awkward as Dymondo was not expecting the old man to accept his offer. Nevertheless, he had promised.

"Sterferep, accompany Lorca to the hall of pleasures and ensure all his desires are fulfilled. Stand guard outside until dawn, after which you shall accompany him home…to his wife," commanded Dymondo. Lorca stared at the ground embarrassed at the mention of his wife.

"Kor, ensure that Lorca's son is safely seen home to his mother."

"Yes, my King," both spoke in unison.

"Lorca, have you told your son about our conversation—that he is to keep his mouth shut?" Dymondo asked.

"Yes, my King."

"Great. You may go."

"One other suspicious point," said Lorca.

"What is that?" asked Dymondo.

"After your birth, your uncle Marahud and the royal physician Ramos were sent away from the kingdom to carry out a task—what task, no one knew. But they did not return. Some say they were banished. Months later, news arrived of their deceased remains. It seemed as though they had been devoured by some creature. They never returned."

Dymondo nodded but kept quiet. Mysteria covered her mouth with her hands.

"Do we know what creature?" Dymondo asked.

"It could not be said for sure, my King. People at the time said it could have been a giant snake. Pieces of snake skin were found nearby. But it would have had to have been a giant snake. Still, no one knew for sure. But…"

"But what?"

"Forgive me, my King."

"Say it, Lorca!"

"I never witnessed it myself, but I believe your father, from time to time, sought aid from powerful creatures."

"What creatures?"

"Those were peculiar times, but I would not be surprised if some of those creatures still exist."

Dymondo thought. "I have heard stories too of talking animals."

"Precisely! It came to my knowledge that King Balathaar would often ride to the lake on the banks of River Krool whenever he had a discrete task that needed completing. The creature from the lake was a giant, hooded snake. I may have even heard its name. Sanpsarp."

"My father gave tasks to a giant snake?!"

"Yes, my King"

"What kind of tasks?"

"My King, such tasks are not spoken of. These are only known to the King or, as you say, to his confidants. I was not a confidant of King Balathaar."

"Who were his confidants then?"

"They no longer draw breath."

Silence had now taken over the room. Dymondo mustered the courage to ask the scholar directly what he didn't want to ask.

"Lorca...did my father have this snake kill my uncle and the royal physician?"

"There is no evidence of this, my King? Nothing to prove it. But the only people that knew what happened on those holidays were your father, your uncle, the royal physician and Queen Ohio, and it is plausible that King Balathaar may have thought it...beneficial...to have less people knowing the truth of what happened."

"What is this great secret, Lorca? What exactly happened on those holidays?"

"That we do not know, my King. Your mother, Queen Ohio, might be able to tell you."

Dymondo nodded again.

"Who else knows about the fact that Father knew this snake and often sought its aid?"

"As I said, all his confidants are now dead."

"How do you know this?"

"Forgive me, my King, but in my youth, I was the best young politician of my time. Often I would be invited to meetings by the King. His confidants would be there, too. No one spoke anything directly, but I was clever enough to pick up subtle hints during those meetings. I absorbed knowledge and kept quiet. I assure you no one else would know this apart from me."

Dymondo nodded.

Lorca bowed and left the chamber and Sterferep followed him. Kor followed them out and headed for Lorca's office where Lorca's son had been asked to wait after court.

Back in his chamber, Dymondo took a deep breath.

"It has been a long day, hasn't it, my love?" asked Mysteria.

"Yes, my lovely. Would you be able bring me some sweet red wine?"

"Of course." She poured wine in a goblet and brought it to him.

"Join me."

She smiled and poured a goblet for herself and went up to him. He stood staring at the ground with one hand against the wall.

"One can never fathom the inner desires of man," he said.

"Everyone has their own principles, my King. You must not let this news trouble you so."

"I'm speaking of Lorca, my lady. Look at him! A man his age? He can hardly walk and he speaks with difficulty, yet he desires womanly pleasures!"

119

"What has *that* got to do with age?"

"I thought he'd have more wisdom by now."

"Human longings are natural, my King."

"I know that Mysteria, but—"

"My King…" She placed her hand on his face and turned it towards her. "…We have our own principles and people have theirs. Some people follow their principles strictly. Some do not have any to follow. People are free to do what they wish. We cannot control that. That would be act of tyranny. We can merely ensure that we follow our own principles and do not question other people. In their eyes, they may be correct, just as we are in ours."

"But Mysteria—"

"Ssh! You walk on your path of righteousness and let others walk on theirs. Everyone knows what is good and what is sin."

Dymondo nodded and softly embraced her.

"I have to speak with my family," said Dymondo. "I must seek an audience with my mother, and I must then speak with my brothers."

"Do you believe him?"

"Not entirely, but he has no reason to lie."

"Why set him the task if you were not going to believe in his findings?"

"I was not expecting him to find anything, Mysteria. I wanted him to say 'all is well and everything is intact.'"

"I can understand."

CHAPTER 19

THE THREE KINGS

The next day Dymondo went to seek advice from his mother, but she had committed to a private seven-day prayer which she had held in her chamber and had strictly warned she not be interrupted or disturbed whilst she conducted the ceremony ("in the name of God Aquinious"). Dymondo initially decided to hold for seven days, but ultimately, he could not bear the wait. He was getting restless. He had to speak to someone in his family. Thus, he invoked the Call.

The Call was only to be invoked in emergencies and circumstances of the direst importance. The Call was signalled by the blowing of a large horn from the post at the shores of Fourtfor across the seas to posts at the shores of Doosranfor and Forprimiera. An acknowledgement is then sent back by the Primieran and Doosran posts and the Kings of those islands are informed immediately.

Upon receiving the Call, it was customary for all three Kings to meet at the Forkshetra Battleground in Fourtfor, so when Dymondo received acknowledgements back from Shilathaar and Grygerious, he headed for the battleground. Shilathaar brought along a battalion led by the commander-in-chief of the Primieran army, Retchia Snapp, and his chief courtier, Orpictus Rali. Grygerious too rode in with a battalion with Gray Sylon and Karnigol Aparata as the leaders. Dymondo rode in with his battalion, headed by Lance Sterferep Unknown and Lance Kor Grayish. The battleground was vast. Many battles had been fought there and won by Landsfor.

"Brother Dymondo!"

"Dear Brother Shilathaar!" the two brothers greeted each other with an embrace. Grygerious too greeted his brothers in the same manner. Retchia and Orpictus got off their horses to stand beside Shilathaar. Karnigol and Gray and Sterferep and Kor did the same for their Kings.

"Tell us, Brother, why did you invoke the Call?" What is so important?" asked Shilathaar.

"Dear Brother, how are you and Sister-in-Law Silvenia? And Brother Grygerious how are you and Sister-in-Law Gilgenia?"

Shilathaar paused. "Well! Both her and I are well!"

"All is well in Doosranfor. Gratitude for asking," replied Grygerious.

"And Mother?" asked Shilathaar.

"She is well. She is holding a seven-day prayer right now."

"Great! So why do you call us? Let's not delay," urged Shilathaar.

"I agree. I do not wish to camp any longer than I need to," added Grygerious.

"Right... well, Brothers, I am going through a dilemma."

"What dilemma?" asked Shilathaar.

"Can we ask our battalions to move back so they cannot hear us?" asked Dymondo.

"We will not! This is for the security of the King!" interrupted Retchia, Shilathaar's commander.

"And he is safe with me, I am his brother!" shouted Dymondo.

"Whoever it may be," Retchia responded.

Dymondo's eyes burned with anger. "I stand here willing to lay down my life for my brothers if need be, and you show mistrust towards me?" Dymondo unsheathed his sword.

Retchia pulled out his sword. Sterferep and Kor did the same.

"Retchia!" shouted Shilathaar. "Show respect to Dymondo!"

"Apologies, my King," trembled Retchia and sheathed his sword.

"Retchia and Orpictus are my trusted ones, Dymondo. Let them be!"

Dymondo nodded and put his sword back. Sterferep and Kor did the same.

"Likewise, I trust Karnigol and Gray." Grygerious's throat was dry after having seen so many swords freed from their scabbards.

"Fine then! Battalions move back ten paces!" roared Shilathaar.

"Karnigol ask the battalion to go back ten paces," Grygerious whispered to Karnigol. Karnigol did as he was told.

"Move back ten paces!" commanded Dymondo to his battalion. The soldiers were now far enough back they could not hear a word of the conversation.

"Speak now, Dymondo! What is it that bothers you?" Shilathaar said.

"Dear Brother, I have heard some terrible news!"

"What news!"

"I had my chief scholar do some research on our lineage."

"Why would you have that done?"

"I wanted to know the great history of the Rain dynasty and about every Rain King who had ever reigned, Brother."

"Ha-ha! You need to go on holiday, Dymondo. Why don't you go over to Grygerious's island? It is filled with all kinds of pleasures!" laughed Shilathaar.

"Of course, come over any time you like, Dymondo. My island is just heaven!" laughed Grygerious.

"Dear Brothers, I do not jest. Please, I request you listen."

"You are very tense, Brother. What did your scholar find?"

Dymondo then mentioned the findings of Lorca to his brothers. Shilathaar's face displayed fury, but he swallowed his pride. Grygerious was shocked and placed his hand upon his face with his mouth hanging open. Though they responded with soothing words, by the time the story finished, Shilathaar's eyes were red with anger and Grygerious's eyes shone with evil intent.

"So let it be, Dymondo! Do not let such stupid findings and conclusions cloud your mind. We are brothers! No matter what anyone has to say," assured Shilathaar. "But gratitude for telling us this." Shilathaar placed his hand upon Dymondo's shoulder.

Grygerious placed his own hand on Dymondo's other shoulder. "Do not worry," he said. "Go back to your palace and have some fine wine, and all that worries you will flee. I would take no notice of such things."

"Nothing can be proven!" Shilathaar added. "Unless Mother tells you otherwise, and if she had something to tell us, she would have done it by now. People will say anything to break up our family. But as the royal family, it is our duty to remain united." Shilathaar's words were comforting, but his eyes said otherwise.

"I still believe we are brothers after what I have heard," said Grygerious, his own treacherous tongue pouring its sweet nectar.

"Gratitude my dear brothers, I too share your sentiments. The burden has lifted from my heart," said Dymondo, though he was not convinced of his brothers' reactions. Something was not right.

"Let's all head back home," smiled Grygerious.

The brothers said their goodbyes and headed home in their respective directions.

123

CHAPTER 20

MOTHER

D ymondo headed straight for the baths after he returned and then to his chamber. As Mysteria was away from the palace and again back at her house with her mother, the King found another maidservant at his service. Dymondo changed into comfortable clothes and sat in the arm chair at his desk with his elbow propped on his armrest and his hand upon his cheek and stared outside his window. He tried to put all the pieces together—the reason behind Oromi's attack and the attack on her. *What could be the secret?* He decided he would ask his mother himself as soon as her prayers were over.

Queen Ohio was overwhelmed with joy to see her son enter her royal guest chamber after her prayers had finished.

"Oh, Dy, my boy!" She said in her firm voice.

Dymondo strode up to her and held her. "Mother! How do you fare? And how did your prayers go?"

"I am well, my son, and yes the prayers too went well. Come…come and sit near me." She grabbed his hand and held it tight and took him over to two soft chairs where they both sat down.

"Dymondo, you look great. Starting to look like your father now!" she smiled. Dymondo's smile fled, and he lost his words.

"Why do you look at me like that? You are beginning to look like him, really! Now what will you have? Grape juice? Or Pomegranate?"

"Grape would be fine, Mother," Dymondo answered.

"You won't be getting any wine, young man," she smiled.

Dymondo smiled, too, and both shared a goblet of the finest grape juice in the land.

"Just as I remember it, from when we were children!"

"Yes, you should drink more of this, instead of that sweet wine."

"I will do."

"Tell me, Son, have you been forgoing meals? You look slightly slender."

"No, Mother. I have just been training more."

"Don't forego meals, my son. I don't like it when my boys don't eat properly."

Dymondo smiled.

"Your mind seems elsewhere, dear. Are you tired? Do you need rest? You are not still worried about that stupid young woman, are you?"

"No, no, not at all."

"Well it sure seems that way," chuckled Ohio. "If it would help, then go get some rest or a hot bath because your mind seems occupied."

"It is not rest I seek mother. I seek answers."

"Answers to what, my son?"

"Answers to my questions." Ohio's smile faded.

"Then go get your answers, Son."

"That is what I came here for."

"Here? Answers from me? What kind of answers do you seek from me?" asked Ohio, feigning surprise; however, deep inside she had started to grow worried.

"Mother, you know—"

"I do not, Dymondo. Now I have always told you, your brothers and your sister, to ask your questions directly. I don't like to play games," she scolded him.

"Mother, I don't know how to ask this."

"Just ask, Son."

"I have been told that my brothers are not my blood brothers. Lorca found the missing entries in the scrolls of royal births."

"Oh that? That is nothing."

"It is not nothing, Mother. I require an explanation."

"I don't have to explain anything to you, my son."

"What happened to Uncle Marahud? I want to know everything, Mother!"

"I have answered your question. I will not entertain another."

"No, Mother, you have to tell me!"

She sighed. "What do you want to know?" She sounded annoyed.

"Mother please, I beg you. You must tell me."

"Some conversations are best not had, my son. They will only bring pain and destruction. Let it be."

"No, Mother, you must tell me; I beg you."

"You are my good son, the most understandable and intelligent. If anyone should know, it is you. But I implore you not to mention this to your brothers or anyone else. It seems enough people know already."

"Then tell me, Mother. I wait for your words." Now Dymondo was worried.

"Why do you wish to know, Dymondo? Is there something you hide from me? There has to be a reason."

"There is."

"Then say it!"

"First answer my questions."

"Then you will tell me?"

"Yes. I will tell you everything.

"Well then, you leave me no choice!"

CHAPTER 21

CALL THE ROYAL PHYSICIAN

O hio spoke softly, "I will narrate you the story of your birth, Dy,".
Dymondo moved off the chair and sat at her feet. She placed her
loving hand upon his head and ruffled his hair.

"It started the day when my King called upon the royal physician, who
had informed him that he may never father a child..."

***

"Greetings, royal physician," said Balathaar.

"Greetings, my King," replied the royal physician, Ramos, as he bowed
and knelt before the King.

"Come and sit down, there is much to speak about," the King replied
politely. "Leave us!" Balathaar ordered. The guards and the maidservants
bowed and knelt and left promptly.

"I pray to the Gods that all is well with the King," said Ramos.

"Quiet! Not a word from your mouth or I shall place my blade in it!"
shouted the King. His behaviour had changed as soon as the guards and the
maids had left the chamber.

"Forgive me, my King, where have I erred?"

"You were given instructions to follow. You were asked to perform the
cure and provide the remedy! I am still waiting," snarled the King.

"I have carried out all the necessary studies, my King, and have tried all
the remedies to my knowledge. The lack lies with you, not the Queen, my

127

King."

The King's eyes turned red in anger. "You dare to utter such words?!" he exclaimed.

"My King, I dare… only because it is the truth. I am the best physician in the land. In the past, you have sought advice from many other physicians. None of them ever came close to discerning the reason behind Queen Ohio being without child. Perhaps some of them did, but they were too afraid of your wrath to say it. But, my King, I serve this land and I serve you. I will not speak untruths. You can never father a child."

"Silence!" shouted the King, striking the outside of his left hand across the physician's nose. The healer crashed to the ground and his nose began to bleed profusely. He held his nose up and slowly got to his feet. As he did, the King walked over and grabbed him by his garments and shook him violently.

"This cannot be! This cannot be! You lie to me, you wretch! How can this be?! You must deal with this! I don't know how, but you will fix it!" roared the King and threw the bleeding physician back on the stone floor.

The bald, plump physician lay on the floor in pain and disbelief.

***

"You see, Dymondo," Ohio explained, "King Balathaar was powerful, but his seed was weak. He could not impregnate me after many attempts, and since the fault lay with him, it mattered not if he took another Queen. He could not accept this."

"Is that when your brother, Uncle Marahud, offered his advice?"

"Lorca could not have known that through his investigations, my dear Dy! How do you know this?"

"All I know, Mother, is that after our births, Uncle Marahud and the royal physician were sent on a task and never returned. I wish to hear about it from you, Mother."

"Very well. Your uncle, my brother, Marahud…" Ohio began to cry as she mentioned his name. Dymondo rose and put his arm around her and consoled her.

"My dear sweet brother. I only wish he had not suggested anything!" She wept more. After a while she stopped and continued:

"Marahud recommended that I use the boon which I had been blessed with when I turned nineteen."

"What boon?"

"A chant whispered into my ear by a great sage, from whom my father and mother sought advice from time to time. He no longer lives. But he did say that whenever I uttered the chant, a son would be granted by the Gods themselves—born with all their qualities and goodness!

"The sage, who was he?"

128

"Sage Shilajeet. But as I said, he no longer lives. Well, as it happened, your father and I decided to go far from the kingdom to a beautiful yet remote place. Physician Ramos and your uncle, Marahud, accompanied us there. I woke up one morning, bathed and cleaned and put on my finest clothes. I sat on top of a high hill and chanted those divine words…and I saw a golden light appear in the sky. It was truly divine. But then I saw the sky turn dark like nightfall and within moments the golden light reappeared and there stood before me the God of War, Terradeus. He smiled and raised his hand and a sharp bright beam shone from his hand directly at my womb. And then I was with child. After nine months, my first son, Shilathaar, was born by the grace of God Terradeus.

We returned to the palace after twelve months with an heir. The citizens were overjoyed with their new prince, but no one knew our grave secret. After a year had passed, I said to the King that I wished for another child. The King refused as he had begun to love Shilathaar more than his life. But I kept insisting, so we returned to that place. Again, I followed the same ritual and our second son, Grygerious, was granted with the blessings of the God of Love, Ishq. It was just like before. A divine golden light appeared in the sky followed by darkness; then followed by the golden light again. A light shone from the God's hand upon my womb, and after nine months, your brother, Grygerious, was born. We returned to the kingdom with our second son. Then after another year, we returned again. This time we were blessed with you. But during your conception, the experience was completely different."

"Different, how?"

"This time, when I saw the golden light, no darkness followed. Just more light: silver light, red, blue, green, yellow and many other marvellous colours. It was just light after light, and no darkness, until standing before me was…"

"Who, Mother? Whom was I blessed by?" asked Dymondo.

"My dear Dymondo, you were born by the grace of the King of the Gods himself, Topus, the supreme being."

Dymondo was stunned. He paused to think for a while. Why did his mother see darkness in the sky during the births of his two elder brothers?

"Every year," Ohio continued, "the King and I would go away and every year we would return with a child. The citizens were told each time that the King and Queen were on holiday, but after three sons, we decided not to go anymore. We were too occupied with bringing you up."

"So King Balathaar is not my father?"

The Queen patted his hand. "You and your brothers are the blessings of different deities, and you all are different from one another. But I gave birth to you all, my son. When the light from the deity's hand shone upon my womb, I became pregnant and you and your brothers were born in the natural way after the usual nine months."

"Then what happened?"

"Tongues begun to wag in the kingdom that there was some mysterious secret surrounding the births of the children. Your father dismissed all the speculation, though it disturbed his sleep for many nights. But after some time, the citizens stopped talking and the rumours dissipated. Only Marahud, my brother, and Ramos knew the truth. Your father reminded them that they could never tell anyone the secret. Then one horrid morning, your father sent them away from the kingdom on a task."

"Why did Uncle Marahud have to leave? He was family. Was Landsfor not his home?"

"Of course it was his home! I belong to a rich, noble family, Dymondo—the reputable Gash household. When your grandfather, Komodothaar, was King, your father was crown prince. I used to attend court with my father, mother and brother. King Komodothaar was always very kind to us. Your father would always want to dance with me at court, and I with him. We began to grow fond of one another, and eventually King Komodothaar and my father gave us their blessings. My father's health deteriorated fast after my marriage. Then he left for the afterlife. My mother could not bear the shock, so she too soon followed. Marahud was left alone in our mansion. So your father and I decided he could come and live in the royal castle, which was at the time situated in Fourtfor. Marahud sold the family mansion and took everything he owned and moved in with us."

"Where did Father ask them to go?"

"I do not know. But Marahud and Ramos left together. That was a horrendous day for me. I wept for months after he left. He was my best friend. I could talk to him about anything."

"Did you not object?"

"Well, I did not think anything of it. Of course, I would have if I knew he was not going to return. But who could refuse the King's orders?"

"Then what happened?"

"Months went by and my tears had finally dried up, until I heard the news which plunged me back into darkness for another two and half years."

"The news that Ramos and Marahud had been killed by a large snake near the river Krool."

"So you learned of that, too. Yes, my eyes did not dry after that. Your father was very kind to me during those two years even though I refused to lay with him during that time."

"That was the least he could do!" said Dymondo staring straight into his mother's eyes. His mother looked right back at him, confused.

"Why do you say that?"

He did not know how to answer her. Did she know that King Balathaar ordered the killings of Ramos and Marahud and she too was a part of it? Or was she oblivious and innocent. He decided not to mention it…at least not yet.

"First, tell me of Nilharia's birth," he said.

"Ah, the lovely petal. She brought new happiness into our lives. She was born three years after you. I finally came out of mourning, and your father and I conceived her naturally. Her birth was an additional blessing as she was born in Fourtfor in front of the citizens; therefore, all those who doubted the previous births went completely quiet. The secret was forever buried. Nilharia was the apple of everyone's eye, especially yours, Dy."

"She still is," smiled Dymondo.

"Yes, I know," laughed Ohio.

"Gratitude for telling me, Mother. I appreciate it."

"Your father was a decent man, a good King, as are you, my son. I am proud of you." She hugged him tightly.

"I love you, too Mother!" said Dymondo, returning the embrace.

"Can you tell me one thing," she asked after Dymondo sat back down.

"What is that?"

"Why did you say that it was the least your father could do during my mourning?"

Dymondo looked away and evaded eye contact.

"Dy, do not look away from me. I have told you everything there is to know. If you know something more, you must tell me. Why did you say that?"

"Mother I do not know how to tell you this. I'm not even sure it is true."

"What is it, Dy? I must know!" His mother was becoming firm now.

"Father may have ordered your brother and the royal physician killed. That snake that killed Uncle was named Sanpsarp. Father apparently knew the creature and often gave it tasks."

The Queen crumpled back in her large chair with her jaw open and her eyes wet. She could not believe what she had just heard. *He knew the creature!* So what she had always feared and didn't want to admit was true. Her own husband had her brother murdered!

Ohio began to cry loudly, beating her fists against the armrests of her chair. Dymondo held her as she sobbed loudly.

"I'm sorry, Mother. I was not sure if I should tell you this."

Ohio cried for a long time, and Dymondo held her until she finally gathered herself.

"You must get some rest now, Son," she said weakly. "We shall meet at dinner."

Dymondo nodded and understood she needed to be alone. He quietly got up to leave.

"I did not want any of you to become aware of the secret," she said. "Shila and Gry do not know, and I want it to remain that way. If they know the truth, they will move against you and seek war. But Dymondo, you know everything, and I know you will still pray for their wellbeing and seek peace."

Dymondo lowered his head.

"Dymondo?"

"I have already spoken with them about this, Mother."

"What? When? Why would you do that?"

"You were busy with your prayers. I had to speak with someone."

"Could you not have waited?!" she shouted.

Dymondo had no reply.

"Oh my Gods, help this family! Dymondo I am disappointed in you!"

"What have I done wrong?"

"You have set the wheels in motion for the Rains to fall! Now they know they are not your brothers and have all the reason to move against you!"

"But why would they do that? They have assured me we are brothers and nothing will change."

"And you believe them? Have you not known your brothers all this time, Dymondo?"

"But..."

"No buts Dymondo! Leave my chamber! Now!"

Dymondo left her room in distress.

***

The next morning Queen Ohio sent for her son, and without haste, Dymondo came and presented himself before the Queen in her chamber. The Queen kissed his forehead and held her son tightly.

"Dy! Forgive me for losing my temper. You are a good boy. Both your brothers are the stupid ones! I will speak with them. At least now you understand why all of you are so different," she smiled.

Dymondo nodded again.

"Absolutely, Mother."

"Dymondo, make arrangements for my travel for I wish to visit my eldest son, Shilathaar, in Forprimiera."

"Of course, Mother. Your wish is my command. I shall make the arrangements right away, but..."

"But what?"

"Forgive me, Mother, but why do you wish to go there?"

"Can a mother not visit her son? Must I provide a reason for everything I do?" snapped Ohio.

"Of course, not, mother. You do not have to explain anything to anyone, but you mistake my intent. I do not ask as King but as your son. If you see fit then answer; otherwise, I shall take your leave and begin arrangements for your chariot and ship and send word to brother Shilathaar."

Ohio did not answer and turned her back to him. She was not happy. In fact, she was very upset. The conversation from the day before was still eating her up inside. Dymondo noticed and refrained from questioning her further.

"I take your leave," bowed Dymondo.

"Dy…" she spoke.

"Yes, Mother."

"Come here and sit down."

Dymondo went over and sat on the couch, and she came and sat down beside him. "I did not mean to raise to my voice again, Son," she said, putting her soft hand on his cheek.

Dymondo smiled. "I know, Mother, but I am worried. I know you're worried, too."

"And how do you know that I am worried?"

"I can tell from your face."

She smiled at that, nodded and closed her eyes.

"Mother, lift this burden from your heart. Tell me the reason for your concern."

"My son, I am heartbroken! Heartbroken to see my own children quarrelling so!"

"You do not need to have any concern from my side, Mother."

"Yes, you have assured me. I just wish to hear the same from Shilathaar and Grygerious."

"Mother, you cannot take a plea from me. That would be a display of cowardice. Do you wish for the world to see me as a coward?"

"No, I do not intend that. I only wish to reason with my son, like I have reasoned with you."

"What do you fear?"

"I fear he will raise an army to overthrow you."

"Brother Shilathaar would not—"

"He is capable, Dymondo, and the sooner you digest that, the better it will be for you. The other one Grygerious is no better. If it ever comes to the point where you all wish to end each other, how can I bear that? I did what was best for our family, and I will continue to do so now and into the future, with or without your consent," Ohio was growing stern again.

133

"No, Mother, you are wrong. I do not wish to end anyone's life. But if brother Shilathaar is preparing and brother Grygerious is plotting, then I cannot sit idle. I will strengthen my defences. If they prepare their armies, then I will prepare mine. I will not attack, but if either of them attacks, I will defend my people. I have no other choice."

"But you promise that you will not launch an attack first?" asked Ohio.

"I can promise you that, and I have promised you. But if anyone attacks my people or hurts anyone I love, then that person will perish!"

"And if Shilathaar says the same to me and so does Grygerious, then no one will attack anyone. Hence there will be no battle!"

Dymondo smiled at his mother's innocence.

"Am I, not right?" she asked again.

"Yes, you are, but do not plea on my behalf."

"I will not. I will simply talk sense into them and convince them to maintain the peace."

"You may go, Mother, but I believe it will be futile. Brother Shilathaar only does what his heart desires."

"I cannot have my children quarrelling over land. I will do all I can to prevent a war. Send word to Grygerious that I travel to Forprimiera and that he too should be present there when I arrive as I wish to see them both together."

"It shall be done," Dymondo said, "yet I fear this shall be misinterpreted by them both. It will appear as if Gammafor and Fourtfor are weak and do not have the strength to answer their onslaught. I assure you, Mother, that is not the case."

"I know, Dymondo, and I know you wish to prevent me from going, but—"

"Mother, you are safe here in Gammafor. If we are to fight, then that is destiny."

"Quiet! It is our actions that decide what seeds we sow for our future. Yes, we have less control over the outcome, but we must not stop acting to prevent calamity. I cannot sit idle when I have a chance to prevent a war. My decision is final. I shall seek peace and harmony. I shall do my part."

"I do not feel right about this. I fear for your wellbeing."

"I am going to see my son, Dy. He will not harm me in any way. I am his mother, too."

"Yes, of course. I know brother Shilathaar is capable of many things, but I agree he would never hurt you."

Ohio nodded in response.

"I am a mother. For a mother, all her children are the same. She cannot see anyone of them hurt. May she have two or may she have ten, her heart will weep equally for all."

Dymondo lowered his head and took a deep breath. Ohio put her hand on his strong shoulder.

"There now, I shall not be gone for long. And when I return to Fourtfor, I expect you to bring this lovely young lady I have been hearing about to my castle for a formal introduction."

Dymondo's face turned red. "Mother, how do you know?"

"There is sweet whisper around the land that the King has fallen in love with a beautiful young woman. Is it true?"

"Well...I..."

"What is her name?"

"Mysteria."

"A very nice name. Where does she hail from?"

"She is not a princess like my brother's wives, Mother. She was my chambermaid."

Ohio smiled. "What difference does that make? She has managed to win your heart and you love her."

Dymondo smiled. "I will bring her to see you very soon."

"You must! I have always wanted for all my children to find their loving partners before I go to the afterlife."

"Mother, do not speak of such things. There is much time for that yet."

"I am not worried about Nilharia so much. I know you will take care of her, and her friend Velvia is there for her, too. I was concerned about you, but now my heart is at rest. But for now, I would like you to heed my command and arrange my travel."

"Yes, Mother, I shall arrange everything. I will send many guards with you for protection."

"You can do that, Dy, but I wouldn't bother. Landsfor is mine. All of it. The land, the air, the water. It is all mine."

Dymondo hugged his mother tight. "Come back soon, Mother." He still seemed very concerned.

She ruffled the hair on the back of his head and smiled, holding her tears as did he.

"I will be back to my castle soon, Son. But if this is my last journey, you must bring me to Fourtfor for my cremation," she laughed.

"Mother! Do not say that!"

"Alright, alright, no inauspicious talks." They looked at one another and smiled.

"One more question, Mother, if I may?"

"Yes?"

"Do you know why the skies went dark during the birth of my brothers?"

"No, Dy. If I did, I would have told you."

Dymondo smiled and did not question her further. "Then I shall take your leave. I will have Lance Tamaris personally make all the arrangements for your journey to Forprimiera."

"That is fine. Go rest now, Son."

CHAPTER 22

DEMONIC INTERVENTION

Queen Ohio had been well looked after by Dymondo, and his Lances, Sterferep, Kor and Tamaris during her stay. Dymondo was pleased with the time he had spent with her. He felt he was closer to his mother now than ever before. Dymondo ordered Oromi to be restored to the guest chamber now that his mother was leaving, but he did not get an opportunity to exchange words with her whilst Ohio was still preparing to leave. Oromi too wanted to talk with Dymondo and was getting restless. Mysteria returned back to the palace as well, but with all the arrangements, Dymondo did not get an opportunity to introduce her to his mother, thinking it be best to leave the meeting for the formal introduction in Fourtfor. At long last, the arrangements were made, and Dymondo bid farewell to the Queen as she headed for Forprimiera with her heart filled with emotions.

When Dymondo returned from bidding his mother goodbye and re-entered his chamber, to his surprise, he found a beautifully-dressed Oromi standing by the window gazing down on the courtyard. Mysteria was there, too, standing in the corner with her head down.

"Oromi!" Dymondo was shocked.

"Ah! Greetings, my King!" said Oromi. "I must say that you looked so valiant when you rode through your streets just now!"

"Gratitude."

"No, Gratitude to you, my King for giving me back the guest chamber."

Mysteria lifted her head slightly in surprise, and Oromi's smile faded. A deafening silence followed.

"Lady Oromi, I am tired and I desire sleep. If there is something you wish to ask or tell me, then please do so promptly. Otherwise, I promise we can talk at length some other time."

Oromi's face fell, yet she maintained her smile and slowly moved forward, coming close to Dymondo and pushing her bosom against his armour.

Mysteria seethed.

"I too am restless. I have been since you left things unfinished, my King. Why don't we draw the curtains, shut the doors, send away this maidservant, and you and I take to the bed. I shall hold your head in my arms and you can sleep." She placed her arms around his neck and brought her lips very close to his.

Mysteria kept her head down, but her eyes rolled in anger, and fear. Dymondo too rolled his eyes, but for a different reason.

"My Lady," he snapped, violently removing her arms from around his neck, "I only desire sleep!"

"And you shall sleep, my King," she replied as she put her warm hand on his stubbly beard, which needed a sharp blade and oil. She thought he looked handsome this way, too.

"You shall sleep peacefully for I shall place your tired head between my warm, naked bosom."

Mysteria looked up without raising her head. If looks could kill, then Oromi's head would have been rolling at her feet. But Dymondo, caught in Oromi's mesmerising eyes, said nothing. Oromi realised this and knew she now had the upper hand. She smiled.

"Oh yes," she said, looking down at her own bosom, "... I forgot...you loved them last time when you touched them, didn't you?"

Mysteria clenched her eyes shut. She wanted to shut her ears, but she could not. Oromi pushed herself farther into the King's armour, displaying yet more of her cleavage. Dymondo gathered himself and gently moved backwards and turned. He walked over to his desk, leaned on it with his hands and took a deep breath.

"My lady, I humbly request you retire to the guest chamber. Once I have shed my fatigue, then I shall speak with you."

Oromi did not know what to say. She was vexed, but she could not throw a tantrum. She was still branded a criminal, and the King had been kind to give her another life. She gathered herself and obeyed with a forged smile.

"My King, your wish is my command. I shall take your leave now."

Dymondo rose from the table and turned to her. "Gratitude, my lady. Thank you for your understanding. Remember, Oromi…"

"…Yes?"

"I know what we agreed upon. But it will never happen again. I love Mysteria. And you came in her and insulted her. Because she is a warm person, she decided not to say anything to you, but that does not mean you may trample over her feelings."

Mysteria smirked slightly with her head down.

Oromi lifted her head high and gave Mysteria the most livid look in return.

"Now you may leave, my lady," Dymondo said, "and forever remember you will not enter the royal chamber again!"

"My eyes will be forever set on the guest chamber's door, my King. The condition we set is yet unfulfilled. If you wish to know the name of the conspirator then you know what you have to do," she said and curtsied.

"No, Oromi, I have had enough of this. I cannot play this game anymore. You have taken it a step too far, hurting Mysteria like this. I care nothing for our arrangement, now. It will never happen."

Oromi felt disgusted and forlorn.

"Then you will never know who conspired against you!"

"So be it! Now leave, at once!"

She turned in fury and began to walk out, then suddenly walked back.

"Why would you not have me?! Not man enough?!"

"Oromi!" Dymondo's anger and voice had reached its peak. "Get out of my chamber! Before I reverse my commutation of your death sentence!"

Oromi's blue eyes turned red and she huffed out in anger. When the chamber door closed, Mysteria slowly moved towards Dymondo and began to remove his armour.

"You let her in?!" shouted Dymondo.

"She's your guest, my King, and I am your chambermaid. I could not stop her."

"So now anyone can skip into the King's chamber? Outrageous!"

Mysteria yanked his armour from him in a huff and glared at him. "I thought you would first correct me on calling myself a chambermaid…like you always do." She carried his armour towards the large cupboard and loudly placed it inside.

Dymondo realised his mistake and walked over.

"Mysteria, you know you're not a chambermaid. So why do you call yourself one, and why do you need me to keep telling you you're not?"

"Because I am your chambermaid!" she turned and shouted, and angrily wiped her tears.

Dymondo walked up to her and held her in his arms. She fought him at first, but he did not let her go. Eventually, she held him, too.

"There, there, my daisy! Do not cry." They both embraced at length and took deep, satisfying breaths.

"That woman! She is poison!"

"I am aware, Mysteria. I do not want her. I long for you. I have been waiting to return to your arms—to the arms of my Queen." Mysteria smiled as the last tear rolled down her beautiful, soft cheek.

"Dymondo, why did she say the condition was "unfulfilled"?"

"I thought you did not want to speak about the arrangement," Dymondo smiled.

"I didn't but…"

"…but now you do?"

"No…yes…no…I…"

"My flower, I had to do what I did for it was my promise as the King. I do not wish to discuss the details because they will do nothing but hurt the both of us. But if it helps at all, then, no, I did not go through with it."

Mysteria smiled but then she thought of Oromi's bosom against Dymondo's armour and found it hard to quell her anger.

"Then why did she say what she said? You like her breasts more than mine?!"

"Heaven's no! She was playing her usual conniving game. She does not love me and I do not love her."

Mysteria lowered her eyes.

"Tomorrow at court I am going to banish Oromi from this land," said Dymondo.

Mysteria looked up at him. "Banish?"

"Yes! She may go wherever she wishes, but she may not remain in my kingdom."

Mysteria cared little for Oromi, but her heart was soft, so she thought about what it would be like for her.

"But what if she goes into a kingdom where they believe in slavery? She will suffer."

"No, I will give her a rudis—a wooden dagger with an engraving stating that she is a free woman. So, unless she decides to sell herself, no one can forcefully condemn her to slavery."

Mysteria breathed a sigh of relief. "It is best she left. But she has not told you who sent her?"

"True," Dymondo said.

"Then?"

"I don't know," Dymondo said, turning and removing his over garments. He stood with his back to Mysteria as she looked upon his bare bottom. He then got into soft cotton bottoms and began tying the drawstrings. He turned towards her and smiled. His shirt was half untucked and untidy.

"Hear, give me your shirt. It's dirty. I'll shall give you a new one," Mysteria said as she walked over to him and extended her hand.

"You ask for too many things from me, Mysteria, yet you do not give much in return," he smiled, standing there with his arms folded.

"Well, you said yourself, my King, that a servant must know her boundaries," jested Mysteria.

Dymondo untucked his shirt, then strutted towards her. She stood firm and straight watching his pectoral muscles and his fine abdomen moving under the cloth. He had lost some of his muscle over time, but he still had a solid frame, very much to Mysteria's liking.

"A master should know his boundaries, too," he said, "But I am not sure of any boundaries between us."

"Which is incorrect. There should be."

"Well, if I am to reinstate the boundaries, I will only break them a few moments after."

Mysteria laughed.

"What do you want for your shirt?"

"Your dress." Her eyes lit up, and a flame ignited in her heart. Her thighs began to moisten, but she continued to jest.

"This cloth? It is not worth much, my King. Your shirt is worth much more."

"I believe it is a fair deal."

She raised her head again and slowly unclipped her dressed and removed it. Naked, she placed the dress on the bed, planted her right hand on her hip and extended her left towards him. "Now...the shirt!" she said, raising her eyebrows.

He could not take his eyes off her. He untucked his shirt, removed it and handed it to her. She quickly turned and walked over to the cupboard and placed it inside. Dymondo's eyes followed her every movement.

She turned around after she had put it away and placed both hands on her hips.

"Would the King like anything else?"

"Yes."

"What may that be?"

"Mysteria."

"Me?"

"Yes."

She walked over to him and stood very close, her breasts almost touching him. She lifted both arms in the air and Dymondo grabbed her and threw her on the bed. They both giggled and disappeared underneath the soft, royal bedsheets. After making love, Dymondo fell into a deep sleep for a few hours. Mysteria woke up before him but decided not to awaken him from his slumber. She got out of bed and picked up her dress from the ground, brushing off the dirt, but it was now so crumpled that she gave up on it. She pulled out another dress from a small, brown, wooden chest placed in the top right corner of the chamber. The dress was made of warm cotton and fit her perfectly. She put away the crumpled dress, walked over to Dymondo and ran her soft, long fingers through his thick, silky hair. He flinched slightly, so she stopped and went over to the window to watch the last of the sun go down. She heard a knock at the door, turned and swiftly walked over to prevent a second knock. She adjusted her dress in the mirror and gathered Dymondo's clothes from the ground before opening the door. It was Sterferep.

"Ssh! He is asleep," she whispered. Sterferep paused.

"My lady, I just came to check if the King is well."

"Do enter, but please be silent."

Sterferep smiled and went inside. Both spoke under their breath to avoid disturbing the King.

"So how is my future Queen doing?"

Mysteria smiled. "She is fine, but worried for her King."

Sterferep sighed. "Yes, aren't we all."

Mysteria closed her eyes and shook her head.

She grabbed Sterferep's strong forearm and dragged him over to the table and gestured him to sit down. She poured him some fresh, cold water from a golden jug into a golden goblet and gave it to him. He drained it in one gulp.

"The Gods will show us the path," said Mysteria. Sterferep nodded and smiled as he placed the golden goblet on the wooden table.

"Did you meet Zircornia?" she asked, referring to Sterferep's love, a match the King had helped arrange.

He shook his head looking down onto the table. She walked over to the other side of the table and sat down in front of him.

"My blood boils to see this, my lady. I cannot see him unhappy."

"You love him like a brother, so you feel his pain."

"Though he doesn't say it, it hurts him to know what he has to face."

"You and Kor know him well enough to observe this."

"As do you."

Mysteria nodded.

"We live in horrid times," Sterferep said.

"The King once told me about the gladiators. I was horrified."

Sterferep smiled and nodded. "Gruesome, isn't it."

Mysteria shook her head. "And the slaves and how they are used for sex."

"That too is true. In parts of the realm, such things take place."

"Go meet Zircornia. She must have missed you while you were away."

"I have missed her."

"Then go see her...unless you think her father will throw you out of the house?" she laughed.

Sterferep smiled more. "He couldn't even if he tried. I wouldn't even have to punch him to remove him from my path."

"There now, he's your father-in-law to be."

Sterferep smiled again and looked away.

"I shouldn't mention it, but the King has decided to banish Oromi from the kingdom."

"Good. He told you this in confidence?" he asked eying her.

"Yes," she said, lowering her head.

"My lady, what he says to you here must stay with you." Sterferep was stern.

"Forgive me. I stepped out of line, but this is the first and last time. It will not happen again. I am only mentioning it to you because you are his best friend. I only want to ensure it happens."

Dymondo moved under the sheets and both went quiet until they were sure he was still asleep. Mysteria then turned back to Sterferep.

"Make sure that bitch gets to court tomorrow, and make sure the King banishes her." Now Mysteria was stern.

"What happened?"

"She came into his chamber," she whispered, leaning in, "waited here for him to arrive from his seeing off the Queen and was the first to greet him. She tried to comfort him with her bosom."

"How did she get into the royal chamber? Was there no one outside?"

"I don't know, Sterferep. I was here. But I have not been officially declared by him yet, so I could not say or do much. But the fact was, she was here enticing my man in front of my eyes and was the first to greet him. *I* wanted to be the first to greet him, not some dirty whore from the dungeons!"

"I understand. What else did she do?"

"Everything! Pressing her breasts up against his chest, running her filthy hands all over his face and body, and openly inviting him to bed!"

"Now, I see the reason why you inform me of the King's plans."

"Sterferep, if the King did not wish me to be part of his life, then I would have happily parted myself from it. But the fact is we love each other. I cannot withstand her being near him. Agreeing to that... arrangement...was like drinking poison. I cannot bear it anymore."

Sterferep nodded.

"If you see me as a friend, then ensure the banishment takes place." Sterferep again nodded.

"Get that bitch as far away from here as possible." Mysteria was clasping the wooden table very hard.

"I'll personally fetch her from the guest chamber in the morning. I'll make sure she is at court."

Dymondo began to stir in his bed and his slumber broke. He rubbed his eyes and sat up awake. Mysteria and Sterferep assumed he had not heard any of their conversation.

"My King," Sterferep said, getting up from his chair.

"Sterferep. How do you fare?" asked Dymondo, still half asleep.

"Well. I just came to check if the King was well and if he required anything. My lady was kind enough to invite me in and offer me some water and a seat."

"Thank you, Mysteria, for a great person like Sterferep deserves such hospitality." Mysteria and Sterferep both smiled and looked to the ground. "I am well, Sterferep. Just a little concerned about what may be coming our way. However, there is no reason to ponder over it anymore. We must act."

"Great to hear that, my King. I look forward to your orders. For now, though, I must take your leave. Tomorrow will be a new day."

Dymondo smiled and nodded. Sterferep bowed and knelt to him and nodded at Mysteria. She smiled back.

Sterferep was about to leave the chamber as Dymondo called to him.

"Sterferep!"

"Yes, my King?"

"Fetch Oromi from the guest chamber early tomorrow morning and ensure she is at court. First thing tomorrow morning I will banish her from this kingdom."

Sterferep and Mysteria glanced at each other.

"Certainly, my King. It shall be done."

"We need to ensure we get that bitch as far away from here as possible!" said Dymondo and smiled at Sterferep. He then looked over at Mysteria with a twinkle in his eye.

Sterferep looked at his King in amazement and then at the King's future Queen. A smile emerged on Mysteria's face. Eventually they all smiled at one another and Sterferep left the room. Mysteria walked over to Dymondo.

"So, you heard what I said?"

"A King must be alert even in sleep," smiled Dymondo as he leaned back onto the headrest and put his hands behind his head.

"Forgive me, my King. I should not have mentioned that to Sterferep. Apologies"

"None required. You did what you had to do to remove another woman from your man's life. That is understandable. However, let me remind you of your own words. This is the first and last time this happens."

"Absolutely, my King."

"Good. Now…come here and sit by my side." Mysteria smiled and sat on the side of the bed and then got in and cuddled up next to him.

"My King, may I suggest something?"

"Of course, you may."

"I feel there are yet unanswered questions in your heart."

"True, Mysteria, you are right."

"What are they?"

"Why are my brothers so heartless?"

"We can't know such things, my love."

"No, we can. Lorca was correct."

"About what?"

"My Mother confirmed it. We are boons of the Gods. We were born by their blessings and each one of us is a son of a deity."

"So, you are not brothers? And you? You're a…?"

"You mustn't utter a word of this to anyone, Mysteria. Our mother gave birth to all of us, but by the grace of three different Gods—a different one each time. But there is a perplexing detail. The skies went dark when my brothers were conceived, but they did not go dark for me. Why? Is that why my brothers are so evil?"

"It is strange, my King. You all have divinity in you, so they should be as righteous as you are."

"I am not a saint, Mysteria, but I am not a tyrant."

Mysteria sat up to face him. "You must get your answers from God himself. Lorca has told you how the birth scrolls did not mention your births, and now your mother has told you the truth. Yet, my love, you still seek answers. No one else but God can help you."

"That would be marvellous, Mysteria. But what would you have me do, just ride up to his door and seek his audience?"

"Yes!"

"I beg your pardon?"

"Your brothers are evil…demonic. Clearly there has been some demonic intervention."

Dymondo too sat up, shocked to hear what she was saying.

"Mysteria, how do you know such things?"

"My grandmother… she was very spiritual. She would sit in the temple for the entire day upon the grey hill, from early morning until nightfall, and then return home. She did this more after my grandfather passed away. My mother and father would scold her for doing so and express worry when she returned home so late. She would listen to their harsh words and just retire to her room. I felt she needed someone to understand her. But first, I needed to understand what she was doing. So one night, when she returned from the temple, I got out of my bed and went into her room. She was lying on her bed with her back towards her door, and I could tell she was sobbing softly. I quietly called out to her, and she turned and gestured for me to come over. She got up and wiped her tears and told me it was late and that I should be asleep. I asked her why she was crying and where she went every day. She said she went to the temple on the grey hill—that it was the temple of the King of the Gods. She said she found peace there and…"

"…and?"

"…that she found God there."

Dymondo was dumbfounded, so Mysteria explained further.

"She said to me that if we called out to God with the true belief and from our hearts, then God will manifest before us. She said she had unanswered questions which she asked of God, and that when he answered them, she was more at peace with everything. She also said that she had a few more questions and as soon as all her questions were answered, she would retire to the afterlife."

"And you believe all that?"

"I did at the time. I was a little girl. But I was too scared to go and try it myself, and as I grew older, these memories became a blur. I never thought about asking anything from God. I was content."

"You said there may be some demonic intervention. Why?"

"As days went by, my grandmother got older and felt too weak to climb the grey hill, so instead, she would stay in the house. Every night for a few moments, after mother and father had gone to bed, I would go sit with her. She would sit me on her lap and tell stories of Kings and Queens. It was during one of these narrations that she once told me a story which sounded just like the history of your family. My grandmother went stone cold after she finished. I asked her what had happened. She replied that I must not tell anyone that particular tale, because it was true."

Dymondo listened with a keen ear. "Please tell me, my dear."

"At the time of your birth, my grandmother was in her middle age and, unlike the kingdom, she did not think much about it. But as you and the other princes grew older, she grew more intrigued by your separate natures. Every citizen knew of the princes' personalities, but where they came from was often a mystery. My grandmother, in her visits to the temple, asked God about them, and God eventually answered her. He told her something about a…. demonic intervention."

"And what is that?"

"I do not recall much, my King, but you asked why they are so evil? Your question jolted my memory. I remember that once my grandmother told me a story of three brothers, whom were sons of the Gods. Two were evil and one was righteous. The righteous brother was righteous because he was a son of the Gods, and the evil brothers were evil *despite* being sons of the Gods. Their evil came from a demonic intervention."

"Tell me more," Dymondo said.

"That is all I know, my love. I think if you want more answers, you will have to ask God, himself.

CHAPTER 23

TEMPLE IN THE JUNGLE

Dymondo had a restless night after what he had heard from Mysteria. Mysteria did not sleep well either and was up before him. He remained quiet throughout the morning until Kor came to collect the King for court. Sterferep was absent as he had gone to fetch Oromi. Dymondo kissed Mysteria and left with Kor.

Dymondo responded less to Kor's jovial nature and humour on the way to court. Kor eventually resorted to silence. Once there, Dymondo went directly to work, promptly dealing with any petty tasks first. The key task was to banish Oromi, but for some strange reason Sterferep still had not appeared with her in court. Dymondo used the time to send word to his brothers Shilathaar and Grygerious about Queen Ohio's visit, telling Grygerious that he was to travel to Forprimiera to meet with their mother there.

***

Meanwhile, Sterferep was sitting in a large waiting area just outside Oromi's guest chamber. She was getting ready for court, he had been told, but he was becoming impatient at having to wait so long for a prisoner. Her indolent nature was getting to him. After an hour of waiting, he stood up and stomped over to the chamber entrance and boomed at the maidservants:

"This is ludicrous! Where is she?! The King does not have all day! He will not be pleased!" The two maidservants went bright red with fear and hurried inside to notify Oromi. They returned shortly after. Sterferep's eyes were red from impatience.

"You may enter the chamber," they mumbled in dread.

"I have not come here to visit her, but to fetch her!" Sterferep's voice got louder.

"She is aware, and she insists you come inside before she accompanies you to court." Sterferep shook his head.

"Who does she think she is? The Queen?!" shouted Sterferep. He clasped his scabbard and marched inside.

Oromi sat in front of the mirror combing her long, silky, black locks, dressed in just a silk gown. As he approached, Sterferep noticed the gown hardly covered her. He made an effort to look away. Oromi glanced back at him, smiled victoriously and continued combing her hair.

"Lance Sterferep, how do you fare?"

"Lady Oromi, you are to accompany me to court. The King awaits." Sterferep's voice had lowered.

"Lance Sterferep… unswerving as always. I asked you if you were well."

"I am well. I hope you are too. Now can you please prepare for court?"

"It is rude not to face the person you are addressing."

"My lady, you know very well why I evade my eyes."

She took a deep breath and slammed the comb down upon the table in front of her and stood up. She approached Sterferep and used her strength to turn the tall man's shoulder so he could face her. She stood in front of him, wearing an unfastened dressing gown and nothing else. She placed her hands upon her hips so that the gown opened more, concealing nothing.

"Why give me respect now, Lance? Where was this courtesy when I stood chained naked in the dungeons?!" she screamed, her eyes going watery. Sterferep looked away again.

"My Lady, this is neither the time nor the place for such a conversation. What is done is done. Now, I request that you please get dressed and accompany me to court."

"Still looking away. Why? You have seen me unclothed before!" Oromi was wasting his time on purpose. She understood very well the King's desire to be rid of her. The longer she could avoid going to court the better.

"My Lady!"

"Quiet! You know what you all did! It was wrong!"

Sterferep took a deep breath and finally faced her. She stood as before, with her hands on her hips exhibiting her naked body. He kept his eyes on her face, removed her hands from her hips, grabbed the ends of her gown, and wrapped her up decently, yet vigorously. His teeth clenched together hard, and he addressed her once more.

"Lady...Oromi! Get fucking dressed now, or I swear I shall grab you by the arm and take you to court as you are! Enough of your tantrums! I know the King has set boundaries, but I have no problem crossing lines. One more word from you, and you shall be seeing the King in your dressing gown. Now...get...fucking... dressed!"

Oromi's face fell. Her smugness and confidence were shattered. She could tell Sterferep meant every word. She nodded and lowered her head.

"Please give me some moments to get dressed."

"A few moments only! If you take longer, I shall do what I said!"

With that, Sterferep walked outside to wait. Oromi made sure to dress hastily, and she was outside in the waiting area in just a few moments. Sterferep walked her to court.

Dymondo too had grown impatient as all the tasks of court were now complete, and he did not like to sit idly. He ignored Sterferep's apologies and explanations as to why Oromi had arrived so late and got straight to the chore.

"Lady Oromi! For some time, you have been our guest! You suffered a great deal in the dungeons for the heinous act you attempted."

Lorca cursed her under his breath.

"Despite your crime, my magnanimous heart has considered the hardships you suffered," the King continued. "No woman in my kingdom has suffered more pain and punishment, and I have decreed that such punishment shall never happen again to any female criminal. To gain your forgiveness and pardon, I bestowed upon you the luxuries and comforts of the royal palace. Only a guest has ever received these in the past. Yet I completely understand that gesture will not completely remove the scars you have suffered both in the dungeon and during the night when an attempt was made on your life."

Oromi glanced up at Dymondo, then lowered her eyes.

"Even so, justice must be served. It cannot be forgotten that you tried to take Lorca's life—a crime for which you no doubt deserve the death sentence. But I shall be gracious and spare your life. Still punishment must be served. Therefore, Lady Oromi of Fourtfor, I King Dymondo Rain, Ruler of Gammafor and Fourtfor, hereby banish you from my kingdom! You are not permitted to reside on my land or set foot back onto it once you have left. You shall forsake these islands forever. My guards will accompany you to the small island that lies between Haask and Gammafor. There you shall exit the boundary of this kingdom! You will have permission to gather your belongings from the guest chamber and your house in Fourtfor, but my Lances will supervise this activity as you may only take items you own or those that have been given to you during your royal stay. Once you have gathered your items, you will be a free woman and will be given a rudis. My men will then take you to the southern border of my kingdom and deposit you on the island."

"My King, I—" Oromi tried to interrupt.

"This punishment is effective immediately," Dymondo cut her off. "You may go and collect your belongings from the guest chamber and your abode in Fourtfor. You have fourteen days to complete these tasks. If after that period, you are seen in my kingdom, severe punishments will be served. Lance Tamaris, Dan and Dwarpal! Please see this task done!" All three nodded.

"But my King!" Oromi said. Her face went blue, as all her intentions and dreams had just been crushed with this command from her King.

"No more!" The King smashed his hands against his knees, rose immediately and walked straight out of the court. Sterferep and Kor followed as usual. Lorca got up and applauded the King as he walked out, and all the other courtiers and ministers followed suit.

Tamaris was the first to walk up to her. "Right then, Lady Oromi, the punishment as you heard is effective immediately." There was a mocking grin on Tamaris's face as he spoke, which Oromi greeted with a stare of mute outrage.

"We have no time; we should leave," said Dan as he and Dwarpal joined them.

"Wait!" shouted Lorca, slowly hobbling up to Oromi.

The men waited until the minister was standing in front of her.

"You will burn in hell, you filthy spider," he murmured in his weary voice. He did not wait for a reply but just walked off. "Now my heart is at peace," he mumbled to himself as he slowly moved out of the court.

Oromi gaped at the floor in shock, her blood boiling with hatred and revenge. She did not deserve this, she felt. After their moment together, she had dreamt of becoming a mistress to the King, and maybe, one day, Queen. But presenting herself to the King had not won her any affection. She had not expected this. She turned furiously for the exit and began to stomp out. Dan caught up and grabbed her by the arm, only for her to shrug it off immediately. Dan grabbed for it again and this time took a firm grip. Tamaris and Dwarpal joined them and the four walked out of court.

"I am doing as I'm told," she growled at Dan. "You do not need to grab me. You're hurting me!" she shouted.

"Criminals do not give orders to the King's men, you stupid woman!" Dan growled at her. "We shall decide how this banishment is executed, not you. Feel fortunate the King has let you live!"

"I seek just one audience with the King, I beg of you. You are his trusted men. Surely you can arrange this for me."

"Of course, we can," said Dan, "but we shall not as we are going to follow his command to the letter. We shall come with you to the guest chamber and to your house in Fourtfor, so you can take your belongings. After which the guards will sail you over to the island. When you and the guards reach the island, you can ask them to leave straight away or keep them there until you've found yourself a place to live," said Dan.

"Or built yourself a place to live," added Tamaris.

"Surely there is something you want," she pleaded.

"We want nothing from you!" Dwarpal snapped. "It is because of you the King lost his faith in us. You have caused me and Dan much misery!"

"I did? You should have kept better guard!" mocked Oromi.

Dwarpal moved towards her only to be held back by Tamaris.

"Calm!" said Tamaris.

"Oh, you all shall burn! Burn in the netherworld! This kingdom and all its men will burn! A great war is coming! Your mothers will lose their sons and your wives their husbands...!"

"Enough!" shouted Dwarpal. "Shut your foul mouth! One more word out of you, and I shall part your tongue from your mouth!"

Tamaris grinned, whilst holding back Dwarpal. He took Oromi's other arm.

"Come on you! Your play time is over," said Tamaris, moving her along.

Oromi was humiliated. She wanted to scream and cry out loud, but she kept it all in and, through angry tears, went with the men.

Meanwhile, Dymondo hurried back to his chamber and, leaving Kor and Sterferep outside, marched straight in. Mysteria jumped at the noise.

"Apologies, my lady!" he said, throwing his cape on a velvet chair and walking over to his writing table. He pulled out a map of his land from inside a drawer, spread it over the table and began looking at it in earnest.

Mysteria was wearing a rare, summery, light-blue dress that morning and looked rather radiant. Dymondo paid little notice.

"Is everything alright, my King?" she asked as she walked over to him and started looking at the map over his shoulder.

"Where is the temple you spoke of last night, my lady?"

She paused and looked at him, then at the map. "Here!" she said pointing to an area on the map with particularly lush vegetation.

"But that's nothing but jungle! Is that where the grey hill is?"

"Yes. No one has ventured there for some time, so the shrubs and trees grew larger and covered the hill."

"Why don't people venture there anymore?"

"No reason that I can remember, my King. Maybe it's inhabited by wild animals." Dymondo studied her and saw that her response was sincere and returned to looking at the map.

"I need answers to my questions, Mysteria."

Mysteria nodded. "If you go there and ask with a sincere heart and with true belief in the King of the Gods; then you will get your answers," she replied.

He looked at her again and she nodded in encouragement.

"I will go at the crack of dawn," he announced.

"Don't go alone."

"I wasn't going to."

She nodded and walked over and sat on her hands on the bed and began to swing her legs slowly. "Did you do what you had planned to do today?" she asked looking at the ground.

"Yes, I banished her."

She clenched her teeth inside her closed mouth and nodded; still staring hard at the ground. She took a deep breath and fell back onto the bed. "Good!"

"Different shade of blue today?"

She smiled staring at the ceiling of the four-poster bed. "I thought you didn't notice."

"How could I not, my lady. It suits you."

"Gratitude."

He carried on looking at the map and called in Sterferep and Kor.

"Sterferep, make plans for us to travel to this place tomorrow morning," ordered Dymondo pointing at the jungle on the map. Sterferep walked over and looked where the King was pointing.

"The holy hill?" he asked.

"Yes!" Mysteria shouted, bouncing up to a sitting position. "The holy hill! That's what it's called!"

"She says it's a dense jungle," said Dymondo.

"Yes, *now* it is," Sterferep explained. "People stopped venturing there as more temples were built around the city and town. They found it easier to go to those instead of climbing up the hill."

"So, there is a temple there?"

"There was one, so it must be there."

"Then we must go!" Dymondo said. "We will depart tomorrow. You and Kor shall accompany me."

Kor nodded. Sterferep kept mum.

"Sterferep?"

"Forgive me My King, but…"

"But what…?"

"No man has ventured into this area for several years. That place has been deserted for God knows how long. What lingers there, no one knows. It is not safe."

"*You* worry for your safety, Sterferep? *You?*"

"Pardon me, I do not. I am concerned for you. You are our King. Let me and Kor go and complete the task for you."

"No, Sterferep. I must go."

"Very well. Then preparations will be made for tomorrow morning's departure. It will take us some time to reach the hill, so we must leave at the crack of dawn."

"Excellent. See it done."

"As you wish, my King…I would suggest you wear your armour and take along your sword, and perhaps your bow."

"Water, bread, and wine as well, my King," said Kor.

"Water, bread and what?" asked Dymondo.

"Wine, my King? No?" Kor looked at everyone. Mysteria gave Kor a fuming look and placed her hands upon her hips.

"Ok… just water and bread," corrected Kor. Mysteria turned her back towards the three men and went and sat at her dressing table. Dymondo, Sterferep and Kor all looked at one another, smiled and exchanged winks.

"That's right, Kor," winked Dymondo. "No wine."

That night Dymondo dined with Mysteria at the royal dining table. Many of Mysteria's favourite dishes were cooked to perfection, which she thoroughly enjoyed. She wore a striking sapphire-blue gown with sparkling silver and crystal ornaments and matching jewellery. Dymondo wore a deep red jacket with shiny, black trousers. Both looked immaculate and enjoyed their meal, after which they retired to the King's royal chamber.

Mysteria removed her necklace and earrings and placed them upon a newly-installed dressing table made of fine wood and gold-plated handles and framing. Dymondo removed his cape and his red jacket. Underneath, he wore a beautiful, pure-white, linen shirt and sat on the bed.

"You a have a long day ahead of you, my King," said Mysteria looking at herself in the mirror.

"I am aware, dear."

"I forgot to mention something. It is very important."

"What is that?"

"When you go on your journey tomorrow, you must always believe that the temple is there. You cannot lose faith for one moment. Secondly, when you find the temple, which you will, you must enter as a person who is seeking something, and treat God as the giver. Do not enter like a King; be humble and bow before God. It is you who needs what he has. You must ask with great compassion and a clean heart. Remember, we all are nothing before God. If even for one moment, you begin to believe that you are a King or any form of pride enters yours heart, then God will not answer your questions."

Dymondo nodded in agreement. "Yes…you are correct, my lady. I shall remember your words."

"I only wish for you to get what you desire."

"Gratitude, my lady." Mysteria turned around and smiled at him.

"The jungle can be forbidding, and Sterferep is correct: who knows what may dwell there? Be safe and take care of one another."

"We will do. Now let us retire to bed, for I must rise early." Mysteria smiled and both went to bed.

The next morning brought a brisk wind into their chamber, though the sun shone brightly. As usual Mysteria was up before Dymondo. She prepared his kit for his journey, and as soon as Dymondo was ready, Kor and Sterferep, were at the royal chamber door. They entered and waited inside the chamber as the King gathered the rest of his items.

"Ready?" asked Dymondo once he had done so.

"Yes!" they all said at once. Dymondo kissed Mysteria and bid her farewell.

Outside, near the stables, Kor, Sterferep and the King mounted their steeds. Dymondo had not ridden his horse, Badal, for a while, so it was a pleasant reunion as the King had a connection with the animal. The destriers were covered by protective clothing, and the men dressed in strong armour with sharp blades in sheaths hanging from their belts. They carried bows around their shoulders and each had a quiver of arrows upon his back. They carried bread and other staple foods along with water. Lance Kor, meanwhile, had surreptitiously stowed another bottle containing strong liquor, as he was known to do on long journeys.

Just before they departed, Tamaris, Dan and Dwarpal showed up with Oromi. They were headed to Fourtfor so that Oromi could collect her items from her house. Oromi was now cuffed and chained.

"Headed out nice and early!" called Kor.

"Good. She'll be good riddance!" added Dymondo as he looked down on her from his horse.

Oromi gave him the most repulsive glare with her sharp, blue eyes.

"The magic of your blue eyes will not be working today, my lady," mocked Sterferep. The men laughed at the remark.

"You are making a mistake," she said.

"I most certainly am not! Tamaris take her away at once. We are going to the temple in the jungle and I need to remain calm," said Dymondo.

"The holy hill?! The temple of the God of the Gods?!" Oromi asked.

Everyone was stunned into silence.

"You know of it?"

"Yes, I even know where it is."

"Another ploy. Let's go!" shouted Sterferep kicking his horse gently.

Oromi knew this was her last chance to converse with Dymondo.

"My King, I implore you. Please listen to what I have to say!"

"I have lost my patience with you, Oromi! I shall get my answers at the holy hill!"

"But I know where it is. I can take you there."

"How do you know of it?" asked Dymondo.

"She lies again, my King!" interrupted Sterferep.

"I do fucking not, you bastard!"

"Easy there, Oromi! I shall not have anyone speak to Sterferep like that," corrected Dymondo.

"Trust me, my King I can take you there in no time! I have seen the temple!"

"Tamaris take this whore away from here!" commanded Sterferep.

"Come on, you!" Tamaris pulled her back from the conversation.

"I beg of you, my King! You have to trust me! Please trust me!"

"Wait!"

"Oh Dy, for God's sake, man! Get a grip! We have a long journey ahead of us!"

"Calm, Sterferep, let me reason with her."

"You do not need to, you're her King!"

"Sterferep, please."

Sterferep waved his hand at him and looked the other way. Dymondo moved his horse closer to Oromi. She was still being held by Tamaris.

"Why should I trust you? You have told me nothing."

"I am scared for my life. Someone already tried to rob me of it! I ask you; what do you think would happen to me if I was to tell you what I know?"

"My King, apologies but we have long way to travel," interrupted Tamaris. He was keen to see Oromi punished.

"Yes, my King. Do not entertain her fibs and lies any longer," added Dan.

"Let us take her," said Dwarpal.

"My King, give me the chance to prove my worth to you. I am trained in warfare; you have seen it with your own eyes. Let me come with you to the temple. At the very least, I will get you there quicker."

"My King, we too are getting late!" spoke Sterferep.

"I want to know who sent you!"

"Someone in your family," she replied.

"Who?! Tell me the name!"

"You promise not to kill me if I tell you?"

"Yes. You are already being set free!"

"No, I am being banished! I'm as good as dead!"

"Fine. I do not need you, Oromi. I will find my answers in the temple."

"God decides what questions to answer, and God will not answer those questions known to living beings from whom you can obtain the answers easily. He will only answer those questions to which only God has the answer, and only after we have searched everywhere and found nothing. Only then can we seek the help of God. And not just for any question. So when you're knelt before God, I suggest you question wisely. As to that one question, I am prepared to tell you. All you have to do is give me some affection, which you refuse to do."

Dymondo was now deep in thought. Even Sterferep was quiet. The question around his birth was more important than knowing the culprit behind Lorca's failed assassination. Yet he wanted to know both.

"What do you want, Oromi?"

"Let me be your guide to the temple. There you can ask your important question, whatever it may be. Then I will return to the palace. You will fuck me and I shall tell you the name of the conspirator!"

The King weighed his response.

"You may journey with us," he finally said, "and if you indeed prove helpful, I will consider our earlier arrangement."

"Mysteria will not be pleased, Dy!" warned Sterferep.

"My King, with all due respect, this is getting beyond a jest," Kor said.

"Why are you letting this stupid woman dictate to you?" asked an annoyed Tamaris. Dan too was getting frustrated, as he wanted to fulfil his duty and see this woman banished.

"Quiet! Everyone, please. You are my Lances. So please, let me go with my instinct and support me."

"We are always here for you, my King!" assured Sterferep and took a long breath. "Very well. Tamaris arrange a horse for Lady Oromi and unchain her. Lady Oromi, you will lead the way. But let me warn you now: If you even contemplate misleading us, I will not hesitate before slicing off your head!"

Oromi's sharp blue eyes fixed upon the tall Lance in anger.

Tamaris flapped his arms in discontent but did as told and walked inside the stables to fetch a horse.

"Dan and Dwarpal, for today, resume your normal duty. No travel for you," said Kor.

"May I come along at least?" asked Tamaris, bringing the horse,

"It won't be necessary, Gratitude," answered Kor.

The three nodded and helped unchain Oromi and placed her atop her horse, then bowed to Dymondo, Sterferep and Kor before they departed.

"Do I get a blade to defend myself?" she asked Sterferep once they were gone.

"What do you think?" growled Sterferep.

"I see you carry an extra. If the need arises, you can throw it to me."

Sterferep thought for a while and nodded.

As they turned their horses toward the palace gate, Oromi grinned at Sterferep.

"Why the grin?" he asked.

"The magic of these blue eyes always works," she whispered and winked at him before riding into the lead.

They rode through the city, still very quiet at that early hour. Those who were around, waved and bowed as the King and his Lances passed, wondering after the mysterious woman who accompanied them. After riding for some time, they caught sight of the mouth of the jungle in the distance. At a convenient place, everyone stopped to hydrate and have the first meal of the day, then after another short interval, they finally reached the entrance to the jungle. It was early afternoon, and the sun was still high in the sky, but the punitive biting gale kept the temperature low.

Now facing the jungle, Dymondo did what Mysteria had instructed. He relaxed his mind and cleared any doubts and any form of arrogance. He focused on the temple within and expected to find it. Keeping all those thoughts going, he got off his steed. Besides the four of them, there was not another soul in sight. Dymondo thought for a moment and then turned to the others.

"Kor, you remain here with the horses, watch that path, and make sure no one else enters the jungle," commanded Dymondo.

"But we may need all the men we have inside, my King," suggested Sterferep.

"I agree, my King," added Oromi.

"No. Kor will remain here," was Dymondo's response. He stared at the tall trees looming before them and did not look back at Sterferep and Oromi for an answer. Kor nodded in obedience, while Sterferep and the Oromi exchanged stares of discontent, yet remained mum. Sterferep drew his shinning blade from its sheath and walked right to the entrance of the jungle.

"No, I shall walk in first!" Oromi exclaimed and strode into the jungle ahead of him. Dymondo then entered, unsheathing his own sword as he moved in after the both of them. Oromi led the way with Sterferep right next to her using his blade to clear the shrubs, bushes and branches as he made a path for his King through the jungle. *Clang!* He battled the dense trees, swinging his sword right and left, and made distinct cuts in some of the trees in order to remember the path back. Many small creatures and insects ran up his arms and across his feet as he worked, but none of them bothered Sterferep.

The three ventured deep into the jungle, battling the thick foliage all the way. Then came a sound from a shrub. Sterferep stopped and raised his hand, but the noise ceased as the three halted their advance. Dymondo gently drew an arrow from his quiver and took his golden bow from around his shoulder. He placed the arrow upon the rest, but did not string it. Sterferep inched ahead and the shrub again rustled violently. Sterferep again stopped but this time, the rustling continued.

Suddenly, a large black cat emerged from behind the thick, green foliage. It had yellow, malicious eyes and pearly-white fangs—it was a black panther. The panther snarled at the men as it moved cunningly towards them. Sterferep swung his blade in the air and prepared to strike. Dymondo knocked his arrow. The silky black panther halted his own advance and sat.

"Stay," spoke Sterferep placing out his hand towards the large feline. The black panther turned its head.

"Ah, stay should I?" the creature asked in a coarse yet deep voice. It sounded as though it were struggling to speak. Dymondo, Sterferep and Oromi gaped at hearing the animal speak. Dymondo relaxed his bow and removed the arrow. He used its sharp end to point at the black panther.

"You can talk?"

"Yes…I can," replied the panther.

"I know some animals can talk and…"

"…You've met one before…have you?" the panther said, completing his sentence.

"Tremendous to have met you."

"Yes, tremendous to have met you too."

"But we must be on own way."

"And why should I let you do that?"

"We seek the temple. Let us pass in peace. We will not harm you, and you shall not harm us!"

"Very kind, for not harming me…but I shall not harm you? Who are you to dictate such terms?"

"I am King Dymondo Rain, the ruler of Gammafor and Fourtfor, and I…" Dymondo paused and stopped to think, recalling Mysteria's words about ego and arrogance. "…I seek your forgiveness, O panther, for I have erred."

Sterferep and Oromi looked at Dymondo. Dymondo placed his arrow back in his quiver and laid down his bow upon the ground and knelt before the large cat.

"I am no one to command you," the King continued. "I hope you will not hurt me and my friends."

"Perhaps!" snapped the panther.

"Right now, we just need to get to the temple."

The black panther sneered at Sterferep and Oromi, then turned back to

Dymondo.

"Ah, so you are a King, you say?" asked the panther, slyly moving towards Dymondo.

"No, I am no King. I am a mere beggar before God, and I seek His help." The panther was now face to face with Dymondo.

"Dy, what are you doing?" Sterferep crunched his words.

"God? Which God?" asked the black panther purposefully, opening his mouth wide to exhibit his jawline. The mouth was close enough to Dymondo's face that he could feel the cat's breath upon him. Surprisingly, it did not smell.

"There is an ancient temple in this jungle. I must find the temple and pray to God."

At the mention of "God," the panther's eyes went red. He moved his mouth nearer to Dymondo's face and shouted:

"There is no God, you fool! There is no temple here! I have lived here all my life, and I have not come across any temple! Go back! For it is futile to continue. All you will find is more cats like me, and they do not talk and reason as I do. They will pounce out of the bushes and dig their shiny, white fangs into your throats before your hand can reach for your arrows. Go from here or else I might change my mind and devour you myself."

Dymondo remained on the ground. Sterferep stood at the ready to swing his blade if he needed to. The black panther slinked around the kneeling King and looked at Sterferep's aggressive pose and grinned. This only infuriated the Lance more.

"One swing…." said Sterferep.

"One leap…" replied the panther. The panther abstained from giving any more attention to the man with the blade and looked back at the man on his knees. He was still humbled.

The panther growled, a deep guttural sound that grew angrier by the second. He rushed toward Dymondo again, trying to intimidate the pilgrim. "Why…will you not go?!" he yelled.

"Because God is here and I have faith. I will find the temple! If you try to stop me, then I will have no choice but to fight you," replied Dymondo. He did not flinch. The panther flicked his tale and turned back, eyeing the courageous intruder.

"Have you seen the temple?"

"No! But as I said I have faith it exists. Only those that have belief get to behold divinity!"

"Ha-ha! You make me laugh, King," mocked the panther.

"Let me slice off its tongue, my King!" yelled Sterferep.

"You couldn't if you tried!" replied the panther.

"My King!"

160

"Yes, King... tell your friend to slice out my tongue!" laughed the panther.

"Sterferep! Put down the sword! And I have told you I am not King of anything. He at the temple is the King of the Gods!" The panther paused and gazed deep into Dymondo's eyes. He saw dedication and determination.

"Very well," said the panther, "I will let you go on one condition!"

"What is that?" asked Dymondo.

"That I come with you."

"Never!" shouted Sterferep.

"Very well, then prepare to die!" said the panther and positioned himself for his launch upon Sterferep.

"Wait!" Dymondo intervened. "Why should we take you along with us?"

"Because I want to see this temple, too. I want see your face drop, when you discover no such place exists!" the panther laughed. Dymondo took a deep breath, picked up his bow and got back on his feet.

"Very well, but you will walk ahead of Oromi and we will walk behind you."

"You speak as though I know the way to the temple. No, your friend here will take the lead and I will walk beside her."

"She is not my friend!"

Oromi looked at Dymondo with emotional eyes.

"Whoever she may be."

"Fine."

"He may lead us to a trap!" said Sterferep.

"Trap? Are you serious? Look around you! There are traps everywhere. This is a jungle!" shouted the panther.

"No. We offered him the lead and he could have led us anywhere. But he refused. I say we can trust him," said Dymondo. "What is your name, Panther?"

"People call me many names for I only answer to those that truly call out to me and seek my help, but for formality sake, my name is Cattus."

"Cattus. Fine, great Cattus. I am Dymondo. This is my friend, Sterferep, and this is Lady Oromi.

"Pleasure!" Cattus remarked sarcastically as he finished giving Sterferep his taunting gaze. "Let me hold you no longer."

The four continued into the jungle. As they sliced their way along the path, Cattus would deliberately brush up against Sterferep to irritate him—sometimes with his tail and sometimes with his body—then follow up with an insincere apology. Sterferep tolerated this behaviour throughout the long journey.

After much walking, they got to a point where the climb became steeper and the way more difficult. Though they had stopped for breaks, they were tired, and the hot, steep climb only made their hunger grow stronger.

Finally, they crested the hill and found a ruin at the top—a stone-tiled courtyard with four tall, stone pillars at each corner. The structure was in bad shape. Pieces of broken rocks and stones along with many twigs, leaves and branches, covered the ground. In the middle was a large stone statue of the King of Gods, Topus. Dymondo and Sterferep gaped at each other then went running toward the statue and knelt before it. They had found the temple.

"O great King of Gods Topus! Please help me for I have come to you to seek answers to my questions."

The black panther walked around the ruins as Dymondo prayed. "It's quite old, this temple is not, King?"

"Cattus please, I am trying to pray, and as I said, I am no King."

"Good! But the temple can do with more people visiting, correct?"

"Cattus…please…But yes, you are correct. I shall have a road paved out from the jungle entrance to this temple, so people can come and pray."

"But what of all the wild animals? The lions, the wolves, the bears," laughed Cattus looking over at Sterferep and Oromi.

"They will not be harmed. I shall have my strong soldiers guard the path to the temple, protecting pilgrims from the animals. I shall have a large wall built that will divide the path and the jungle."

"Why not burn the jungle and destroy the carnivorous animals?"

"No, Cattus, I cannot take them out of the jungle because this is their home. Instead, I can separate the temple and its path from the jungle, so the animals can live in peace, and the people who wish to visit this marvellous and pious place can do so without fear and in safety."

"But the temple is very old…"

"I will get more stone and have it remade. This place will have small shops where people can rest and find food and water to ease their journey." Cattus smiled and nodded. "Now if you will let me pray, please, Cattus." Dymondo turned and closed his eyes.

"O God," Dymondo said. "I am in despair. I have come here to seek your help, O God. Why is it that the sons of Ohio, Shilathaar and Grygerious, my brothers, are epitomes of unrighteousness? Why is there so much evil in their hearts despite being the fruits of the Gods like me. Why is it so, O God? Please answer me."

"You came here to ask this? Ha-ha!"

"Cattus!"

"No, tell me. You know that they are the blessings of the Gods. But you also know every person has a different personality and aspect. Some people are calmer than others and some more aggressive. Some people are kinder

162

while others are more vicious. Your brothers are aggressive and vicious, King."

"No there is more to this, Cattus. Blessings of the Gods cannot be like this!"

"Fine! I will tell you. The first time round when their mother Ohio used the blessing, she was tricked by a demon, who intervened in the proceedings. It was the demon, Koll. He exerted his powers upon Lady Ohio before God Terradeus manifested and blessed her. Why do you think the skies went dark? Shilathaar, who you know to be the son of God, Terradeus, is also born by the grace of this demon. God Terradeus struck down demon Koll, but the damage had already been done. The God of War gave all his powers to Shilathaar, but he could not eradicate the evil implanted in him by that demon. The same happened with Grygerious, who you know to be the son of God Ishq. Ohio again became victim to a demon, this one Amor, who exerted his powers upon her before God Ishq could manifest. This again explains the darkening skies. Likewise, Amor was struck down by the God of Love, Ishq, but along with God Ishq's powers, Grygerious received the evil from the demon. The third time round, Ohio invoked the King of the Gods, Topus. This is when you were born. With your conception there was no demonic intervention. You received only the powers of your father, and now you kneel before him today...right at this moment."

Dymondo, Oromi and Sterferep gaped at Cattus in amazement.

"My father?! What do you...How do you know all this?" asked Dymondo.

Cattus smiled and gradually grew large and took the stunningly beautiful form of God Topus himself. Rays of divine light emanated from him. He was true perfection dressed in brilliant white and red. It was difficult for the party to fix their gaze upon him, he was so radiant and pure. Dymondo, Sterferep and Oromi could not believe how tall he stood. They were as miniatures before him. But more than that, they were overwhelmed by the indescribably pleasant experience of being in his presence.

"Oh God, forgive me, for I did not recognise you!" cried Dymondo as he bowed and knelt again.

"Forgive me, too, O God!" spoke Sterferep dropping to his knees.

"Rise, Dymondo. Rise, Sterferep. I came here to examine your will and determination. And you passed my test. Sterferep, you are a great and brave warrior and a loyal servant. Dymondo is fortunate to have you. And you, Dymondo, you are a great person and great opportunities await you. There are difficult times ahead though, my son. Be brave and always walk on the path of righteousness, and victory shall be yours," spoke the lord in a loud booming, yet heavenly voice. "Do you have the answers you seek, my son?"

"I do, my lord, and gratitude for giving them to me. But I have just one more. Can I ask about Nilharia?"

"She was miraculously conceived naturally by your earthly parents. You must seek forgiveness from Lorca for he tells the truth," With those words, God Topus disappeared.

CHAPTER 24

OROMI'S KING

The task was a success. Dymondo and his companions returned safely from the great temple back to the entrance of the jungle by nightfall and met up with Kor.

"Let us camp for the night. We shall move towards the city at day break," said Dymondo.

Everyone agreed. Sterferep and Kor set up camp with two tents and lit a fire, and everyone sat around it to enjoy its warmth. Oromi was still feeling cold, so Dymondo went over to give her his shawl. She took it with a smile.

"My King, you will catch a chill. Gamman winds at this time of the year can be fierce," warned Sterferep.

"Share it with me," suggested Oromi. Everyone went silent. Dymondo did not accept and merely sat down next to her.

"Doesn't sleep beckon you, Sterferep?" he asked.

"No, my King. I will remain awake and keep guard throughout the night."

"I shall, too," said Kor.

"No Kor, you should get rest, so you can lead the way back tomorrow," advised Sterferep.

"I agree…Good night everyone," Kor said and went to sleep in the smaller of the two tents.

"My King you too must take rest," Sterferep recommended.

Dymondo nodded and stood up to go to the large tent. He held his hand out to Oromi and she took it, rose and started walking with him to the tent.

"My King, I insist—"

"Sterferep, setting aside the notion of Kings and Queens and Lances and Knaves; we are human. Oromi is a young lady. No matter what training she may have received or crimes she committed, she is still a woman and it is important for any man to provide a woman safety. That is all I am doing."

Sterferep did not have a reply to this.

"Good night, my King."

"Good night, Sterferep."

Inside the tent, Oromi made herself comfortable, and Dymondo again sat beside her.

She began to stare at him and he too could not take his eyes off her.

"Life hurls one situation after another."

"Why do you say as such?" she asked him.

"Never mind. Thank you for helping us find the temple."

"I can understand what it must be like going through what you have, and what you are still going through."

Dymondo nodded and lay down. She too lay down beside him and took him into the shawl.

"Gratitude, my Lady," he said as he placed his arm upon his eyes. "A request... if you'd entertain?"

"Yes, my King."

"Please can you keep the secret to yourself and not mention it to anyone."

"You have my word."

"Gratitude."

After a few moments, she asked him: "What about our bargain? It doesn't have to be at the palace."

Dymondo lifted his arm from his eyes and looked at her.

"My lady, Oromi, that is not something I would do out of choice, let me remind you."

"I know that, my King and it hurts to know that. But you can at least try, can you not?" Oromi got close to him. "Am I not attractive?"

"Ha-ha! My lady only a fool would consider you unattractive."

"Then why the hesitation. Kings run through women like they change their tunics."

"I am not like most Kings. I have a woman, one I dearly love."

"Yes, you said that, too. Does she know of the condition I set?"

"She does."

They fell silent.

"Fine, I will not have you carry out the deed if you do not wish to, my King. And rest assured I will not proclaim to anyone that you did not hold up your end of the bargain. No matter what you decide about tonight, I shall tell you who sent me tomorrow morning."

Dymondo's head lowered. He suddenly felt guilty for not keeping up his end of the bargain.

"You do not owe me anything," she added, "so do not hold it in your heart that you did not meet our arrangement. It was stupid of me to ask in the first place. You are free to do what your heart desires." She turned her back to him.

"Wait."

Oromi turned and faced Dymondo.

"Why do you wish to lay with me?" he asked.

"My King, as soon as I got caught, I knew that it was going to end in death for me. I was adamant I would never speak the truth and that, eventually, you would order me executed. And if by chance I did end up saying the truth under torture, you'd kill me off anyway. But..."

"But what?"

"I saw a man in you that I have never seen in any other. You were strong and courageous, but also kind and caring. You poured water over me to clean me and averted your eyes. You wrapped me in a cloth, had me bathed, fed me and shared with me your luxuries, all despite me being a criminal."

"You are a woman, my lady, and all women must be respected."

"Precisely! Which is why you are the one man any woman would desire!"

"No! That is not true! There was one woman who rejected me!"

"Impossible!"

"I tell the truth!"

"Then there is only one explanation."

"Which is what?" Dymondo was intrigued.

"You are aware that there are such men that desire men, and not women?"

"Of course, that is natural and a part of life!"

"Likewise for women..."

Dymondo's eyes grew large in shock.

"Yes, my King...she must desire other women! Again, as you said this is natural and a part of life," smiled Oromi. Dymondo put his hand on his head and ran his fingers through his silky hair again and then placed it on his mouth.

"Remember this forever my King. *Every* woman in Landsfor desires

167

you."

"You use the name, Landsfor?"

"Ha-ha, you do! And so does Queen Ohio! Anyway, as I was saying, women desire you everywhere, in Landsfor, Blee, Orakray…News of your valour has even reached Haask, so even women of Haask now desire you! So if you know a woman who does not, then she does not desire men. Mark my words!"

"Enough." Dymondo's mind was muddled.

"I have not finished! As I was saying, if I am to die, then so be it. And this is how I felt as your captive, so, I thought, why not strike a bargain with the most desirable man in the realm. He would have to bed me in exchange for the information he required. And I've won! You are here," she nudged him, "but I know you are a good man and do not wish to hurt the one you love. I cannot put you through that. If you still feel compelled to keep your end of the bargain, then I would no doubt welcome that, but come to me willingly not begrudgingly. Otherwise, my great King, you are free from obligation." She again started to turn away again.

"No, wait Oromi," said Dymondo. This time he placed his hand on her shoulder to turn her toward him. "I will keep my end of the bargain," he smiled. Oromi's heart was ecstatic. She could not believe it.

"When you get back to the palace, though," he added, "after you have had some time to rest and prepare for your journey, you shall leave Gammafor and Fourtfor and never return. Agreed?"

"Agreed."

Dymondo nodded, but he could not help but think about Mysteria.

"There is no rush, my King," said Oromi. "We can talk for a while if you wish."

But there was no more need for talking. Dymondo moved closer to her and placed the side of his hand on her soft cheek and she shut her eyes. He removed the clips from her hair and her straight locks fell over her shoulders. He ran his fingers through them to straighten them out more. He then held her face in his hands and kissed her softly. She smiled as the short kiss turned into a long and passionate one. When Dymondo finally ended the kiss, she moved back and began to remove her shiny, royal blue dress.

He too started removed his armour and clothes.

She beheld the figure before her—the King of the Gods, Topus himself. After the vigorous trek through the jungle, each muscle was visible. His body shone like a clean-shaven, oiled gladiator poised in the arena.

He too beheld a grand beauty. Her skin was fair and her lips a luscious pink. Her shoulders were cut to perfection and her breasts were large and round with lovely erect nipples, all the more pert from the slight chill in the tent. Her waist and stomach were perfectly slim and muscular, and her thighs too were tight and firm from her day of riding. Dymondo recalled the time she stood before him nude in the dungeons, when her lovely body had been covered with muck and unwanted hair. Now all her sensitive areas were smooth-shaven and every inch of her body was desirable.

"From now until dawn, just as you desired my lady, we shall take our time."

"And what of dawn until dusk?"

"We've lost most of the day in the jungle."

"Let us make the most of what we have," she said as she pulled him inside her.

CHAPTER 25

DEEP WOUND

D ymondo did not question Oromi the next day and she too did not
say anything in return. As they rode back to the city, Dymondo
occupied his mind with thoughts of having discovered the
overwhelming secret of his birth, but as they neared the kingdom, guilt
from having laid with another woman crept into Dymondo, making him
forget why he did it in the first place. Oromi for her part could only think
of how she could get another opportunity to spend more time with him
once they were back at the palace. Sterferep and Kor kept quiet and just
exchanged pleasantries and knowing glances.

When they all returned to the kingdom, Dymondo dismounted his steed
and started towards the palace.

"My King," Sterferep called after him.

"What of her?" asked Sterferep gesturing towards Oromi.

"Yes! Lady Oromi, I believe you have something to tell me?"

"I do, my King, but not here in the open in front of everyone. We are all
tired. Rest a while, then, come see me in the guest chamber…that's if I
still…?"

"Of course, you are welcome! As I said, you will be allowed to rest for a
few days and then you will depart. Let us talk in private this evening."
Oromi smiled seductively. Dymondo ignored the look.

"Sterferep, see to it that Lady Oromi is safely escorted back to the guest
chamber."

"My King."

Dymondo turned and went in. Kor started unloading the horses.

Oromi's face fell as she watched the King walk swiftly away.

"Shall we, my Lady?" Sterferep asked.

"Gratitude," she said.

Oromi and Sterferep walked toward the palace together and Oromi thought it a good opportunity to make amends to the stern Lance.

"I would like to apologise for calling you a bastard," she said. "The King is lucky to have a friend like you, Lance Sterferep Unknown."

Sterferep stopped walking and looked at her.

"I too, my lady, have not been pleasant either."

"Is that your way of apologising?" smiled Oromi.

Sterferep smiled in return.

"Lance, may I ask, why 'Unknown.'"

"I am adopted. My foster parents brought me up. I do not know my birth parents." Oromi put her hand over her open mouth.

"I sincerely apologise, Sterferep, for I did not know. I did not—"

"I know you didn't know. Perhaps you just have a talent for cutting remarks," he winked.

"That must have been difficult."

"Nothing to be concerned about," he said. "Shall we?"

"Yes, but before we do; I just want to you to know that I am in love with the King and have great care and respect for him."

Sterferep nodded.

"I understand, my lady, but he is to marry Mysteria. With all due respect, you stand in their path. What has that young woman done to you to deserve that?"

"Nothing. Nothing at all. But I do not have control over my desires, Sterferep."

"No one has control over the emotion called love, my lady, but if Lady Mysteria finds out that you're still here in the palace, then she will be extremely angry with me and the King."

"Why you?"

"She set me to the task of making sure the King carries out the banishment."

Both went silent.

"Tell me, Lady Oromi, that night when you were attacked, did you manage to extract anything from the attacker?"

"I did not. Did you identify him?"

"No. We removed the mask, but no one was able to recognise him."

"I fear the person who sent me feared disclosure. They likely, sent someone to silence me."

"We can speculate as much as we like. But we won't find out now."

"Only if you had taken a moment or two longer to arrive, then I would have got him to confess. He agreed to tell before you all filled the room."

"To know who sent you would definitely help," smiled Sterferep.

"Do not worry yourself, Lance. I will tell him this evening."

"I believe you owe him that much."

Oromi said nothing and both walked on towards the guest chamber.

***

That evening Dymondo visited Oromi with Sterferep. After pleasantries were exchanged Dymondo asked her the question:

"Tell me, lady Oromi, who sent you?"

"Before I tell you, can I make a request?"

"You have made enough already, don't you think? And I have granted them all."

"Just one last one, my King."

"No. I want the name."

"I promise. Last one."

"Be quick then."

"Please do not banish me and let me stay here."

"I have announced your banishment in court, Oromi. You too have agreed to go. I cannot go back on my words and neither should you."

"But that was before what happened last night."

"That was an arrangement."

"Oh, leave it will you. Arrangement? You could not get enough of me. You wanted me, my King. You'd have me now! Even you don't want me to go."

"No, I do not."

Oromi was pleasantly surprise and Sterferep's eyes showed discontent towards his King.

"But I am King. I will make the decision that is beneficial for the realm, not just for me, so your request my lady has been rejected."

It was Sterferep's face that had the smile now and Oromi's faded away. She gathered her courage and began to speak.

"Very well. I suggest you sit down to hear this."

Dymondo looked over at Sterferep and took a seat on a soft chair.

"May I enter, my King?" There was someone at the door.

"Lance Tamaris! Do enter. What brings you here at this time?"

"Gratitude my King. My duties bring me here. My loyalties to Gammafor and Fourtfor."

"Tamaris, we are in the middle of an incredibility important conversation. If it can wait then the King will see you afterwards," said Sterferep.

"Yes Tamaris, please head on, and I shall summon you."

"May I remain here and wait?"

"No, you may not. I would rather have this meeting over sooner rather than later, so I can get some rest."

"I believe this lady was banished, my King?" asked Tamaris.

"I see, so you have come to find out when you can take to her banishment?"

"Precisely."

"Soon, you shall get the opportunity to do so, now I request you to leave."

"Of course, but pardon me, my King, my throat is parched, may I get water before I leave?"

"No you may not, Tamaris, now leave!" replied Sterferep sternly.

"There now Sterferep, our Tamaris is thirsty. The least we can do is give him water. Yes Tamaris. We all shall have some water. Why don't you and Sterferep pour some for us all?"

Tamaris and Sterferep walked over to the small table upon which the decanter sat. Sterferep placed four goblets on the plate and extended it towards Tamaris.

"Here, you hold the plate, I'll pour," said Tamaris

Sterferep thought Tamaris was behaving rather strangely. Nevertheless he let the Lance pour the water into the goblets and waited for him to place the decanter back upon the table.

"Shall we?" he asked as he took over the plate.

"For the lady first," smiled Tamaris. Oromi hesitantly took a goblet from the tray but did not drink first.

"Then the King!" Dymondo appreciated this and took the other goblet.

"I shall take the next and the last one for our dear Lance Sterferep." Everyone took their glasses but no one dared drink first.

"Cheers everyone!" said Tamaris and drained the goblet in one go. Then everyone raised their glasses to their mouths and began to drink. But as their attention was diverted, Tamaris drew a dagger and swiftly ran it into Oromi's lower back, twisted the weapon to cause as much internal damage as possible. Oromi screamed and began choking on the water she was drinking as blood came into her mouth.

"No!" shouted Dymondo.

"What the...!" Sterferep clinched his fist and drove it into Tamaris's face. Tamaris flew backwards and landed upon the ground, leaving the dagger lodged inside her. Oromi collapsed to the ground, but Dymondo caught her in his arms before she did so.

"Oh dear! Oh dear! What has happened? Tamaris! Why did you do this?" shouted Dymondo.

"Guards!" The room filled with guards within moments. "Surround and seize Lance Tamaris!"

The guards did as they were told but surprisingly Tamaris did not resist arrest. His face was blue where Sterferep had struck him. Sterferep walked up to him and clenched his fist again for another taste, but Tamaris had tears in his eyes and raised his chin like he was welcoming Sterferep's blow. Sterferep stopped midway and shook him vigorously.

"Why? Why, Tamaris?! Why do this?!" he asked him.

Meanwhile, Oromi lay in Dymondo's arms struggling in agony as the blood poured out from her back. Dymondo placed his hand upon her deep wound.

"Don't worry, Oromi, nothing will happen to you! Guards, get the apothecary!" A few guards ran out to fetch the man.

"My King, my King, it's too late. The time has come for me to go!" said the breathless Oromi.

"No! No!"

She was struggling to speak and breathing heavily.

"You can try, my King, but I...I...I do not think I shall survive this."

"You will, Oromi. You will. You are strong. Your wound will heal."

"I cannot keep my...my...eyes open..."

"You must. Stay strong. Hold on tight. I have you! Don't close your eyes."

"My King...I must fulfil my promise! I am not a bad woman, I was bound by my loyalty towards... my Queen."

"Queen? What do you mean? A Queen of another kingdom sent you?" asked Dymondo thinking instantly of Silvenia.

"No...my King. As I...told you, I hail from... Fourtfor. I speak of... Queen Ohio."

Dymondo hands went cold and his jaw dropped. A chill went down his spine and his stomach tightened. He could not believe what he was hearing. Dymondo's clutch loosened in shock.

"You lie!" Dymondo was angry.

A tear came to her eyes followed by a sympathetic smile.

"No, my King. It was your mother. She sent me to finish off your chief researcher. She did not want you to know of the secret."

"No! No! This cannot be!"

"It is, my King."

"You accuse my mother of such deception?!"

"It was for your own wellbeing. Some secrets must be kept as secrets," she said. Her face had now turned a ghostly white and her lips were turning blue.

Considering what acts his father had been driven to maintain the family secret, what Oromi said made some sense. Whoever sent her may have also sent the attacker to finish her. If it was his mother, then it would explain the absent maidservants and guards that night. But his own mother? It couldn't be.

"No! I cannot believe this! Why would mother do this? Does she wish ill of me?"

"No, my King! She loves all her children, especially you and your sister. That is why she had me intervene."

"I shall ask her!" he snarled, trying to hold back his tears. "If she denies it...you die!"

"I will die anyway, my King. I have broken my Queen's trust, and she will have me executed. That is why I asked you to lay with me. I wanted to be with you before I departed from this life. There, now you have it all."

The apothecary arrived with his helpers, took Oromi from the King's arms and tied a strong cloth bandage around her wound and began to take her away.

"I love you, my King!" she cried.

Dymondo, forgetting his anger, rushed to her and kissed her on her lips. The taste of blood and tears was distressing to him. "You'll be alright, you hear me! Promise me you will fight!"

She nodded as she began to pass out.

"Take extra good care of her!" he commanded the apothecary. "I want her alive!"

The thin apothecary bowed and hurried Oromi out of the room. Dymondo pondered her words with his head in his hands, running his strong fingers repeatedly through his thick hair.

He then turned to Tamaris.

"Tamaris! Why, man?!"

Tamaris was weeping. "Forgive me my King, for I did not wish to do this, but I was bound by instructions!"

"What fucking instructions! I give the instructions around here, you idiot! Whose instructions could supersede mine?!" his voice echoed in the entire room.

"There can only be but one, my King."

"No! No! You lie, Lance."

"Have my head if you wish, but it is the truth. Queen Ohio sent me to finish her."

Dymondo stepped back and fell into a chair. Oromi told the truth. The Queen wanted her dead. He looked up and found the faces of the four guards staring back at him in concern.

"Not a word of this to anyone, you hear me?!" roared Sterferep.

They all nodded.

"Now take him away to the dungeon." The four guards started to take a devastated Tamaris away.

"Remember…" The King spoke. "Tell the dungeon master he must not forget that Tamaris is a Lance. He is to be treated as one!"

"I do not deserve that my King," cried Tamaris.

"Tamaris, you have hurt me. …Nevertheless …just go…"

"Forgive me!" Tamaris shouted as the four guards took him away. Sterferep walked up to him and put his hand on his shoulder to console the fuming King.

***

The following day was heavy for Dymondo. The events and revelations of the prior evening had crushed him. His mind was in turmoil. He felt exhausted and frightened. He adjourned court for the morning, but having spent the entire morning in his room, he decided to divert his attention and summoned his royal builders and architects to begin work on resurrecting the Temple, including building a wider path and walls with minimal disturbance to the surrounding jungle life.

Oromi was still battling for her life but reports came that she was still breathing. Mysteria had not yet returned from home. Meanwhile, a Lance, one he loved as a friend and a brother, languished in the dungeons, living evidence of the severe accusations raised against his mother. Dymondo, Sterferep and Kor worked hard to maintain integrity and not disclose the incident between Oromi and Tamaris to others in the Kingdom. Dymondo wanted to speak to Tamaris himself first before making any decision about his future. But he did not deal with this straight away as he himself needed time to digest the overwhelming revelations about his family.

After another glum day or two, Mysteria returned from her home. Sterferep, Kor and Dymondo decided not to tell her that Oromi was still in Gammafor; instead, Dymondo made a decision to dispel the black clouds of conspiracy and eradicate the deathly taste of pessimism from his mouth. He needed to bring radiance back to Gammafor, so he decided to announce Mysteria publicly as his future Queen.

***

There was a general sense of joy and happiness at court that day as Dymondo made the official announcement and unveiled Mysteria to the courtiers. Her remarkable beauty was that of a Goddess. She was easily the most gorgeous Queen in the realm. The couple also appeared to the people of Gammafor on the royal balcony. Mysteria's mother was ecstatic at the news, and she too was asked to come and reside in the royal palace.

This announcement of their match was well-received throughout the land, though a few people silently raised their eyebrows, expecting a royal alliance. Nevertheless, good wishes flowed in. Gifts arrived from

176

Forprimiera, Doosranfor, Blee and Orakray. Surprisingly the kingdom of Haask too sent a trifling, yet beautiful gift. Everyone was astonished to see Haask taking part in such formalities, and no one knew the reason why. Some speculated that Haask sent the gift after hearing the countless praises sung throughout the realm of the great King Dymondo Rain. After all, Dymondo's praises had reached to every corner of the realm, and far beyond. But still, to receive a gesture of good will from Haask was a great achievement for a King Dymondo's age. Dymondo reciprocated and sent a personally handwritten scroll of gratitude to the King of Haask, along with a custom-forged sword made of pure gold.

Dymondo's chamber looked entirely altered as it was redesigned to accommodate his new Queen. The beige silk drapes were replaced with the royal colours of blue and purple with subtle whites introduced to compliment the finish. The chamber was expanded, so Queen Mysteria could have her own dressing area where she could spend time with her ladies in waiting: Glimer Kasturia and Shona Van der Hill. Dymondo's work desk was replaced with a finer wood model, consisting of golden handles.

The bed remained the same as the colours matched the new desk, wardrobes, drawers, and dressing table. A selection of at least one thousand dresses were sent to the royal chamber for the new Queen Mysteria, all handpicked personally by the King for his new love. Dymondo also chose the finest fabrics, trinkets, and jewels to be presented to Mysteria to become part of her new jewelry collection.

When Queen Ohio got news of the announcement via messenger bird whilst on her journey to Forprimiera, she sent immediate word of her subsequent visit to Gammafor. She wanted to meet her new daughter-in-law at the first possible chance. In the meantime, she sent another messenger bird to Fourtfor to her servants, asking them to send Mysteria even more dresses, these ones in shades of orange, red, and mauve, handcrafted by the greatest weavers in Fourtfor.

Mysteria was loved by everybody: the guards, the Lances, the courtiers, the Noblemen, and the maidservants, for they all saw her warm and caring nature. Nilharia too was pleased for her brother and immediately welcomed Mysteria into the family. After that regrettable day in the chamber, Velvia never met eye to eye with Dymondo and Mysteria; however, she did show respect to the future Queen and performed her duty. Dymondo and Mysteria acknowledged her quiet and expressionless gestures, and Velvia was content that Dymondo no longer had feelings for her and that she had mended her relationship with Nilharia and was spending time with her again. Dan Smoten no longer pursued his interest and relationship with Nilharia. There was no official severing of ties. They just stopped and never spoke about it again.

Mysteria was not yet accustomed to royalty, but she soon acclimated herself to her new role. She began to help her King before he left for court and advised him from time to time on matters of state. Soon there were talks of a grand royal wedding, where all the families from Forprimiera, Doosranfor, Orakray and Blee would be invited, along with the royal family from Haask.

CHAPTER 26

UNMERCIFUL DEMON

The day after she sent her messenger birds to congratulate Dymondo on his engagement to Mysteria, Queen Ohio's ship approached the shores of Forprimiera. Fluttering high on the main mast of her magnificent sailing vessel was the blue and purple flag of Landsfor with its striking golden lion. She shook her head as Forprimiera's own flag came into sight—a purple flag with a fierce red dragon embroidered at its centre. *Dragon*, she thought. *Why a Dragon?* She appreciated that Shilathaar at least held to the traditional colour of purple.

As she neared the shore, she saw another ship already moored closer to land—another large vessel with a gigantic light blue flag with a white dove sewn onto it. It was Grygerious's ship. He too had just arrived. Ohio saw Shilathaar and the conniving Silvenia welcoming him on shore. Grygerious and Shilathaar exchanged pleasantries, and as usual Grygerious's lips received a large kiss from his sister-in-law before the three of them laughed and carried on. Unlike Dymondo, who would find such overtures awkward, Grygerious enjoyed the greeting. *Despicable*, the Queen thought.

It was not long until her ship too came to shore and all attention diverted towards receiving Queen Ohio. Shilathaar hugged his mother, as did Silvenia. Ohio grabbed at the young Queen's dress and adjusted it violently to cover the girl's cleavage, which again was on display.

"It is cold near the waters. Don't want you getting ill," Ohio said and

179

went over to greet Grygerious.

Silvenia's smile turned into a repulsive glare. She pouted and rolled her eyes as Ohio turned her back towards her.

Grygerious too embraced his mother. Ohio looked behind him and saw his maidservants. The attractive Cresenia stood closest. Angry at her son's lack of decorum, Ohio asked about Gilgenia. Grygerious lied and said she was not well. Ohio decided not to question him any further. Instead, she met them all with a stern attitude, and after more pleasantries were exchanged, they all rode on chariots into the kingdom.

Ohio gazed upon all the military preparations in Shilathaar's city and a cold chill went down her spine. It deeply hurt her to witness it, but it was clear that Shilathaar was preparing for war. He and Grygerious still resented their brother for becoming King of the two islands and had not let the issue rest. The fires of jealousy still burned within them. Dymondo was right to be concerned.

At dinner that evening, Queen Ohio mentioned to her sons that she wished to talk to them later about something important. Shilathaar laughed at her comment, ignoring the gravity of her tone. He in return said that she should rest for a few days and that they would discuss the matter later. This pleased Grygerious as he just wanted to relax. Ohio insisted it was important, but Shilathaar still managed to postpone the meeting.

Queen Ohio did not enjoy her time in Forprimiera as sleep became a stranger. She wanted to speak with her sons, but Shilathaar found more reasons to delay. As for Silvenia, she merely fulfilled her basic duties towards her mother-in-law and nothing more. She did not wish to be in the old Queen's company any more than Ohio wanted to be in Silvenia's; therefore, the two avoided each other and rarely spoke.

***

During their stay, one evening, Cresenia entered the guest chamber where Grygerious was staying. She was wearing a dark purple dress and silver ornaments and looked ravishing.

"My King," she said.

"Is it done?" he asked, placing his hand on his face.

"Yes…" Cresenia gave an evil smile and they both started laughing. She came closer to him and they kissed. "I spoke with Karnigol about the…poison damsel," she said, whispering the last two words. "Before we set sail from Doosranfor, he informed me he was able to locate one."

"Great! If only Mother hadn't called me over to Forprimiera, then we could have started sooner!"

"I know, but just have patience, my King. The difficult part was to locate her."

"You're right."

180

"The victory shall be yours, my King,"

"Indeed, victory shall be ours!"

Cresenia's eyes lit up in delight when he said that, and the two lovers kissed each other deeply.

***

Frustration had started to settle in as Ohio waited and waited for an opportunity to discuss the topic of war with her sons. Eventually she had to resort to summoning them to somewhere private where she could speak to them. She chose the secret chamber down one of the darkened halls of the palace.

Queen Ohio waited impatiently for her childish sons to arrive. They entered the secret chamber laughing, but their laughter came to a sudden halt as they saw their mother sitting on the chair waiting for them in anger.

"What took you both so long? I summoned you hours ago! I expect you to show respect to your elders!" she shouted.

"We apologise, Mother. We came as soon as we heard," Shilathaar said, trying to be polite.

"Yes Mother, and now we're here," added Grygerious less tactfully.

"Take a seat! The both of you!"

Shilathaar and Grygerious sat down on seats on either side of Queen Ohio's chair.

"Yes, Mother? Are you enjoying your holiday?" asked Shilathaar.

"I certainly am!" Grygerious interjected. "The pleasures of this palace are without equal!"

Ohio glared at Grygerious, then turned to Shilathaar. "I am and gratitude for that, Shila, but I need to speak to you about something more pressing."

"Of course! What is it?!" he boomed.

"Are you headed to war?"

"War? No!"

"Shila, tell me then, why you are making preparations? I saw the training grounds as we entered the kingdom?"

"Oh that! You need not concern yourself with that, Mother. That is just general preparation. I am a leader to my people. I need to be prepared at all times!"

"I have seen war preparations before, my son. There is nothing routine about what I witnessed!"

"Mother, I am not your little boy anymore. I am now King. I heard rumours that other kingdoms are planning to move against me, so I decided to tighten up and make my own preparations. That is all. It is just everyday precautions and training. Do not be worried!"

"Shila, I have been a sovereign much longer than you! I do not need a

181

lesson from you on how to rule! No one is moving against you! Orakray is your ally, and I cannot see dear Grygerious or his in-laws on Blee making that mistake! And Haask has never attacked anyone, ever! So, who is this new enemy?"

"Move against brother Shilathaar?! Never!" Grygerious protested. "I will stand by his side forever!" Grygerious was filling his brother's ear with nectar, and Shilathaar ate it up. Ohio shook her head at both of them.

"Right enough! I am going to say it you straight!" she shouted. "You have to stop this, Shilathaar!"

"Stop what?" said Shilathaar feigning ignorance.

"Admit you are preparing to launch an attack and tell me against whom!" Ohio was getting angry.

"No one!" shouted Shilathaar.

"Watch your tone, with me, Shilathaar! I will not tolerate such rude behaviour from my children!"

"Mother, leave this be. Enjoy your holiday and rest. Listen to the harp or have my actors enact a play for you. But leave the politics to us. We are not children anymore!"

"You and him! You will always be children to me! And politics?! If you were a great politician, then your *subjects* would be happier!"

"Mother!"

"Yes, I know you call them citizens, but they are not free, Shila. Since I arrived here, I have not seen one happy face!"

"If they are unhappy, it is their own fault! They have everything!"

"They have nothing! You are a bad King!"

"Mother! Do not—"

"Shut up! And listen, the both of you! You both are unfit to rule!"

"And what have I done?" Grygerious asked in monotone.

"You are a womaniser!"

"Mother!" Grygerious put his hand over his mouth.

"Oh, spare me, Grygerious! Act like a man! You are King, and you do not even know when you last spoke with your wife! Gilgenia is a great woman. You are lucky to have her."

"I do not dispute that, Mother! She is wonderful!"

"Then why is it that you do nothing but sing, dance, and bed your mistresses?"

"Because I am excellent at delegation. All my affairs get handled by my great ministers. There is little left for me to do!"

"Rubbish! The both of you talk rubbish! I know what you're up to!"

Shilathaar was reaching his boiling point. "Oh? What are we up to, Mother?!"

"I will tell you! You are moving against Dymondo!"

"Truly, Mother, if you already knew, then why did you bother to ask?!" shouted Shilathaar rising from his seat.

"Because I did not want to accept the truth!"

"And what truth is that?!"

"That you are not fit to be King!"

"Mother!" Shilathaar raised his voice as loud as he could. Now his pride was wounded.

"You are my first born, Shilathaar, but your father did not have the spine to tell you that being first born is not all it takes to be King! It is not enough!"

"Mother, stop!"

"No! I shall not! You now move against your youngest brother, but he is the true and worthy heir of Landsfor!"

"Do not say that name!" boomed Shilathaar.

"Landsfor! And your brother is the rightful King!"

"He is not! I am the first born! I am the heir! I should rule all four islands!"

"All four, huh? And what do you think of that, Grygerious?" But Grygerious said nothing. He shuddered in fear as the titans clashed.

"Mother, stop this talk at once!" Shilathaar commanded. "If you are not happy here, then I shall gladly make arrangements for you to sail back to your castle!"

"No Shila I will not stop! You have crossed all lines! Breaking ties with your brother, distancing yourself from him, and being jealous of his progress, purely because he is worthy and tolerable. But to raise an army against him so that you can overthrow him?! I will not allow it. Not whilst I live! Shila, Dymondo is kind! If you asked him to give you his kingdom, he would do it tomorrow... with a smile!" Queen Ohio raised her voice as she stood up. It was louder than Shilathaar's.

"I do not want his charity! I don't want alms!" Shilathaar railed, his large frame looking down on the old lady, who was proving she had more power than him.

Shilathaar turned his back to her and started to walk away. Ohio sat back down.

"Come back here at once!" she cried. "You do not walk away whilst I am speaking to you!"

"Mother, my anger has reached its pinnacle! I cannot hear anymore! I shall not be deterred from my intentions. Try as much as you wish! I am going away!"

"Here is a true example as to why you're not worthy! You have no patience, no humility. You certainly do not have respect, and you are blinded by power and driven by greed! You are a still a child!"

Shilathaar turned back to face her, his eyes seething with rage. "I am the true heir! Period! This kingdom is mine! All of it! And I can choose to do what I wish with it! Not even the Gods can deter me from my path, let alone you, Mother!"

"How can I explain it to you, son? I am trying to tell you what is right and what is wrong!"

"I know what is right! Right is what I say is right, and wrong is what I say is wrong."

"Shilathaar!"

"Fine! You're right! You have read my thoughts, Mother! I will launch an attack on Dymondo and seize from him my birth right! I should have done it long ago, when father left for the afterlife! But I wanted to build an army so strong and powerful that it struck fear in the hearts of the Gods themselves! Now I have the power of Orakray and its fine generals. I have the power of Blee behind me!"

"And Haask? Do they support you? No! They are the most powerful kingdom in this entire realm, yet they observe their humility! They are strong yet peaceful! You should learn from these rulers, my son. Become like your brother Dymondo and run your kingdom like Haask."

"Haask does not support your darling Dymondo, either!"

"Then why did they send an appreciation gift to Dymondo for his coming wedding. Never has this happened before in my lifetime! If Dymondo seeks aid from them, Haask will answer! I can promise you that! And all those warriors and kingdoms you mentioned, they shall all crumble under the power of Haask and Dymondo's army!"

"Enough! I shall not hear praises of my enemies!"

"He is your brother, you idiot!"

"Are you certain of that mother?" Even Grygerious now gave Shilathaar a surprised stare. His eyes became filled with fear. What if he was next after Dymondo? Shilathaar noted the concern on his face.

"How dare you?!" Ohio accused. "You three are my sons. Hence you are brothers!"

"Mother! You enrage me! I was going to be merciful and let your little boy live! But all shall perish now! Anyone who has the audacity to stand in my way will die! I will crush Dymondo's kingdom under my feet and kill them all!"

"Never!" Ohio's voice reached up to the heavens and down to the netherworld. "This shall never happen! As long as I draw breath, I shall never let you succeed in your motives! Before you face anyone, you will have to face me! You will have to cross my corpse!"

"Mother! That is enough! Return to your castle! I promise you my men shall not hurt you or your beloved memories as they march through and invade!"

"You are a coward, Shilathaar! It is true. You are not fit to be King! You never were and never will be! You are not my son! You are not his brother! You are a demon!"

"Mother!" In a rage, Shilathaar unsheathed his dagger and launched it directly at his mother. The dagger pierced straight through her heart and the tip came out her back.

The old woman collapsed onto the lush carpet and took her last gasps of air until her eyes turned upwards and her body became still. All that was left of Queen Ohio was a stiff corpse lying in pool of her own blood.

LANDSFOR
QUEST FOR THE FROZENFIRE

Excerpt

PROLOGUE
THE KEEPERS

Long ago in a distant realm, an unrighteous Lord rose from the south and advanced north towards the Kingdom of Landsfor, crushing any other lands and Kings that stood in his path. Those were terrible times for the Kingdom of Landsfor. A great evil had befallen the realm and its four islands.

The King of Landsfor, King Solothaar Rain, sought aid from the God of the Gods, Topus, in the temple upon the holy hill. God Topus heard his prayer and answered him by showing him the way to defeat the evil Lord from the south.

The answer was the Emispear, the unsurmountable power of the Frozenfire—a mighty battle spear made up of four parts: three blue, red and green gleaming rods and a yellow blade for a spearhead said to contain the power of the sun. When all four parts were joined together, the weapon shone a luminous white.

The God of Gods Topus bestowed upon King Solothaar this divine weapon so he could defeat the evil Lord and protect humankind. The weapon was only to be used against the forces of evil and for the preservation of righteousness. It was a formidable weapon any King would have been determined to keep. But once the weapon had been used and the evil forces defeated, the weapon was to be dismantled once again and its four pieces returned to their keepers.

King Solothaar, being a righteous and responsible King, accepted all

186

terms and adhered to them strictly. He used the weapon to defeat the evil Lord along with the help of the four keepers. Then after the war against evil was won, King Solothaar returned to the holy hill as promised and returned the weapon to the God, expressing gratitude for his aid. Though God Topus did not manifest, the four guardians were there to collect their respective parts for safe keeping.

The first keeper was the great fire breathing golden hawk, with feathers of sharp blades. The bird was the keeper of the spearhead. Solothaar placed the weapon upon a rock and a sharp yellow beam shot from the hawk's eyes and separated the head from the staff, and the spearhead resumed its place as one of the feathers of the bird.

The second guardian was a great red bear. He took the red element, one of the three elements comprising the staff, the one known to contain the powers of fire, and held it near his large, white belly until the staff disappeared inside him.

The third keeper was a large blue bear. Similar to the red bear, he took the blue part of the staff, the one bearing the powers of sky, wind and water, and held it near his large, white belly until it too disappeared.

Finally, the blue bear picked up the final green piece of the staff and threw it into a moving green shrub with red berries. The green rod, representing the earth, vanished inside the leaves of the bush.

With that, King Solothaar paid his respects to the keepers before they all went their separate ways. The Emispear was never to be invoked again, unless a similar calamity one day befell the Kingdom.

CHAPTER 1
SLEEPLESS NIGHTS

For King Dymondo Rain of Gammafor and Fourtfor, the wound of losing his mother was still fresh. Though her eventual demise was expected her sudden death came as shock to the entire family.

Dymondo tossed and turned in his bed, his lips shivering and his pillow wet from the cold sweat that had formed on his forehead. It was the same nightmare—a memory that had haunted him all his life—an inner guilt that devoured him from inside. The more he tried to forget it, the more it returned to terrorise him in his slumber.

His Queen, Mysteria, awoke to his mumbling and forceful movements caused by his nightmare. She had experienced this many times now and was quickly becoming used to her husband's troubled sleep. She took him in her arms and slowly and gently rocked him, trying to calm him down whilst being careful not to wake him to prevent further shock. It was no use.

Dymondo shot up, momentarily released from his nightmare, but in shock. He was breathing fast, his heart racing like a charioteer in a grand contest. His eyes were wide and his hair drenched with sweat.

"My King," said Mysteria, putting her hands gently upon his shoulders.

Dymondo jumped at the touch, but she held tight.

"It's alright…It's over…"

Dymondo nodded and wiped his sweat-filled forehead. He got out of bed and headed for the water flagon. He did not bother with any goblet or glass but drank straight from the container.

Mysteria came out from underneath the bed sheets and covered herself with her gown. She went towards a wall lamp and lit it to allow some light in the room.

"Blow it out, my dear, for I am going back to sleep."

"No. We are talking about this."

"About what, Mysteria?"

"About your nightmare."

"I am not having any nightmares," lied Dymondo.

"You hide what you see from me. Why?"

"It is nothing at all, dear. Just a nightmare. Nothing to be concerned about."

She walked up to him and turned him to face her. She had her other hand upon her gown to hold it in place.

"Mysteria, please. I wish to go back to bed." Dymondo wiped the sweat dripping onto his neck from the back of his head.

"You cannot hide such things from me, my King. You'll have to tell me."

"I shall, but not now."

"Why not now? This isn't the first time I've seen you run for the water jug in the middle of the night."

"I know. Perhaps I miss Mother."

"Oh dear, come here." She extended her arms out to him. He walked up and embraced her.

Her gown flung open and she held him tight and close to her skin.

"That was a terrible loss for us all. I didn't even get the opportunity to meet her as her daughter-in-law. But you must be strong, my dear."

"Others may have accepted her unexpected departing to the afterlife, but I am still in mourning, Mysteria."

"I understand…But everyone gave her a great send-off, didn't they?" Mysteria added, trying to apply balm with her words.

"Yes." Dymondo withdrew from the hug. "No doubt. Brother Shilathaar raised the Call straight away after her demise. He preserved her body in a large container filled with oils and other medicines and when we met up for the Call, he had already placed her in Fourtfor castle, where she wanted to be."

"Yes, that was kind of him…surprisingly."

"She was his mother, too," defended Dymondo.

"Of course, my King but… she seemed, as you say, fine and healthy before she left for Forprimiera."

"Yes, Mysteria, but her death was due to natural causes. She was found sound asleep in her chamber."

Mysteria nodded.

"Now she is reunited with Father in the afterlife. May her soul rest in peace. We all gave her the best send-off we could with the great royal funeral in Fourtfor, but I still miss her, Mysteria."

Mysteria held him again.

"I know how much you loved her and how you could confide in her. But that doesn't mean there is no one else you can speak with. You can always speak with me. Tell me…what did you see in your dream?"

"I see…"

"Go on."

"I see my childhood. Three princes of Landsfor playing atop the mountains just outside the jungle. I see myself. I am ten. I see my brothers. They too are children like me. I see another child playing among us. He is the son of the Prime Minister, the one at that time. Syterius, I think his name was. A very talented child, a genius. He'd beat us all in any game or competition despite being younger than all of us—a rare talent. I see us all playing a game in which he defeats me and Brother Grygerious. One turn is all that remains of the game and he and Brother Shilathaar are all that's left. He beats Shilathaar. The game gets played again, over and over, and every time, he wins. This makes Shilathaar very angry. Both Grygerious and I know that Shilathaar is going up to strike him, and I can stop him, but I respect Brother Shilathaar... and fear him."

"Then?"

"Then I see Grygerious looking on with a wicked smile, as if this is all entertainment."

"Then...?"

Dymondo stopped and gazed at her not wanting to continue.

"Please, Dymondo..."

"Then...I see Shilathaar grabbing Syterius by his neck and he starts to push him towards the cliff of the mountain..."

"Then?"

"He did not stop. I ran after him and so did Grygerious, but Grygerious was enjoying himself, clapping his hands, spurring Shilathaar on to hit Syterius. I was shouting... "No! Stop, Brother! No!""

"Then..."

"He did not stop... Shilathaar pushed him to the point where there was no ground. The poor boy fell over the edge and dropped far below, into the tall trees of the forest...to his death."

"Oh my gosh! Is this incident true...?" Mysteria put her hands over her mouth,

"Yes...it happened, but only the three of us know the truth. Everybody else thinks Syterius slipped by accident."

***

Around the same time, Lance Sterferep, King Dymondo's most trusted aid, was sneaking into the home of Zircornia Matchiwada as her secret guest. Zircornia Matchiwada was a very beautiful young woman belonging to a privileged household as her father was an influential nobleman at King Dymondo's court. The Matchiwadas lived in a beautiful house with all the luxuries of the royal palace, situated in a prime location in the Kingdom. With her parents sound asleep, Sterferep snuck into Zircornia's chamber and spent the night in her bed.

Zircornia resembled a Goddess and had long, blonde, silky hair with light blue eyes. She would often dress in long, blue and white dresses and rarely chose another colour to wear. A decent, twenty-five-year-old woman she was with much respect for herself and her mother.

She adored Sterferep and he loved her, but this was the first time Sterferep had stayed over at her home, so the brave Lance was feeling slightly apprehensive.

After having made love, they lay together quietly in each other's arms unclad. The skies outside starting to turn from black to red. Sterferep noticed this and got up.

"Oh, stay a little longer," she said quietly.

"I must leave, it is nearly daybreak. I will be wanted back at the palace."

"A few moments longer…?"

He moved to her and kissed her on her lips.

"As much as I'd love to, I must go before anyone gets up. Your father will definitely not be happy to see me here," he said and started to get dressed. She too got out and put on her silky gown.

After he had donned his trousers and boots, she embraced him and could not help but notice the engraving on his shoulder again. It was as if the mark was part of his skin—a mark for life given at birth.

"So, what is this little creature doing here? I have wanted to ask you before, but I never did," she said stroking it gently.

Sterferep put his hand over his right shoulder and sat on the bed with his back to her.

She went over to him and embraced him from behind.

"Tell me. What is it?"

"I've had it since birth. You must not mention this to the King, Zircornia." Sterferep was serious.

"Of course not, but you must tell *me* Sterferep. What is it?"

"It is the Cecrops—a depiction of a man with a serpent's tail."

"I can see that, but why is it there?"

"I don't know, but my parents say it must have been with me since birth."

"Must have? Surely they must know…"

"…No! I was adopted. My parents found me by the riverbank of Krool, and though they were poor, they took me in and raised me as their own. I don't know who I truly am, Zircornia. Hence the reason everyone refers to me as Sterferep Unknown. But my father always asked me to hide this mark and not let anyone know of it. It was like he knew something but never shared it with me. He died when I was eighteen and my mother two years back. As for the mark, I have kept it hidden my whole life. I had forgotten about it, actually…until now. No one else knows about it apart from you.

Can I trust you?"

"Of course you can, my love. I am yours and you are mine, along with all your secrets. But…"

"But what, my lady?"

"Three years ago…King Shilathaar came to Gammafor court and brought his wife…Queen Silvenia. I did not look closely then, but…" she paused to think. "I believe…I have seen the same mark on her right shoulder."

"How…?"

"We were all dancing and Queen Silvenia of Forprimiera is known for her loose clothing, as you know. As usual, she was dancing freely. I cannot fathom why she dresses like that."

"Yes, her bosom is often on display," smiled Sterferep.

Zircornia opened her mouth and hit him gently on his bicep in jealousy.

"Where were your eyes?" she asked.

"Ha-ha! You know her, my dear! How could I not see?"

"True, and that day she was wearing a lovely thin silk dress—too thin; her entire figure could be seen. I saw her right shoulder and….it had the same mark. Maybe there is a connection between you and her?"

Sterferep went quiet and Zircornia rubbed his shoulders in consolation.

"I'm sorry to have caused you more concern."

"Its fine, Zircornia. I have been running away from this all my life. Perhaps it is now time to solve this mystery once and for all."

Zircornia smiled and kissed him.

"Just remember, I am always with you. But how will you find out?"

"Gratitude, Zircornia," smiled Sterferep, kissing her. "I'll seek the help of my friend, the King. I just need the right moment."

Zircornia nodded. "We can always trust him."

"But I cannot disturb him about it right now. He is occupied with important matters of state. But I will look for a chance to speak with him."

"You must."

"First, I must get back; otherwise, your parents will not be pleased to find me here."

Zircornia's face dropped and Sterferep finished getting dressed and left through the window from where he had come. Zircornia watched him jump into the bushes, making sure he landed safely and waved him goodbye. He waved back and then silently ran off toward the palace.

ABOUT THE AUTHOR

Raj Bansal was born in Southampton Hampshire and currently resides with his wife in Hounslow Middlesex. Gourav is an IT consultant by profession, but writing is his passion.

Thank you for reading his book. If you enjoyed it, then please take a moment to leave a review at your favourite retailer including Amazon. Also, please take the time to leave me a review over on Goodreads too.

www.ingramcontent.com/pod-product-compliance
Lightning Source LLC
Chambersburg PA
CBHW071238170626
46809CB00014BA/1015